PENGUIN BOOKS

WARPAINT

COCHRANE

JUN 1 2 2014

Alicia Foster grew up in Yorkshire and lives in Kent. She has a PhD in Art History and, when she's not writing, she teaches art students. *Warpaint* is her first novel.

Warpaint

ALICIA FOSTER

PENGUIN BOOKS

PENGUIN BOOKS

Published by the Penguin Group
Penguin Books Ltd, 80 Strand, London WC2R ORL, England
Penguin Group (USA) Inc., 375 Hudson Street, New York, New York 10014, USA
Penguin Group (Canada), 90 Eglinton Avenue East, Suite 700, Toronto, Ontario, Canada M4P 2Y3
(a division of Pearson Penguin Canada Inc.)
Penguin Ireland, 25 St Stephen's Green, Dublin 2, Ireland (a division of Penguin Books Ltd)
Penguin Group (Australia), 707 Collins Street, Melbourne, Victoria 3008, Australia
(a division of Pearson Australia Group Pty Ltd)
Penguin Books India Pvt Ltd, 11 Community Centre, Panchsheel Park, New Delhi – 110 017, India
Penguin Group (NZ), 67 Apollo Drive, Rosedale, Auckland 0632, New Zealand
(a division of Pearson New Zealand Ltd)
Penguin Books (South Africa) (Pty) Ltd, Block D, Rosebank Office Park,
181 Jan Smuts Avenue, Parktown North, Gauteng 2193, South Africa

Penguin Books Ltd, Registered Offices: 80 Strand, London WC2R ORL, England

www.penguin.com

First published by Fig Tree 2013
Published in Penguin Books 2014
001

Copyright © Alicia Foster, 2013
All rights reserved

The moral right of the author has been asserted

Every effort has been made to trace copyright holders and to obtain their permission
for the use of copyright material. The publisher apologizes for any errors or
omissions and would be grateful to be notified of any corrections that
should be incorporated in future editions of this book

Typeset by Jouve (UK), Milton Keynes
Printed in Great Britain by Clays Ltd, St Ives plc

Except in the United States of America, this book is sold subject
to the condition that it shall not, by way of trade or otherwise, be lent,
re-sold, hired out, or otherwise circulated without the publisher's
prior consent in any form of binding or cover other than that in
which it is published and without a similar condition including this
condition being imposed on the subsequent purchaser

ISBN: 978-0-241-96277-0

www.greenpenguin.co.uk

MIX
Paper from
responsible sources
FSC
www.fsc.org FSC® C018179

Penguin Books is committed to a sustainable
future for our business, our readers and our planet.
This book is made from Forest Stewardship
Council™ certified paper.

To John, Madeleine and Isaac

PART ONE

December 1942

MINISTER OF INFORMATION, THE RIGHT HON.
BRENDAN BRACKEN, M.P., SENATE HOUSE,
MALET STREET, WC1

Copy To: Black; Sir Kenneth Clark for War
Artists Advisory Committee

I have just left an all-night meeting at
No. 10. The Boss has asked me to impress
upon everyone, as a matter of urgency, that
the end is nowhere in sight. We must each
do our utmost if we are to prevail: productivity is our watchword. There is no time
or money left to waste. Those sectors that
do not comply will be terminated.

Chapter One

A motorcycle made its way down a country road in a winter dawn, through grey mist and between brown hedges. It growled and snorted along the short high street of Aspley Guise – shops and houses still and silent at this hour – then left the village behind. A mile out, surrounded by fields and woods, it turned off down a narrow lane, jolting over a pothole, almost bouncing the rider – a small figure, slender as a child – out of the seat. The machine slowed, turned back the way it had come for a few seconds, and stopped.

Struggling to balance at a standstill – with toes barely touching the ground – the rider rummaged in a haversack and pulled out a map, propping it up on the curve of the petrol tank. The thin beam of light from a pocket torch illuminated clean, logical lines of black on white, which barely seemed to correspond to the surrounding Bedfordshire farmland – fields of ochre and dun, blurred and merged by the early fog, sketched over with haphazard tracks and the smudged tracery of bare copses. The motorcyclist shivered: belting along quiet lanes at top speed was fun, usually, but this landscape was eerie: rather than opening up in front of you, it felt as if it were closing in.

And the destination was a blank. Someone had drawn a red line on the map from Bletchley Park – eight miles away, where the motorcycle dispatch unit was stationed – to the middle of a wood, but there looked to be no building here at all, although was that a narrow track? On the map some sort of pathway led from the lane to the red-ink cross in the middle of vacant space where, apparently, the message had to be delivered. A turning had been missed.

The rider dismounted, kicked down the stand underneath the motorcycle, bracing one foot against it, tugged hard on the handlebars with a grunt of effort so that the machine lifted, rocked and came to rest, and left it there in the middle of the lane, engine running, to walk back, searching. Only on foot would you notice this entrance, partially concealed by a row of laurels allowed to grow high and thick. The drive beyond it was enclosed on either side by hedges; it veered off at a sharp angle to continue parallel to the road. All you would glimpse as you rode along at pace was an impenetrable green wall.

Uncertain as to how far there was left to go, the rider steered the machine slowly up a winding drive. At the end, in a clearing among trees, shrubs and long grass, like an apparition in this isolated spot, stood a villa. Pulling the motorcycle on to its stand again, this time switching off the engine – so loud in the silence – the motorcyclist stood, head tilted back, taking it all in: a substantial Victorian pile with deep bay windows, a steep pitched roof of fancy tiles, and rows of tall brick chimneys in patterns of spirals and diamonds. Above the Gothic point of the front door was an elaborate window of stained glass as tall as a man; this was a house with pretensions, home perhaps to a prosperous country doctor or vicar once upon a time, although with the blackout blinds down and the overgrown garden it had the look of being abandoned, shut up for the duration of the war.

Looking over the map once more to make absolutely sure, the rider felt around in the haversack for the memo. For a second it could not be found and there was panic, but then fingers closed around it. It was sealed in a blank envelope – the instructions had been to memorize the name, *Samuel Thayer*, and title, *Head of Black*, and to deliver it to him only. There would be hell to pay at the depot if a mistake were made. A deep breath: there was nothing for it but to knock on the door.

Leather-gloved knuckles on the wood made a soft, thick sound . . . but no one came. There was an ornate enamel and brass doorbell, but no ringing could be heard when you pressed it; this might be because of the heavy door, but you couldn't be sure; another push, still no response. Standing back to look at the windows, the motorcyclist saw that all the blinds remained down, but perhaps behind one of them there might be a maid or a cook, already up, readying things for the day?

Holding the blank envelope right out to make the purpose of the visit obvious should anybody appear, the small figure walked round the villa, past dark windows, between the remains of a kitchen garden gone to seed and a row of outbuildings, to the back door. There was no answer there either. Peering through the adjacent window, the rider gave a low whistle – a shiny cooker and refrigerator were the modern, expensive backdrop to an astonishing array of food, laid out on the table ready to be prepared and carried through to an elegant dining room for breakfast, no doubt. There were pots of jam and marmalade gleaming like jewels, a loaf of fine, white bread, a red and silver tin of coffee, a mixing bowl piled full of eggs and a golden pat of butter. Past the table, a larder door was open on to shelves crammed with boxes, packets and bottles. Through another door, you could see a cool room with white tiles, where a fat stack of bacon rested on a butcher's block; hanging above were loops of dark, blood-coloured dried sausage and a whole ham. All of this abundance here, and breakfast at the depot had been a tin mug of weak tea – there was no sugar – and one dark, gritty crust spread with margarine. Even that was better than at home, where you'd be lucky to get the tea.

After knocking once more, the messenger waited, then tried the handle – tempted by a sudden thought of slipping inside and pocketing an egg, a jar, a packet – but the door was locked. Turning away, looking past the straggling fruit bushes and sprout stalks you could see into the garage: within was a most beautiful car, a black Rolls-Royce; the shape was unmistakable even before you saw the silver mascot on the front. The car lured you towards it to have a closer look. Then there was a sound from somewhere at the front of the villa.

Hurrying back round, the motorcyclist found the Gothic door ajar – but there was no one there. Pushing the door wider open you could see into the hall; no lights on, dark paintings in gilt frames, a crowded hatstand, a table with ranks of newspapers neatly arranged – so there was life within. Then a man's voice came from somewhere: 'Can I help you?'

'This is for a . . . Black,' the dispatch rider said, just as they had

6

been instructed to at the depot. If there'd been any sort of mix-up and the address proved wrong it would look as if 'Black' were merely the surname of an individual, a Mister or Major. The motorcyclist knew that 'Black' was not a person, but had no idea of the truth.

'Black? Yes: Black,' the man said.

The eyes of the messenger adjusted to the gloom, and the dimly coloured light from the stained-glass window in the hall picked out a tall figure, thin and rangy, wearing spectacles with narrow wire frames: 'bookish' was how he would be described later, when the motorcyclist told the story of the war years.

'Well, don't look so worried, you've come to the right place. Let me take it for you,' he said, reaching out for the envelope.

'I need your name.'

'I see.' He let his arm drop and looked annoyed, but only for a second, and then his face worked itself back into a pleasant smile. 'Charles: will that do?'

'Sorry, no. I'm looking for the Head: this is for no one else.'

'Of course, of course. But they're still abed; never up at this hour, and we had rather a late one last night. Top of the stairs, turn right, and then first room on the left. Off you go, then. And . . . good luck.' He smiled again at the rider. 'But perhaps you won't need it.'

Chapter Two

Sam Thayer surfaced from deep sleep to find his favourite fantasy had come to life: a girl in her late teens, and in uniform, had materialized right by his side of the bed. He opened his eyes further to see long, slender thighs emerging from tight-laced, knee-length leather boots; above that, a grey dispatch rider's jacket buttoned over a tidy figure; at the top, a fresh, appealing little face and blonde hair set free as a crash helmet was removed. His wife, Vivienne, was already awake, and looking at the girl with a hostile expression. Sam turned away from Vivienne, on to his side, to conceal his growing, rising, strengthening interest in the courier.

The girl stood, unsure as to how to proceed, holding the sealed document out towards Sam, awkwardly. Vivienne huffed and burrowed back down under the covers, until only the top of her head with its dark curls was visible.

Sam reached for his watch and then sat up, straightening the top of his pyjamas, clutching for his cigarettes and lighter. While he arranged himself the courier glanced around, taking in the room: a velvet eiderdown and matching curtains with silk tassels; a gauzy evening dress thrown over a chair, zip undone and skirt crumpled; stockings dropped on the floor as if they were ten a penny; a mirrored dressing table with photographs in frames and an array of scent bottles – more than she had ever seen outside one of those city department stores, some with their stoppers left off; long-stemmed crystal glasses – smeared, with liquid still at the bottom – on the nightstand; an extraordinary display of luxury to her eyes, and treated so casually.

Above the bed were eight framed prints in two rows, of people from the olden days disporting themselves in white wigs, men with breeches around their knees, members erect, launching themselves on to prone women who spilled out of muslin gowns, plump legs

8

open, private parts exposed. As she gazed, fascinated, the motorcyclist became aware that the man in the bed was watching her, lying back on his pillow, one arm behind his head, a cigarette between his fingers. She looked down at the toes of her boots, feeling that perhaps she should pretend to be abashed – it didn't do to appear too forward – but she found his scrutiny irritating so she looked straight back at him, and spoke.

'Your name?'

'Mr Samuel Thayer.' He said it formally, mocking her attempt to be curt and authoritative. The motorcyclist looked at her boots again – this time she flushed pink.

She handed over the envelope. He put his cigarette between his lips, tore the letter open, and held it with one hand as he smoked and read.

Sam could feel the chill emanating from his wife. Not his fault that they sent such a pretty girl to wake him. But he would make a point of asking for the same courier next time, when, hopefully, Vivienne would not be around.

'One minute. Ah . . . Oh. So . . . Yes. No reply . . . I said, no reply.'

Chapter Three

The girl flashed a mutinous look back at Sam as she left: he had dismissed her so abruptly. She'd have to learn: playing dress-up in uniform meant that she could not expect the courtesies due to a lady; all of these young women, rushing out into the real world at the sound of a gun, would soon retreat to the niceties of the drawing room – to doors being held open and bags carried for them – when the war was over.

Sam turned to Vivienne to explain about the message, but she lay on her side, blankets still pulled up around her face, eyes shut: asleep, or pretending to be.

An hour later Vivienne sat up. Sam had been waiting, smoking, needing to talk. As she ran her fingers over her hair, patting it into place, he put the memo on the bed in front of her.

'Bracken's on the warpath about money. We've to prove ourselves or we're for it. And this isn't a ruse to buck us all up: they mean it.'

'What'll happen to us?'

'God alone knows. But I'll be damned if I let them disband Black *before* we've lost the war. We must carry on till the bitter end, no matter what. We're their best hope, their only hope; why don't they realize it? They make such a hoo-ha about Bletchley Park, but it's useless without us. Chasing codes on its own gets us nowhere, they change 'em as soon as they're rumbled. What we do with the decrypts makes a much greater impact.' Sam's voice was louder now. 'Psychological warfare, sowing doubt, generating fear – that's the modern way. No point fiddling around trying to decipher the Nazis' next move and only then trying to stop 'em, point is to chop 'em off at the root, bring Hitler down once and for all. For that to happen you've got to get inside people's minds, their hearts. And it's not dirt just for the sake of it, as some of the high-ups seem to think, noses in the air with disgust whenever I appear. People love smut, it's the spoon of honey with the medicine, and if you give them a taste of what they like they'll swallow what you want them to without thinking. As if you can win a war playing by the rules: English-fucking-gentlemen will be the death of us all.'

'Stop shouting, I'm right next to you. You'll wake everybody,' said Vivienne.

Sam was at his most vehement in two areas of his life: the pursuit of women, and the defence of Black, the organization he had conceived and created after a youth spent in Germany – he spoke the language like a native – and then success as a foreign correspondent. When hostilities began and Sam was casting about for some way to carry on working in a manner he could enjoy, he had managed to persuade the newly formed Ministry of Information to give his idea a try, to let him hand-pick a small band, and over the intervening years three other men had come to live and work at the villa with Sam and Vivienne. Between them they had the daring, skill and imagination (unhampered by taste or decency) to produce covert propaganda, documents, images and broadcasts designed to undermine the Nazis, to be circulated behind enemy lines to spread mistrust, disloyalty and chaos.

Black's creations were always mendacious, often cruel and obscene, and the government wanted nothing, *officially*, to do with them. Most of the material the unit produced simply appeared to surface behind enemy lines; nobody could trace its origins. Only a few men, right at the top, knew about Black, about the villa. Which was unlike the overt face of the Ministry of Information, trumpeting out its wholesome, rousing message from Senate House, a tower in the centre of London, and unlike that other 'secret', Bletchley Park, the centre for code-breaking that had become by this third full year of the war almost a new town with a population of many thousands. The Park – a Tudor mansion built by a Victorian tycoon, eight miles from the villa – was now crowded with Nissen huts. Cars, buses, bicycles and motorcycles went to and fro day and night, choking the country roads, carrying a strange cargo of military intelligence officers, librarians, chess masters, mathematicians, linguists, crossword addicts, rare-book dealers, dons and Wrens. After work this motley congregation would gather at the Park's own social clubs, bridge and chess tournaments, dances and dramatic productions.

Sam turned round on the side of the bed, scratching his head, stubbing out his cigarette. 'I'm telling you, Vee, compared to the M of I, compared to Bletchley, we're a model of bloody efficiency. They won't get rid of Black without a fight. But if they do, and then the Germans win, we'll be for it, first up against the wall,' he said grimly. Seeing the look on her face, he relented. 'Don't pop a suicide pill just yet. Carry on with your drawing for the Greek campaign: the Hausfrau having a bit on the side while *lieber* Fritz is away fighting. Greek situation is terribly dicey: unless the enemy loses momentum and the resistance holds we can kiss goodbye to the Med. And the more Black churns out the better, at the moment. We need to be seen to be contributing.'

Sam took Vivienne's hand and pressed it to his lips without looking at her. 'I'd better be going. Got to dash over to Bletchley and back, and then up to London for a meeting; was going to skip it, but important to be visible. I'll try to make Bracken see sense.' He picked up the memo from the bed and dropped it on the dressing table on his way to the bathroom.

Vivienne lay back on her pillows and let herself fall into a half-sleep. Sam came in again; she did not open her eyes or speak. She smelt his Italian cologne – sharp and delicious, lemons and cedar wood. She heard the rattle of coat hangers as he chose a suit from the many in his wardrobe, and then quiet while he selected his customary bright silk handkerchief and tie. The door shut gently behind him. Alone in the bed she found herself smiling, thinking about Frido, her fellow worker in Black and her lover, asleep in the room just across the corridor. Perhaps today, once Sam had gone to London, she could spend some time alone with him.

Chapter Four

Sir Kenneth Clark, Head of the War Artists Advisory Committee at the Ministry of Information, received Minister Bracken's memo while standing at the window of his marble office on the seventeenth floor of Senate House, Bloomsbury. From this art deco monolith, high above the lean houses and green squares, Clark looked down over a peaceful vista: no flames or smoke rose from the capital, but previous air raids had left here and there a dark crater in a row of buildings, like a missing tooth.

Senate House was supposed to be a beacon of hope and truth in these troubled times. From here the Ministry of Information tried to transmit a message of British pluck and virtue across the nation, to inspire optimism and the bulldog spirit through the paintings and drawings it commissioned and the films, pamphlets and posters it produced. The Ministry wished to dominate the cultural landscape, just as its home, Senate House, in its gleaming vastness, could be seen for miles around. Black Operations, out in Aspley Guise, was, then, the Ministry of Information's dark other: its shadow, creeping and vaporous, conjuring up the malign elements of human nature – lust, envy, fear and hatred – from the hidden villa in the wood.

Clark read the memo twice. It was as if – out of this quiet morning – a grenade thrown by his own side had landed in his office. He stood frowning, a narrow figure given manly shoulders by his Savile Row tailor. As always when he was thinking, Clark smoothed one hand over his brow, high and wide as that of a baby. He had to find a way to stop them sniffing around WAAC, perhaps even closing the whole thing down. Such a shadow over his achievements brought to mind the scandal that had marred his directorship of the National Gallery. There had been accusations of financial mismanagement, and insinuations that his own talents were for high living and high-handedness, rather than high office. He had survived that onslaught, but he might not do so a second time. Clark moved towards his desk and picked up the telephone to summon his secretary: a blonde, the best kind, yes, but over the hill, thirty if she was a day, and not fragile enough for his taste – he preferred them like snowdrops, pale, slight and uptight, there was more sport in it. He had used to compare his wife to just such a tender flower at the beginning, before she'd gone inexplicably haywire and made their home life such a misery with her rages and her tears. He'd thought she understood about his lady friends, about the horribly bourgeois nature of monogamy, but apparently not. And so the days when she would wait for the man to refill her glass were long past. Little wonder he had been forced to spend so much time at work, and regularly seek out consolation elsewhere. He sighed deeply with the pity of it all and then remembered the receiver in his hand and spoke to his secretary, sending her to fetch an underling.

Ten minutes later there was a knock and she was back, a second figure close behind her.

'Janet, you've found him? Ah, there you are, Smith. Do come in. Now tell me, our Minister, Brendan Bracken . . . have you met him?'

'Yes . . . that is, I mean, no.'

'Red-haired; finger in every pie. You know the type.'

'Absolutely.'

'The thing is, dear Brendan's got the PM's ear – his heart, even. The old boy's completely smitten. Seems it's purely paternal, perhaps precisely that. You've heard the gossip? . . . Bracken senior away from Ireland, apart from his wife, nine months before her baby – now our esteemed Minister – is born. Meanwhile, a young and vigorous Winston *was* there and sowing the seeds of accord all over the place, apparently. Not got a clue, of course, Bracken, about the job, and to cover that up he endlessly talks up his big idea – "productivity"; as if he invented the word, as if our artists are busy "producing" turnips, not paintings.'

Smith made an effort to maintain an attentive but cool expression, not to appear too eager, too fascinated by the famous personage in front of him. Sir Kenneth Clark could certainly not be called handsome. Even though he was still a youngish man – not quite

14

forty, perhaps – his hair was sparse, oiled and combed from side to side above his forehead; small, deep-set eyes wandered disconcertingly as he spoke, settling on your lapel, your ear, or some other part. But from a wide, thin-lipped mouth crammed with yellow teeth issued words so perfectly turned, so fluid and silky, that when he gave one of his lectures it sounded as if the wireless, rather than a man, were talking to you. 'The top of the *tar* is the seat of Clark's *par*,' the clerks would chant to each other, puffing up and down the many flights of stairs with their memos, the lift being reserved for those too important to use their legs.

Clark sat down behind his desk, leaving Smith and the secretary standing. 'You know what it is that we do here at WAAC? I select artists to work for the Ministry, decide who's worthy of our support. We commission them to make the kind of work the country needs to see: the painter's eye is so much more sensitive, more truthful, than the camera lens. But that can be tricky, we have to tread carefully, steer some of them away from . . . the unsuitable. In return we pay them, make sure they survive; nobody's buying art at the moment, can't have them wasting their talent making munitions, or worse, volunteering for the front – you know how romantic and reckless artists can be . . . And if, by some miracle, we do manage to win the war, we need to have some remnants of an art world left. We're very busy here, as you can imagine, responsible for safeguarding the culture of the entire nation: artists can be demanding at the best of times . . .' He paused. 'Point is, Smith, I need an extra pair of hands for what was a difficult task, and now is a difficult and urgent task.' He looked down at the memo on his desk and grimaced. 'I heard that you'd studied art history, thought you'd be just the fellow. We've two kinds of artists on our books. There are the big guns, on a decent wage: Henry and Graham – that's Moore and Sutherland, of course – and so on. They're all looked after personally by me, no problem there. But then we have a smaller list: our ladies.'

Clark gestured to his secretary without bothering to turn towards her, or to look in her direction, and she handed him a piece of paper.

'The ladies: a particular challenge for us. We pay them per commission. They're sent to cover one subject at a time. Don't think we aren't generous – we give them money in advance, expenses and so on. But they aren't salaried like the men. Should have made them keener to please. However, getting anything out of them is a nightmare. On our balance sheet it looks as if we're paying for nothing; and now . . .' He stabbed at Minister Bracken's memo with a forefinger and pushed it across the desk so that Smith could read it. 'I will not have the whole of WAAC sent down the tube because of some recalcitrant mares. I'm creating with immediate effect a new post to deal with the problem before it destroys everything, and I'm giving it to you. Co-ordinator of Women Artists, how does that sound?'

'Yes sir, thank you very much.'

'Luckily, some days ago I arranged a meeting with the special cases – those who need a strong hand – for this morning: ten thirty. Was going to take it myself, but now it's your job. My advice?'

'Sir?'

'My advice, Smith, is: should you have to swallow more than one toad, down the biggest one first.'

'Sir?'

'I'm afraid you'll be seeing Dame Laura Knight. Ghastly old thing, knows everyone and everyone knows her. Royal Academician. Treat her with kid gloves, but get some paintings out of her! And I've called in Faith Farr: lovely to look at; bloody intractable. Rather a character. Find out what the hell's going on, there's not been a thing from her for what, six, seven months now? No contact at all. Decorative as she is, we aren't a charity. We've written to her, made ourselves clear. Time's run out. Either she comes in today with some work we can use, or she's for the chop. Don't look downcast, man. Not afraid of hard work, I hope?'

'Leave it with me,' said Smith, with a confidence he did not feel in the slightest.

'One more thing: end on a high note – Cecily Browne, she's a terribly nice girl, her father's a friend. I've not called her in because she's a problem: no. I want you to take extra care of her, make sure you pay her on time – actually, now I come to think of it, put her on a regular wage, a modest sum of course, but don't make her mess around with invoices like the other women, and no rough stuff, give her knitting parties, nurses, that kind of thing. Now, I do hope that I've made myself clear? Biggest toad first? Clock, ticking?'

Smith nodded.

'Good chap: gee 'em up, get 'em going.' Clark slapped his hand down so hard on the blotter that his fountain pen jumped. 'The Minister says we've not much time: so I'd better catch up with you again soon, say, a couple of weeks, a month? Remember, I'm counting on you to help me to save WAAC. You know what it will mean if we are "terminated", as Bracken puts it? The death of British Art, no less: *the death of British Art*.'

Chapter Five

Smith followed the secretary along hundreds of feet of corridor, and the scenery changed from marble on both floor and walls to parquet and wood panelling, to linoleum and dull green paintwork, until – her fair hair shining even in the gloom – she opened a door and ushered him in. Smiling to show all of her pretty white teeth she said, 'Don't they make uniforms in your size?' Her heels tapped briskly away.

The office was similar in size to a lavatory cubicle, with a small window high up in one corner criss-crossed with tape in case of air raids. On the metal desk sat a pile of files; behind it one chair, three waiting in front. There was an empty bookshelf. But Smith did not immediately notice the meagreness of his new environment: for him it mattered only that he now had a room of his own with a door you could shut. True, there was a square of glass in the door at head height, but this was clouded and blurry: he was almost certain you could not see in unless you stopped and pressed your face up close, although he would have to test this himself. No matter: the office was a magnificent prize in this age of obligatory sharing and 'all being in it together'.

Smith savoured his moment of triumph. Twenty-one years old and selected from the ranks of Ministry drudges to work directly with Clark – Knight Commander, Director of the National Gallery, Surveyor of the King's Pictures, head of WAAC; brightest sun in the art universe. Clark's committee had been considered brilliant at the start of the war, when the strategy had been to signal huge strength by spending a huge budget. Giving money directly to artists was evidently a stroke of genius: they always charged more than you thought they would, submitted extravagant claims for expenses, and complained throughout that they were being exploited. Crucially, Clark had avoided the problem of 'underspend', which Smith had assumed must be a good thing when he heard the term bandied about. It was soon made clear to him that if you brought things in below budget, all it meant was cuts the following year. The trick was to ask for much more money than you could ever need and always, always, get rid of the lot. Receipts had to be provided – they were strict about that – but most of the time you could get away with writing 'essentials' on the form, as long as the numbers added up. Smith had heard that 'essentials' enabled a certain high-up Ministry man to dine at the Ritz every night and furnish his home in Eaton Square with the latest luxuries, from electric mangle to nylon counterpane. Clark – so they said – ate off gold plate with his cronies, and had lived in great splendour in Portland Place before the war forced him to shut the mansion up. Even in these frugal times he dined with lords and ladies, spent every weekend in some castle or other. Perhaps one day, Smith imagined, such a life might be his? But then his eye fell on the row of chairs in front of him in the small, drab office, on the files on his desk.

Pushing aside the work lying in wait, Smith unfolded a newspaper. He could not face the task in hand, not quite yet and, after all, there was no one to report him to a supervisor for idling. He read the headlines: 'NAZI OUTRAGE! BRITISH SERVICEMEN TORTURED AND SHOT!' Two RAF gliders and a plane had crashed in Norway and it transpired now that all survivors had been executed, even though they were in battledress – the Germans must be so sure of victory they thought they could do whatever they wanted. Next was November's final tally of U-boat strikes, the worst of the war so far, and not only in the Atlantic, in the Mediterranean too, off Gibraltar and Morocco; there would be no dates this Christmas, no tangerines. To the east the news of the Soviet counter-offensive was very confused, both sides were fighting to the death in Stalingrad, and there was no reason for optimism, Smith thought, remembering the terrible stories from the summer, when attempts to push the Germans back through northern France had ended with Allied bodies stacked like sandbags on the beaches of Dieppe. Neither did Montgomery's recent victory at El Alamein alter Smith's mood – the glorious heat of the desert sun was too far away to warm him. Britain was dark, cold and hungry, at the limit of its endurance – people felt as if they were in the middle of a tunnel with no light visible at its end, and in the blackout they walked around in circles, fell into bomb craters, or blundered off the pavement into the traffic . . .

And then, further down the page, Smith saw: '18 AND RARING TO GO – COME ON, BOYS! DO YOUR DUTY!' This explained the secretary's comment: now that the age of conscription had been lowered, to be a young man in civvies you might as well wear a sandwich board with 'defective' printed on it in ten-inch letters. He shuddered. Passers-by in the street would examine him, up and down and all over, looking for his imperfections – asthma, nervous debility and severe flat feet. He would stand out uncomfortably again, just as he had at grammar school because of his name – Aubrey; his mother's choice, in homage to the artist who had provided an escape from a deprived childhood into dreams of sloe-eyed sirens and peacock feathers. The habit among the boys was to use surnames only; they had made an exception in Smith's case. Although later, when studying for his degree in art history at the Courtauld, being an Aubrey made him blend in happily with the crowd of long-haired boys and short-haired girls, not a Jane or John among them.

Smith put the newspaper aside; he would rather make a start. The top file on his desk belonged to Faith Farr, the one who had apparently stopped painting. Someone had written 'just married, check new surname' on the front; perhaps that was the reason for her lack of work? And below that file: Dame Laura Knight's. He knew of Knight, of course, had watched her in the newsreels, seen her in the newspapers showing off at the Royal Academy or one of her exhibitions, a dreadful figure in jangling beads and peculiar 'arty' fabrics, two coiled plaits clamped over her ears like wireless headphones, relics of her youth but now grey as the mooring ropes of Bankside barges. She had made her name painting backstage at the ballet, at the circus; pictures of solid, muscled women in dingy dressing rooms struggling into thick stage tights, their faces daubed with pancake and rouge. Why did she always insist on showing you the sordid, lumpen truth behind the scene, Smith wondered, when what you wanted was the ethereal vision, the nymph or undine, tantalizing, glittering and weightless? He had attempted to read her autobiography, a tedious rags-to-riches tale the width of a house brick, but he'd given up three chapters in, couldn't think for the life of him why it had been a bestseller.

The difficulty of dealing with the women artists would not lower Smith's spirits now that he was in the orbit of Sir Kenneth Clark. Some of Clark's glamour, his authority, would be sure to rub off – and now that he'd seen him close up Smith realized, with a great surge of hope, that it was not physical charm at all but pure power that kept women hovering around Clark at Ministry functions. Some were known to offer him additional services outside of work hours. The rumour was that Clark's wife, racked by his indiscretions, spent her days trying to drink her pain away with whatever was in the nearest bottle, that Clark used the air-raid shelters beneath the National Gallery for his trysts. And now to be in the proximity of such a distinguished figure! Smith looked at his watch: 10.20. The women artists would arrive very soon, he must make plans: he would need a sign for his door, headed writing paper, perhaps a card with his new title upon it? He stretched his legs out under the desk. His future dazzled with possibility.

Chapter Six

The knock on the door startled Smith: although he was expecting the three women he had been lost in visions of his own potential. But only one figure moved into the room and sat down before he could stand up or speak. In fact he could not think of what to say: her appearance captivated him absolutely. She was older than him, twenty-five, twenty-six? But that was of no consequence because she was so very beautiful, with a pale oval face and heavy chestnut hair falling to her shoulders like a Pre-Raphaelite Madonna, a mermaid, a Lady of Shalott – wistful and wan, too fragile for this world. That was the thing about the Brotherhood: frightful painters, to a man, but excellent taste in women. They could definitely pick a stunner, and would have gone for this one, although, looking more closely, Smith noticed that she had obviously fallen on hard times – the toll of the loss of a loved one, perhaps? Not unusual these days, of course, but the effect on this woman had surely been severe. She had made no effort with her appearance – her hair was unbrushed, no lipstick – and her battered hat did not show her wonderful features off to their best advantage; neither did her expression, which pinched the corners of her mouth down and scratched lines on her brow. Under a patched, green coat her dress drooped from her skinny frame and was not as clean as it could have been. There should be some kind of budget to stop a girl as good-looking as this from having to wear cast-offs. You could justify the expense by categorizing it as a morale-booster, keeping the pretty women at their best to lift the spirits.

'Mr Smith? I'm Faith Farr. I was asked . . . rather, I was *ordered* by Sir Kenneth to bring in my most recent work this morning, without fail. But they've told me I'm to see you instead.' Her expression was one of insubordination, her voice definitely below-stairs, the sound of the near-slum two-up two-down, a world away from his own suburban semi-detached.

'Come in, come in,' he said, and then wondered why he had said it. 'Lovely to meet you.'

After a pause, he added, 'Before we begin, Miss Farr – I do apologize, you're now Mrs . . . ?'

'No, Mr Smith. I'm not.'

He glanced down at his list and then back up at her, in confusion, but she did not return his look, and gave him no helpful sign as to how he should proceed while she placed her portfolio on his desk and opened it. He fidgeted in his chair, then stood up and began to examine the sheets of paper.

Only sketches. And although well observed, the subjects were all wrong: women in a café, a Lyons Corner House or some such place, sitting at small round tables, talking, eating, lifting cups to their lips. One fat lady toyed with an éclair. Another was a cruel caricature of a type all too visible in the city these days, in costume jewellery and heavy make-up – in the turmoil dropping her standards and welcoming every opportunity that came her way. There were crowds of people sleeping in the underground. This might be acceptable if Henry Moore had not already taken over the subject, his sketches showing platforms and tunnels filled with his signature monumental figures, whereas, unfortunately, in Farr's drawings the shelterers looked hungry and unwashed, like refugees in their own land. Worst of all were her drawings of seedy men loitering in the street, hat brims down, lapels turned up, and of couples stumbling out of public houses, waiting in line outside dance halls, kissing in the cinema queue.

'These are all very interesting, Miss Farr. But . . . how can I put it? What we need is something that gives people a sense that the *right* kind of thing is going on – and that the *wrong* kind of thing isn't.'

'I'm not sure that I understand.'

He picked up her file and nodded as he flicked through it, as if reminding himself of what he already knew. 'Well, you see' – he scanned the papers quickly for some titles of her previous work – 'um, last year, the oil paintings you did for us – *Concert at the Albert Hall*, for instance – they made people feel better, and what I think we would really like is for you to concentrate on that kind of thing.'

She looked at him but did not speak. He felt obliged to keep talking. 'These are technically excellent, really very nice; the economy of line . . . But – cafés, dances? These ladies – rather unpleasant, aren't they, gobbling up cake when so many are making do on rations? These unsavoury individuals, and couples, you see, doing . . . whatever it is they're doing, with so many men away.'

'It just seems to be what's happening, that's all. I can't bring myself to paint people being happy in a concert hall any more – it feels naive, foolish, given what the world is really like, the wickedness that men are capable of. And, anyway, I thought I was supposed to look around me, *to observe*.'

'Well, yes, yes you are, but it's what you *choose* to observe that's important.'

'Surely, Mr Smith, my job is to record what's there. I mean, look at Dickens – his characters aren't all attractive, or doing good. Actually, Little Nell and Oliver Twist are the least interesting of his inventions.'

'I quite agree,' Smith said, smiling, implacable. 'But what's so important about you and the other lady artists, Miss Farr – is that you're so terribly clever at *finding* the good in all of this: strength, beauty, the things that give men hope. I'm afraid I do need to see something acceptable, something more substantial, from you, and very soon, otherwise . . .'

He stopped talking as she had shut her eyes and leant back in the chair with a look of absolute defeat – white face, unhappy mouth. This was the moment in which he could take charge. He continued more gently.

'If it were up to those above me, I'm afraid we'd be letting you go, today. However, it's not up to them, it's up to me, and I say that you deserve one more chance. I'm prepared to tell them you're working well. But in return you must play your part.'

Faith Farr opened her eyes and looked at Smith, her expression closed. She did not reply. This was too much; she might show some gratitude at least.

He persisted: 'You don't seem to realize the gravity of your situation, Miss Farr. Unless I see evidence of your willingness to turn over a new leaf I'll be forced to act immediately. No further commissions: how on earth will you live? No more expenses: you know how dear decent paper and paint are these days. And I shall have to take back the sketching permit you've been given: an end to wandering about where you will in pursuit of your art. So I'll ask once again: will you, Miss Farr . . . play your part, I mean?'

'Yes, yes . . . Thank you.' She smiled, briefly, warily, but still . . . And then there was an awkward moment when they both sat motionless on either side of the desk, not looking at each other.

The sound of footsteps nearing the office, stopping outside, meant that Smith, glancing towards the door in anticipation, did not see Faith Farr's expression as she began to shuffle her drawings together. Without first knocking someone flung the door open.

'Mr Smith? This is the right office? Are you ready for us?' He recognized Laura Knight immediately. She was followed in by a young woman with mousy hair and a snub nose whose wide-apart grey-brown eyes matched her well-cut, sensible tweed suit, and who carried in pink-gloved hands a large rectangular parcel wrapped in paper. She was pretty, in a quiet, undemanding way, her face was soft in colour and contour and her expression timid. She gave the impression of being childlike, unformed.

Smith was unexpectedly delighted to see the two other women. Faith Farr's truculence had unnerved him, and he was happy to have a distraction. And Knight was quite something, dressed in some appalling cheesecloth blouse covered in crude peasant embroidery – gaudy little men leading horses, or was it camels? Augustus John and his gaggle of well-heeled art-school gypsies had a lot to answer for: it was distasteful for an old lady to draw attention to herself when decorous tones of pearl and lavender would have been so much more fitting.

'Haven't brought anything with me, couldn't carry it all, back isn't what it used to be. Next time! Thought instead I'd tell you all about it. Oh, I am sorry, my dear,' Laura Knight said, smiling at Faith Farr. 'Didn't know there was anything going on in this den.' Her voice was louder even than her clothes, and despite her advanced years and celebrity she had chosen not to amend the vulgar flat vowels that stated her Derbyshire origins boldly, as if she didn't mind people knowing. When she spoke Smith tried not to notice her grey and brown teeth framed by a fleshy, too-mobile mouth, and the smell of cigarettes with a pungent undertone like the smog escaping from a public bar when its door swings open on to the street. Altogether Knight was too large a presence for such a small office.

Dame Laura sat on one side of Faith Farr who, cowed by the other woman's fame, florid appearance and grating bonhomie, surely should have finished getting her things together and gone. But she didn't move. The girl in tweed – Smith assumed that this was Cecily Browne – took the remaining seat, and sat silently as, without waiting for an invitation, Knight launched into a long account of her latest paintings, interspersed with a request for 'real work – I want to paint soldiers, the airforce, not women *all* the time,' and a diatribe on the difficulties of getting hold of enough petrol and paint.

Smith managed to interrupt, eventually. In solemn tones he passed on Minister Bracken's message about time and money running out, and about each of them having to work at her utmost to make sure they sent new pieces for his inspection as soon as possible, in one month at the latest – otherwise they might find that there was no more WAAC left to support them. When he had finished he asked Cecily Browne to undo her parcel. She peeled back the paper nervously to reveal a painting as grey-brown as her eyes and clothes of a row of women struggling into gas masks and capes, every one of them swathed from head to foot in oilskin, not so much as an ankle on show. It might go down very well in the pages of *Woman's Own*, Smith thought, but he did not like it; there was nothing for your average red-blooded art critic to get his teeth into. Still, it would count as productive, collecting a painting on his very first morning in the job. Smith made the right appreciative noises. 'Just the ticket, Miss Browne, just the ticket.' And remembering as he spoke what Clark had said about looking after the girl, keeping her safe, he suggested that she paint a group of ladies engaged in voluntary war work as her next project. He would find her such a subject straight away in a genteel part of the city.

Rising to her feet Laura Knight turned to the women sitting next to her. 'All reports over! I expect you're both as desperate for a cup of tea as I am. Perhaps you'd like to come with me?'

To Smith's great surprise the three left together.

As the door closed behind them Laura Knight took Faith Farr and Cecily Browne each by the arm. 'May I give you some advice on dealing with Smith and his type – horribly patronizing, wasn't he, terribly insincere. Did you notice, I didn't show him anything at all, didn't give him a moment to get a word in. By the end he was so anxious to say goodbye that he didn't have a chance to criticize. Of course it is harder for you two, such young things. I remember quite how it felt. Now, let's see about that tea . . . Miss Farr, you are going to come with us? No, I insist. I know just the place, near the Academy. I have to drop in there afterwards. We'll take a taxi – my treat.'

Chapter Seven

The windows of the Kardomah café in Piccadilly had misted up and it wasn't clear, looking in, whether a table could be found. Laura, Faith and Cecily pushed through to the back, next to the dumb waiter. Some of the customers recognized Laura, moved their chairs aside, followed her progress to her seat with interest. The scent of real coffee lingered from before the war, when you could still buy it. But there was hot tea and a glowing stove; the coats of those sitting near to it steamed gently.

Laura talked about herself. The other two women listened, Faith looking down at her cup, fiddling with the handle, Cecily gazing at Laura, astonished, admiring. The worst beginning: the family fall from owning a lace factory to a life of poverty; an errant, absent father and mother dead too soon; the young Laura left with her sister and without a penny, having to make her way alone in the world. And now – the most famous painter in the country, married to a loving, understanding husband, who allowed her to live and work exactly as she pleased.

'You're wondering why I'm telling you this now. It's not to boast – well, perhaps I am a little. But to show you that you must both persevere.'

'He didn't like anything of mine. It's hopeless,' said Faith.

'Smith? I agree – terribly frustrating,' said Laura. 'Don't think I haven't knocked heads with the Ministry many, many times. I long for a big commission, the front, war at first hand. But until I find a way past them – and I assure you I will – I do what I have to.'

'I love the work, so far,' said Cecily, quietly. 'You see, I do adore painting and I must say I find things tough now that Richard's flying all the time – he's my fiancé. I get so terribly worried, and painting's a wonderful distraction, makes me feel as if I'm some use in the world. Oh I'm sorry . . . sorry, really, what a fool.' She took a hand-kerchief from her bag and blew her nose, dabbed at her eyes. 'Every time I talk about him, this happens. It is tiresome, I do apologize.'

Faith smiled politely. She had not taken to the girl in grey-brown – Cecily, was it? The painting of women in gas cloaks that Cecily had shown Smith was competent but so . . . tame; and now tears in public, too. The girl had clearly been cosseted her entire life and was as soft as her appearance: she kept her blinkers firmly on and did not see what was really happening in London, and in the other cities burning and falling all over Europe. But Faith knew the rules of conversation among women: they must all reveal something, and it was her turn. She wanted the talk to end, now, not to have to tell about herself.

When the awkward silence lengthened and still Faith did not volunteer anything, Laura addressed her directly: 'I'll bet you sit in your room a lot, on your own? You do look peaky. All well and good if you're thinking, drawing . . . but if you can't work it's the worst thing. You need a change – people, some air, a walk, a stiff drink. A night at the pictures? Even if you don't want to – especially if you don't want to.'

She glanced at Faith's ring finger. Faith saw the look and folded her hands on her lap. 'No young man? The good ones aren't easy to come by these days, I suppose. Oh, must you go?' Faith had risen, was shouldering on her coat.

'I have to be somewhere, I forgot.' The lie was obvious and embarrassing but she had to get away, could not bear the intrusion, the advice, for another minute. She began to move towards the front of the café, towards the door.

'Do hang on, don't just run away. Shall we say tea again, in a few weeks?' The volume of Laura Knight's voice, the fact that others in the café were watching the famous artist, meant that Faith could not pretend that she had not heard. She turned back to the two women, tried to smile, and was handed a card, engraved with *Dame Laura Knight, RA* and a St John's Wood telephone number. She tucked it into her pocket. But Laura was not satisfied. 'Here,' she said, passing her a small sketchbook. 'Write your address on that page so I can get in touch with you – just in case you forget.' Faith did as she was asked then disappeared out into the drizzly street. Cecily waited a moment out of courtesy, took another sip of her tea and then she, too, got up.

She hesitated before moving away. 'Dame Laura, I should like to say . . . that I wish you a Merry Christmas.'

Laura was surprised – touched – by the conventional formality of the girl, so unusual in the art world. 'The same to you, Miss Browne,' she said. 'And congratulations: I suppose you'll have a different name the next time we meet.'

'Oh no, not until February – Valentine's Day. Richard's very determined that everything should be just as we always wanted. He's very determined, full stop.'

'You've still some time to wait, then? And he's in the RAF, you said? . . . Well, I wish you both the best of luck, my dear.'

When she was alone, Laura sat thinking about the meeting with Smith. She could not make up her mind whether he was lying about the danger to WAAC. It could be that he was trying to scare his women artists rather crudely into painting flat out for him so as to appear dynamic in the eyes of Sir Kenneth – but it was true that the omens were bad for the country and, Laura felt, for herself. Although she would never admit it – not to Smith, not to the two youngsters who had just gone, especially not to her husband, Harold – she felt terribly old, worn out, and worst of all, afraid. She was afraid that her time was about to run out – if Hitler did not finish her off soon then age certainly would – and that the Ministry would not, in the end, commission the great war subject that would silence those other artists – Moore, Sutherland and their irksome gang – who dismissed her for painting the domestic front, women, the unimportant. Afraid that the power to give her this splendid opportunity, this last great chance, lay with Smith, and that he was too green and stupid to know it, or too arrogant and wrong-headed to allow it . . . Laura pulled herself together: the only antidote to fear was work. She finished her tea and opened her sketchbook at the page with Faith Farr's address scrawled on it. From memory she outlined the girl's face and the way she held herself in her tatty coat, tense and guarded. The pencil moved swiftly over the paper. That was better – she had her. Laura might be sixty-five but her hands were more fluent, more confident, than ever. The drawing was interesting; she would make use of it.

Chapter Eight

Vivienne Thayer, sitting at her dressing table in the Black villa, contemplated a portrait – of herself. A studio photograph, taken in 1936, the year she had married Sam: it had been worked on, of course – the confection of creamy skin and hair glossy as syrup had been conjured by the photographer with lights, filters and touch-up paint. And she *was* tired, woken too early by that annoying dispatch rider with her message, but her face had been so much smoother – only six years ago – the line of her chin so much firmer.

She was still much better than most, could usually bewitch a man when she chose, but then she had started out with greater natural gifts than most – eyes, lips, breasts, legs; all knockout. And a gradual falling off from such a sumptuous youth was the most difficult thing of all to bear. Even though she still tended her appearance with great care, creating the impression of an enamelled surface, exquisitely arranged and impenetrable, over the past year she had found, when she caught sight of herself, that she did not look entirely like a 'Vivienne' any more. She reminded herself increasingly, unpleasantly, of the name she'd been christened, her real name – Myrtle – that she had shrugged off soon after she started art school. A tutor there had said, 'Myrtle reminds one of Sickert at his bleakest – dreary women in dismal bedsits – very old-fashioned. Paris is where everything is happening these days: you'll get further in the art world with something French, and it would suit you much better, my dear.'

She introduced herself as 'Vivienne' when she met Sam for the first time, in the Café Royal in the winter of 1935. She had finished her training that year but nobody wanted her paintings, and so she was clinging on to a life in London by posing as an artist's model. She had persuaded her parents to let her study by telling them that after college she would come back to them in Liverpool and teach, but she had no intention of doing so, or of enduring the same fate as her mother. Her parents had married for love, and 'Look where it got us,' her mother said, bitterly. Her father was away with the merchant navy for months at a time, and when he came back the rows would begin. He never held on to enough to support them, and the smallest bedroom was taken up with his sideline, a menagerie of exotic animals smuggled back to sell on to the circus, or the zoo, but mostly to milliners and makers of ladies' accessories – stoles, handbags, gloves. In that boxroom, being pretty was no protection: the more luxuriant your feathers, the softer your pelt, the more gorgeously textured your skin, the quicker you would be dispatched. Vivienne could still hear the cries, like those of human babies, the frantic flapping and scrabbling, and then silence, as her dad prepared a delivery.

That autumn her father had died. Vivienne returned to Liverpool for the funeral, and lied to her mother about her success in London, leaving again after only a week. In truth, in the studios of Soho she was earning barely enough to eat. Then her mother's letters became frequent, imploring – could Myrtle please come back, to ease her loneliness, to help with the household bills? For the first time, she began to think of going home.

Vivienne was considering such a move – the possibility of defeat – while sitting alone in the Café, trying not to finish the one drink she could afford too quickly, hoping that one of the more prosperous artists there would like the look of her, hire her. She had turned down an advance from a boy with paint-marked corduroy trousers, a pipe and wild hair – she could not afford to waste her time on another penniless would-be Modigliani. A man sitting at the bar had watched with amusement as this little dumb show of rejection played itself out, before he sent a note to her table, asking her to join him in a glass of champagne. A big man with heavy brows and jowls, not at all handsome and much older too, but that was outweighed by the expensive suit, the offer of the best wine and the way he looked at her as she approached, as if he were under her spell. Vivienne felt in control, like a woman in a film, the kind who wore a tight satin evening dress and carried a cigarette holder. She thought herself sophisticated, but she had not yet grown out of expecting people's characters and propensities to be clearly written on their faces, for them to be open and legible.

So when Sam told her of his work as a journalist, beguiling her with his sharp, irreverent accounts of the men who made the world turn, she asked, 'Couldn't you tell, when you met Hitler, what he'd become?'

Sam had smiled at her. 'Adolf? Not immediately: nondescript little man, fat nose, bad skin. But women adore him: powerful weapon, that.' And then Sam kissed her – sitting there in the Café – and she had let him, even though she did not find him attractive and he smudged her lipstick, carefully applied in a fashionable hunter's bow.

Vivienne sighed – only seven years ago, but hadn't her mouth got thinner, too, since then? She coloured it slightly over the natural line. The photograph stared back at her from the dressing table; she would have to move it to a dark corner where it would not mock her every day. Next to it lay the memo from Minister Bracken, where Sam had dropped it that morning. Irresponsible of him to leave it where the maid might see; he must be unusually distracted and worried to slip up on the necessary precautions, even in such a small way, to leave such a document lying around in his absence.

As Head of Black, Sam was often away from the villa, at Bletchley Park or the Ministry of Information's hush-hush London office in St James's (where the most important work went on, far away from Senate House, the Bloomsbury tower which, Sam said, was so conspicuous it might as well have a target painted on its roof to give that final bit of help to the Luftwaffe). He was permitted to wander freely between the different departments selecting gobbets of information that he thought Black might be able to make use of. For security reasons – to prevent documents being mislaid and so that his movements could not be easily followed – he had been allocated his own driver and car, a black Rolls-Royce Phantom III that smelt richly of leather, wood polish and now Sam's Italian cologne.

The Ministry of Information paid for such luxuries, needing the Black team to be content with their life in Aspley Guise. Their ample expense fund meant that Sam could afford what was kept under the grocer's counter for privileged customers, and was also able to use the secret channels he had set up to funnel Black propaganda into Europe to bring back French cheese, German ham, Swiss chocolate and Italian wine and coffee. The larder in the Black villa was full of such delicacies, while the rest of the population reused tea leaves until their pots poured grey water and measured out their lard into matchbox-size pieces which had to last a week.

Black's rich diet – following on from years of journalists' lunches – meant that Sam now topped eighteen stone. Yet so capacious was the Rolls that his bulk did not appear at all cramped on the back seat, wide and well-sprung as a Chesterfield sofa. He would sit in stately comfort, a full glass on the pull-down table cleverly built into the back of the driver's seat, poring over his stack of documents, German newspapers, the text of Goebbels' most recent speech and carbon copies of the latest decrypts that the clever girl clerks at Bletchley made especially for him. So very many pretty young things dressed up in uniform and working alongside the men in this war; so difficult to be a wife.

Vivienne put her photograph face down on the dressing table, brushed her hair and went downstairs. The window on the landing – lozenges of red and purple – was streaked with rain. By the door of the workroom she paused, as a jolt of excitement deep in her belly disorientated her. She put her hands up to the door to steady herself at the thought of Frido inside, sitting over his papers.

Many of the girls at Bletchley Park had a pet German, a Prisoner of War they shared cigarettes, chocolate rations, kisses and strolls around the perimeter fence with. These lovers were captive, tame and grateful, which meant that you would see the most unprepossessing women escorted by men who were as extraordinarily handsome as they were attentive. Vivienne had done better: Frido was not a prisoner but something important in the Berlin resistance, spirited away to safety after an almost fatal encounter with the Gestapo, admired and treated with great respect by his British saviours. He was a free man, and he had selected Vivienne. He could have had his pick of any of the clerks and Wrens: twenty-five years old, tall and broad-shouldered with a fall of thick, straight hair the colour of ripe corn over his brow, he might have been a feted son of the Reich if his fine looks had not been matched by a fine character.

Vivienne pushed open the door. In what had been the drawing room of the villa – still decorated for domestic life with a showy, gold-striped wallpaper and a woollen carpet patterned with swirls and scrolls – stood a rectangle of six desks pulled together to form a large table, with a metal reading lamp at each corner and four more clustered together in the centre. The space above the fireplace, where a painting of a stag on a mountain top or a galleon at sea might once have hung, was now filled by a cork noticeboard, pinned with directives, memos and a poster: 'Bletchley Clubs and Activities – Drama! Country Dancing! Bridge!'

The three others who made up Black were at work. Charles crouched over a document, dabbing around the edges with a fine paintbrush. Tall and angular, he sat awkwardly, legs stretched out underneath the table, elbows splayed at his sides. The pooled light reflected upon a studious face, bespectacled, calm in concentration. A quiet man, he would occasionally, if prompted, talk about his job before the war – as a publisher of school textbooks – but never of how his 'hobby', as a supremely talented forger, had been discovered and had led him to Black. He had arrived at the front door of the villa one day this summer with a single suitcase. Although he'd been there only a few months, as a colleague and housemate Charles proved diplomatic: he anticipated the petty irritations of living in such close quarters and worked subtly to make bad feeling between them cool and dissolve. He managed to keep Neville in check – a poet and critic who had been chosen by Black for his literary flamboyance and the salacious cast of his mind (a verse about rifles became, in his hands, full of innuendo about 'slippery parts'). This morning, as always, Neville wore his green velvet jacket, balding at the elbows, a pipe wedged in its top pocket. His hair was allowed to curl freely, unoiled, in homage to Dylan Thomas, whose devotion to the bottle he also shared.

Over in the corner sat Frido. Vivienne allowed herself one quick look as she greeted the three men. Frido stopped hammering at the typewriter – it was a joke between them all how vehemently he punched at the machine – and took the cigarette out of his mouth to wish her good morning. He frowned back down at his work of correcting the colloquial German in the texts he was given to ratchet up the vitriol or indecency. Vivienne began to sort through her notes, to remind herself of what she had to do, and to restrain herself from looking too much at Frido in the presence of the others.

Chapter Nine

It was no good, trying to work with Frido sitting opposite her: even if she did not actually glance at him, Vivienne sensed him there and caught his scent, not of expensive cologne like Sam's, but the actual smell of his body. In attempting to behave normally, her movements and conversation felt clumsy and artificial.

The door opened and they all looked up from their work to see a smiling young woman come into the room, rather sturdily built, in spectacles and with straight brown hair combed neatly from a centre parting. Her blouse was buttoned high at the neck, but her lips shone scarlet. She was followed by Sam.

'Everyone, may I introduce Angela, found her in the Bletchley Park Drama group – she has *the* most seductive voice. She's here to try out for the role of Lotte Leckerbissen in the new show Neville's just written for us – take a bow, Neville. Thought you could all listen before we give her the go-ahead, put her on air. We're going to broadcast *Lotte* to the enemy – my BBC friends are lending us a transmitter, all on the QT, of course. *Lotte* will be such hot stuff they won't be able to turn off, and when we have their attention, we'll plant our nasty little seeds of doubt . . . grab them by the balls and twist, so to speak . . . We'll do the read-through in English now so you can all understand, and then, Frido, you translate, make additions as you think fit. Angela can cope with anything you throw at her, her German is faultless. That's right, isn't it, Angela?'

The girl began to read with relish and no hint of embarrassment:

'The bigshot officer's room was the last word in luxury, tapestries covering the wall, a roaring fire, a table set with champagne and caviar for two.

'"If you give me what I want, Lotte, you'll find me generous."

'Can I just stop for a sec, Mr Thayer? Did you want him to have a different voice? You know, manly, guttural, I can do that for you, too, might make them laugh,' Angela said.

'Yes, excellent, excellent,' Sam said.

'"Why, Herr Obersturmbannführer, whatever do you mean?"'

'As I said this, I took off my coat. He stared at me, and I looked down and blushed to see how the flames shone through my flimsy blouse, revealing my breasts.

'"When you are as close to the party leaders as I am, you aren't bound by the rules the lower orders must follow. Anything you want I can get for you, Lotte, jewellery, furs – just name it."

'As he said this, he came up close behind me. I could feel his interest.

'"Why, Herr Obersturmbannführer, what on earth are you doing?"'

'"Come, little one."'

'I was so confused, I could not think of how to excuse myself and leave, he was a powerful man, I did not want to offend him. And . . . I am ashamed to say that I was becoming aroused. I thought of my husband, deep under the sea, facing death for my sake, and still I could not help myself.

'"Give me your hand, Lotte, touch here, and . . . now, here. I have such a weapon waiting for you: shall we unload it?"'

'Then cut to music,' said Sam. 'Something exciting: swing, jazz. I'll talk to our American brothers-in-arms; something new, to hook them . . . That was superb, Angela, by the way, really very good. I think a round of applause. If you wait in the hall for me, I need a word with the troops here. We can discuss arrangements in the car.'

When Angela had shut the door behind her, Sam spoke. 'So we're agreed? She's just right, isn't she?'

'Before I begin,' said Frido, 'I shall need to know exactly who I'm writing for.'

'U-boat crews – the wolfpacks who send so many of our merchant ships to the bottom of the sea. How many convoys have we lost? I've even lined up some help for you with the lingo, make sure the slang is right. And as well as the broadcasts we need some cartoon strips to drop over the German ports. Vivienne, that's where you can help – a series, all starring Lotte.' He dropped his voice and looked towards the door. 'Obviously we won't use Angela for the visuals, I'm on the look-out for a suitable girl. Now – to other matters. Can I have your full attention for a minute? Bracken's sent a new directive. We're to up productivity.

'I know,' Sam went on, apologetically. 'It does seem odd, given the circumstances.' He addressed Charles particularly, who was looking around at the others, amused. 'But the country's up against it. And even though we don't exist on the books, they're still paying for us. The money has to be accounted for somewhere down the line. We don't want them sniffing around our expenses, deciding we aren't worth the cost – imagine a future of powdered egg and no bacon. So we'll make a splash. Hence *Lotte*, among other things I'm mulling over. What's the matter, Vivienne?'

'It feels all wrong sometimes . . . Training as an artist, I didn't think I'd ever . . .' She had always held her talent lightly; her appearance had enthralled the male lecturers and students, but her art was not nearly so interesting to them. Even so, as her affair with Frido developed so did a sense of discomfort with her work for Black, a feeling that she was falling short of her standards, of being contaminated and wanting to be clean.

'Tell yourself you're putting your hands in the dirt, to pick it up and throw it at them,' said Frido, looking at her.

'Exactly so,' said Sam. 'And we can do things the others can't. Think about it – if you were working in public, you'd have to hide everything. War artists are kept in the dark about what's really going on, strangled by permits, everything they draw or paint is pored over, to make sure it toes the official line. Because we're secret we can do anything, show everything.'

Before he left the room he took Vivienne to one side, speaking quietly. 'I'll be in London until late. Don't worry if you've gone to bed. I know it's a bore for you, stuck out here.'

A little later the rain stopped, the sky cleared. A brilliant, low winter sun cut through the trees surrounding the Black villa and raked into the workroom where Vivienne and her three colleagues were sitting, lighting up the gold stripes of the wallpaper. Neville pulled himself up in his seat and stretched his arms above his head. He looked at his watch. 'I think some air: helps me to compose.' With only three left behind the room came alive with a secret static between Vivienne and Frido, who kept their eyes averted on their work. Then, a knock on the door: the supplier of specialist papers – for German ration books, passports, leave cards, government correspondence – had arrived a day early, to show Charles his latest finds. The two men went into the dining room to lay the specimens out on the table, undisturbed. On these visits they lunched at the village pub where Neville would also soon be settled: although his daily search for inspiration began in the garden of the villa, it ended, unfailingly, at the bar of the local inn.

Vivienne and Frido, left alone in the room, continued at their tasks until they heard the others leaving the hall, their footsteps moving down the drive and away. There was silence, and an awkward moment, the switch between being at work and the sudden, unexpected possibility of intimacy, and then Vivienne got up quickly, pulling the curtains shut – they could say the sun was bothering them if anyone spotted this from outside. She stood behind Frido, who had not moved; he was waiting for her. She put her hands on his shoulders, she ran her fingers down his arms and grasped his hands. He tilted his head back, eyes shut; she moved around, bent over him and kissed him for so long that she needed to stop to take breath, and then sat on his lap and kissed him again. She took one of his hands and placed it on her breast, and guided the other under her skirt, along her thigh, between her legs.

Afterwards, lying facing each other on the floor, smoking cigarettes, clothes rucked up and the smell of the carpet on their skin, Frido said, 'You know, the more we do this, the more I want to. There are times . . . it's difficult for me to think of anything else.'

'I love you,' came from Vivienne's mouth. She had not expected to say any such thing but the words were out before she could think. She had no idea how Frido would respond, was immediately afraid she had damaged something between them and could not bear to see his expression. She looked down, saw a hairpin and took it up, turning from him to smooth over her hair and push it back into place. Then the door opened.

Charles hurried in. He put a finger to his lips. The shock of his presence in the room drove out the dazed, open lassitude after sex in a second. Her nerves snapping and shrieking, Vivienne put her appearance in order, fingers rushing at buttons, waistband, hem. Charles' expression was impassive, as if nothing untoward were happening; it did not falter as he signalled to Vivienne to sit at her desk. He gave no indication of being affected by what he had come across, of what he might think about Vivienne and Frido. Frido stood, pulling the arms of his shirt down, doing up his trousers, twisting his tie around to the front again. Charles had just moved over to the curtains and was opening them when Sam appeared at the door.

'It seems a shame, that's all,' Charles began, as if the three of them were deep in conversation. 'Sam! Thought you were up in town?'

'Can you believe it? Wrong blasted day,' Sam said. 'Only realized when I went through the paperwork in the car; I'd read most of *The Times* first as well, we were halfway there.'

'Devil of a job working with this bilious wallpaper all around now it's stopped raining,' said Charles. 'Every time the sun shines we have to shut the bloody curtains . . . made it difficult for us all this morning, I can tell you. God knows how your wife copes, with her artist's eye: must be doubly hard for her.'

Chapter Ten

Late that evening – eleven thirty or thereabouts – the usual lavish dinner at the villa had ended and the other members of Black moved into the drawing room with their cigars and brandy. Vivienne, though, said she would stay behind in the dining room to talk to the maid about the food for tomorrow. In truth she needed a moment before she rejoined them, to recover from the torture of wondering what Charles was going to do with his knowledge of her affair with Frido. Charles had given no sign, he behaved that evening just as he always did, the quietest among them but not shy, joining in if he had a point to make, courteous as ever. The atmosphere in the villa had altered, though, as if there were a clinging, invisible web connecting Charles, Frido and herself, so that neither of the men could move, direct a look, or talk, without Vivienne feeling it, and the effort not to show this, to respond as normal to Neville's banter and Sam's stories, was gruelling.

Alone in the dining room, Vivienne sat back in relief while the maid began to clear the table, a ruined landscape of crumpled napkins, dirty glasses, plates and cutlery. Only the flowers were still in order at the centre, although Vivienne noticed one bud, brown and curling at the edges before it had even opened. She snapped it off, irritated. She gave her orders to the girl, and was standing by her chair, picking up her evening bag, about to go through and find the men, when the door opened and Charles came back in.

As the maid, carrying a tray, went past him he said, 'Leave the rest until the morning, please.' He shut the door behind the girl, and stood with his back to it, waiting as her footsteps moved away across the corridor.

Vivienne could not think how to react, what was it he wanted? Eventually she said, 'Thank you . . . for your discretion today.'

'There's no need. We're holed up so close together here, aren't

43

we?' he said. 'Not a recipe for civilized life. You feel uncomfortable about what I saw – a private moment between you and Frido. But I've something to confide in return. Do sit down.'

She hesitated; his tone made it sound like an instruction, rather than a request. But he sat down opposite her so that she felt obliged to do the same. They looked at each other across the wreckage of the dinner table.

Charles moved two glasses away from in front of him, brushed aside some crumbs carefully, and reached into his pocket. 'My job here isn't quite what you think. Cigarette? To be frank, I've been sent to keep an eye on things here. Black's work is of the utmost importance at the moment, but there are doubts about exactly what's going on, about whether information is being leaked to the other side. You can understand the concern? You send things back and forth across the Channel unhindered. Neville is not an issue at all, but Sam – Sam has contacts right at the top of the Reich, Frido has a secret network in Berlin . . . And then I come to the villa, and it feels to me as if games are being played, people aren't quite what they seem. And what do I find today? It's a dreadful tangle, isn't it? You and Sam . . . you and Frido.'

Vivienne tried to appear impassive as Charles spoke, but she refused his offer of a match, jerking her head away. She opened her evening bag and took out her lighter – tortoiseshell with 'VT' in diamonds – a gift from Sam. She put her cigarette to her lips without trembling, but had to click the lighter three times before the flame caught.

Charles pressed the point gently. 'Rather a delicate situation, the three of you.'

Vivienne wanted to say that it was none of his bloody business; she felt exposed, humiliated. But Charles had the power to use what he had seen against her. And while she and Sam had agreed that they might find entertainment in the arms of others, he would not allow her a lover in the same house, the knowledge of it shared among his colleagues. Such things had to be skilfully managed – for a wife. If Charles were to tell Sam, the affair would end immediately, and Frido would be sent away.

'I know that you're worrying that I might inform your husband. But you see, that's not my intention, although unfortunately he's bound to find out about your affair if it's written up in my report. What matters to me is that those above me won't like it if they know.'

'Who won't like it? Who's above you? Do you mean to tell me you work for Intelligence?'

Charles said nothing in reply, just looked at her steadily so that she felt compelled to carry on. 'They wouldn't have set Black up unless they were sure of us, we've all been vetted. And why are we so important all of a sudden? We only make propaganda – pictures, documents, broadcasts – who knows if any of it makes the blindest bit of difference . . .'

Charles watched her face as she talked, as if he were trying to decide whether he believed her. She spoke again, her voice flatter now: 'Do you really have to tell them about me, about Frido?'

'I'm afraid so. I'm under orders to describe exactly what I find here . . . unless . . .'

Vivienne struggled to guess where Charles was taking the conversation, what it was he was about to demand; she must understand in order to know how to respond. He sat, observing her in his usual calm, unreadable way, giving no sign of what he was leading to. But then, she thought, it was probably the most obvious thing. She smiled at him tentatively.

'No, I don't want you, Mrs Thayer. I'm sorry to put it so bluntly. You are a beguiling woman, but this isn't a film, and there's far more at stake than coercing you into bed. Let me explain. What happened today – when I came across you with Frido – it made me think, that we could find a way out of this situation together. If you were to help me I might be able to edit certain things out of my report, give them only what they need – and no more.'

'Help you, how?'

'You look very pale. May I offer you a drink, a little more brandy, perhaps? Good. Take a minute . . . Your husband isn't a problem, as far as I can tell at the moment. I'm pretty certain that he's genuine – his love of his country, his affection for you – even if he is so . . . exuberant that he can appear to be rather a fake. And then, he is so utterly sure of himself. I find his company enjoyable, but others, well, it rubs them up the wrong way. I'm sure that's part of the reason there's a question mark over Black at the moment.'

Vivienne put her glass down, turned her head away and placed her hands on the edge of the table, looking at her fingers.

Charles continued, 'He's actually rather idealistic, isn't he, Sam? Straightforward, not fond of paradox, of complexity, even though he likes to think of himself as a worldly man – a cynic, even.'

Taking her hands from the table Vivienne looked directly back at Charles again. Of course Sam couldn't be implicated, but the patronizing description hurt her. 'He is certainly innocent, but he's not so utterly transparent.'

But Charles ignored her. 'Frido, though, is more of a challenge. I'm not entirely convinced about him. Perhaps he's a little too perfect? And he won't confide in me so that I can get what I need to make a judgement. You, on the other hand . . .'

'Frido doesn't tell me anything important, only small things . . .'

'Yes, but it's the small things that interest us, the intimacies that lovers share in those unguarded moments, you know how it goes – his memories, his friends, his life in Berlin. You might encourage him? He'll reveal far more to you than he would if we were to haul him in to an interr – . . . view. And, however trivial such information might seem, Intelligence can use it, they can check it all, you see, make sure he is what he says he is.'

'No, I can't do it. You're asking me to spy on him.'

'Your belief in the value of loyalty is admirable, Mrs Thayer, but you haven't grasped its implications. What I am going to say to you now will sound rather harsh. I'm trying to make you listen to me for your own good, to avoid having to hand the situation here at the villa over to someone else, who won't have my compunction about the fragile relationships torn apart, the reputations injured, to get to the truth. I am asking you to act, to provide information, *out of loyalty* – to Britain first, but also to your husband and, *yes*, to Frido. Presumably you wouldn't have become involved with Frido had you the slightest doubt about him? I do hope that's the case. But I need proof. I am only asking you to demonstrate your faith in Frido.

If you are right, then he is in absolutely no danger from any material you pass on to me, and it will only serve to vindicate him. Of course there's a small cost to you, the pain of concealing a secret, but then, you are quite skilled in that regard.'

Vivienne remained silent, looking at her hands which lay palm up in her lap and cold, although the lines describing her fate were wet with sweat.

'Let's examine your situation from the outside. You sleep with two men under the same roof. Now I know that you're an artist, you've lived in a different world from the rest of us, studios, cafés, bohemia, the normal rules don't apply. Others have less tolerance, a more rigid view. As far as they'll be concerned, you've betrayed your husband with an employee of his, and a German. Remember, for most people Frido is only that, his shining record doesn't count for much, and if the story gets out somehow, imagine the public outrage that Frido has been living such a comfortable life – not interned behind the wire with the rest of his kind – and enjoying himself with one of our women at the same time. He of course won't bear the brunt of it, there'll be an element of "boys will be boys". It's always the female who takes the blame. All sorts of filthy assumptions will be made about you – you're attractive and have a complicated personal life, which in their eyes means that you are duplicitous, promiscuous and dangerous. There are posters warning the public about such women all over London, aren't there? They'll love hating you, the story will run and run. Where will you go? It's not as if you can leave the country. And Black will be finished, shutting down the villa is the least of it, everyone here will be under suspicion. You see, I'm trying to avoid all of this . . . I simply want to reassure myself, and them, write my report, and be on my way.'

'I have to think.'

Charles rose from the table. 'Please bear in mind, if you do tell anyone about our conversation it will be taken very badly, by me, and my superiors. You'll be obstructing a government investigation, hampering work that's essential to the safety of the nation at this perilous time. We only want to ensure the loyalty of everyone at

Black. You should want to help us. This is a test for you, too. And you know that should you inform Sam or Frido it will be obvious, they're both proud men, headstrong, not cautious, and they'll react immediately, make a huge fuss. That would be a disaster for you, and for them.' He offered Vivienne another cigarette. 'Of course, I'll give you a few weeks. We'll have another chat then.'

Wanting to appear in control she took one, looking at Charles steadily as she did so, but then she fumbled with her lighter and dropped it, heard it land on the floor, and had to bend down in front of him, feeling under the table to find it. By the time she lifted her head he had left the room.

Chapter Eleven

Vivienne lay in bed unable to sleep for so long that in desperation she crept back downstairs when the house was dark and still to drink a tumbler of brandy, and then another two, sitting alone in the dining room with the lights off. Nothing helped, nothing blurred or diminished the scene with Charles which remained sharply, monstrously, defined. Only when the chill had crawled right up her spine did she go back to bed. She fell immediately into an uncomfortable sleep, and woke with a start in the morning, later than usual, a curdled taste in her mouth. Sam was downstairs already, so at least she did not have to face him first thing.

She would go out, into the garden, try to think, calm herself with a cigarette before work. But as she reached the bottom of the stairs, she heard a voice, raised, from the workroom: Frido.

Vivienne crossed the hall and opened the door; there was Sam standing with Frido and Charles, while a man she did not recognize lounged on one of the chairs, balancing it on its back legs, smoking, smiling, gazing about him. He wore a brown uniform and a Military Police officer stood over him. He must be a German POW, thought Vivienne, and quite unconcerned by the argument raging around him as he can't understand it.

'I won't work with him, it's too much to ask,' Frido said. His eyes bright with fury, he would not even look at the seated figure in brown.

'Heaven's sake, Frido, it doesn't matter why he's agreed to tell us about the U-boats, only that he knows his stuff,' Sam said.

'Yes, it does. It does matter.'

'He'll make sure we get the slang exactly right, code names, injokes; it'll make our broadcasts to them that much more effective, really gain their trust, then we can start to plant our stories undetected.'

49

'But that . . . that . . . *shit*,' said Frido. 'He laughed, said he'd enjoy helping us to send them all to the bottom of the sea, because it served them right for demoting him. He lived alongside those poor bastards, most of whom will drown and they know it – *die Glückliche Zeit* is over. They didn't choose their work, the boats are manned by conscripts now – there are so few volunteers. And here he is betraying them for no reason at all, just because they disciplined him. How have I come to be working alongside such a man? How can we be on the same side? I can't accept it, I can't tolerate it.'

'Actually, Sam, I do agree with Frido,' said Charles. 'Does it have to be him? I know he showed willing, but the over-eagerness, the crowing, it's too much. I can see why it's impossible. He's betraying his side out of petty vengeance, he's not under duress.'

'That's the bloody point, we haven't had to force the information from him, he's volunteered it. That's good, isn't it? Oh, oh I see, were we to put the screws on him, it would be better?'

'Not so, not so, but . . . all the same.'

'And then, following your logic, if he supported the wrong side, killed our boys, terrorized his own people, but loved Hitler, steadfast, unwavering, refused to help us, he'd be OK too?' Sam waved his hand, resignedly. 'All right, all right, this is getting us nowhere, take him away. We'll have to find another. But can I remind you, Frido, we've a war to win, we can't afford such niceties of feeling. All that matters is that we get the upper hand, not how we do it or who we ask to help us along the way. You can be sure that our enemies are not so fastidious. You know as much, I'm surprised at you. Wait, you're going straight to Bletchley? I'll come with you, see if I can dig out someone my colleagues here might find acceptable.' Sam left with the prisoner and the guard.

Vivienne spent the day finishing a cartoon to be sent behind enemy lines in Greece. As she worked, she was horribly aware of Charles' eyes lighting on her from time to time; they seemed to graze and prick her skin. His championing of Frido – the charade of it – nauseated her. Charles was trying to insinuate himself, she could see it happening. He distrusted Frido but was pretending – wonderfully – otherwise, to lure him into friendship. But something else about the scene rankled, too. Before Charles' conversation with her, she would have interpreted the altercation about the prisoner that morning straightforwardly, as further evidence of Frido's sterling character. But suppose – just imagine – that Charles were right, that Frido was not who he pretended to be. Frido, then, would not want to have another German around in the villa. If Frido was working for the Nazis he might not be able to 'tolerate', as he put it, having in close proximity a fellow countryman so blithely betraying Hitler. And the prisoner might also become a threat, by complaining to others of his kind back at Bletchley Park about Frido living in luxury, telling them his name, describing him. There was always the danger – remote but still conceivable – that Frido might be known to one of them, that details of a past he wished to hide might thus emerge. If Frido were playing such a hazardous game of double-bluff, he would not want to take the slightest risk of being recognized . . .

Vivienne stopped herself, the whole thing was absurd. She thought of Frido, how they had been with each other. Doubt had been implanted like a splinter of glass now rising to pierce the surface of her thoughts, but she would try to ignore it. She would not let Charles sully what she and Frido shared. But how could she deal with Charles? A few weeks, he had said, before he expected a response from her.

In the late afternoon, when the day's work was over, Vivienne went straight up to the bedroom, excusing herself from tea with the others in the drawing room. Half an hour later Sam appeared at the door and, noticing her distressed face, said, 'Bad atmosphere today, not happy that you should have to put up with it. Right, then, town tonight: the cinema, dinner? Far from this bloody villa. I need to get away too. I'll have the car brought back round to the front.' If he knew his Vivienne, she needed a break from the stifling quiet and stillness of the fields and trees, to be able to breathe freely again among the rush and clamour of the city.

Chapter Twelve

As they drove into London that evening the fog in the broken streets made them difficult to pass through and Sam and Vivienne missed the newsreels and the opening credits. But at least one could watch a film again. When the war began they had closed all the cinemas in the city: the Germans were not to have the satisfaction of wiping out an entire matinée crowd. Several months later, when it appeared that the enemy's master plan did not, after all, involve the destruction of the Odeon, the Gaumont and the Regal, the cinemas had reopened. Although, like everywhere else now, the cinema heaved with people, Sam and Vivienne went up to the dress circle which usually stayed empty, not because of the expense but because the fear of sitting up there in the Blitz was still alive in Londoners' memory. At least up here there wasn't an obstacle course of feet and knees and a chorus of cross sighs to contend with. From above their heads the shaft of light from the projector picked out the crown of Vivienne's hat – tall, with a narrow brim, like a miniature topper, and a net veil gathered behind.

As soon as she began to find her bearings in the gloom – the air as stale and heavy as the blankets they handed out at emergency shelters – Vivienne knew the film wasn't up to much. It wouldn't distract her from Charles and his threat. And Sam was being unusually affectionate, holding her hand, looking at her with concern, making it worse. The same woman as usual filled the screen – the actress might change from film to film but it didn't make any difference: a neat body and flowery frock, flat hair and clipped voice, through which a tremor of emotion was allowed to (hesitantly, occasionally) waver out. She was talking with her husband. The war was just about to begin. He – Vivienne recognized Noël Coward – would be leaving the very next day to ready his ship. Only they didn't really mention it at all. There was no tearful goodbye, no embrace.

Although the wife did bring herself to ask if she could visit him aboard before he left.

'You'll have to, whether you like it or not: my cabin's got to be made presentable.'

'Does the chintz look all right?' she asked.

'Absolutely first class.'

Floating above a plateau of tobacco smoke, the home on the screen radiated calm. Although Noël Coward struck a decidedly false note – surrounded by children and wife on the sofa, he looked about as comfortable as if shoehorned in between Himmler and Goebbels.

Sam squeezed Vivienne's hand again; she could smell his expensive scent, part of the air of ease and affluence that he gave out, which had intoxicated her from their very first meeting, more powerfully than sexual attraction or mutual affinity could ever have, or so she had believed before she encountered Frido. And Sam's infatuation with Vivienne had lasted nearly two years before his attention began to widen its focus away from her alone, to become habitual rather than urgent – by then they were safely husband and wife. He had roared with laughter when he heard her real name – as he had to during the wedding formalities. 'Thank God you chucked it. Myrtle might have put me off . . . No, it wouldn't really, darling, I'm only joking.' He immersed himself in completing her transformation into Vivienne. He dressed her in couture, Vionnet, Mainbocher and her favourite, Molyneux. He arranged for her voice to be improved – stripped of its Liverpool accent. He educated her eye – showed her fine furniture and architecture – and her palate, taking her to chic restaurants where he translated the menu for her, and there was always a party to go on to.

Perhaps thinking about Sam had transmitted itself to him in the darkness of the cinema. His hand brushed Vivienne's knee and started to slide up her thigh. This is what they always did when the movie was a dud. But all that Vivienne desired at the moment was that his fingers return to the armrest of the cinema seat and lie still. She wanted to watch the film, forget everything and everyone: Sam and Frido, what Charles had said, and what she was going to do about it. She put up with Sam's attentions until she'd had absolutely enough and shifted in her seat. Sam said something to her, stung by the rebuff; she felt guilty and started to apologize, he asked her what on earth was wrong, and then they both realized they were not alone up there at all – there was someone in the darkness to Vivienne's right. A voice said clearly, '*Will* you please shut up?'

Vivienne looked around in that direction. In the same row, but about five seats along in the darkness, sat a woman holding a sketchbook. As the cinema screen brightened into an outdoor scene the woman was momentarily illuminated in profile. Vivienne, surprised, recognized her. She had seen her arrive at Frascati's – about a year ago – just as they were paying their bill. Sam had looked her over, as he did every attractive woman who crossed his path. But what had made Vivienne notice her, what had struck her so hard that the woman had stayed in her memory, was that she encapsulated everything Vivienne herself wanted to be, and was not. Vivienne had watched as she sat down. Her dinner companion had not yet arrived – she made the waiter leave both place settings – but she didn't seem perturbed. Coolly, she pushed the cutlery and napkin aside to place a sketchbook and pencils on the table. She began to draw the other customers, intent on her work, a serious artist oblivious to the glances of those around her. And she looked wonderful as she did it, her oval face, chestnut hair and slight figure complemented by a velvet hat with a curve of feathers that shone green and purple like beetle wings, and a black suit buttoned up to the neck where the jet beading caught the light. Set off by the portly Victorian gilt cherubs and blowsy wine-coloured plush of the restaurant, the severe clothes made her appear self-possessed and distinct from all the other women, from Vivienne, so obviously on display, selling herself with her cleavage and bare arms. Vivienne was enthralled and then annoyed, and when Sam looked at the strange woman a second time, she said sharply, 'Darling, perhaps you'd like to invite her over? Just think, she might do your portrait, then you'd have a reason to stare at her.' That stopped him.

And here she sat now, in the cinema after all this time, and drawing again. Vivienne could just make out her hand moving slowly over the paper, tracing the outlines of the rows of people below. She probably had some kind of proper artist's commission. Like that ridiculous old Laura Knight in the *Picture Post* photograph, perched high up on the rubble left by an air raid, balancing an easel and pal-ette, and wearing, of all things, hoop earrings and a frock that made her look as though she was on her way to a costume party as a gypsy, her ugly old face sitting on a frilled collar like a suet pudding on a doily. And her paintings – always the same: plain women in frumpy uniforms pulling together like jolly good sorts on the Home Front. How could she stand to churn them out?

A picture of the drawing Vivienne had finished that day came into her head, the design of a salacious cartoon to be printed on several thousand 'greetings cards' and dropped upon occupied Greece. The Greeks were being starved to death by their German invaders, and any protesters shot without ceremony. Black was trying to help loosen Wehrmacht fingers from their rifles. The German soldiers would, hopefully, stop to pick up the cards because Vivienne's drawing would bring thoughts of sex to them, fluttering miraculously down from the sky: for a moment they could remember and imagine, escape from death, hunger, dirt and fatigue. But the lust would quickly turn – because of the details of the drawing – into fear as to what might be happening back at home, and they would find it difficult to fire with the same zeal. Or that was the idea, anyway.

To attract as many as possible, the 'cards' must fall from the plane like a shower of obscene confetti: their size, and the amount of printer's ink used, had to be carefully controlled so that they remained light. Yet the drawing was complicated: it had to show a foreign interloper (swarthy of skin, large-nosed, obviously not a son of the Reich) taking advantage of a buxom young Hausfrau while her husband was away serving at the front. The couple had to be entangled in a position in which you could see, immediately, what they were up to, but also exactly who they were. This was where it became tricky. Clothes were important, and the figures couldn't be lying down, as one of them would be half-hidden. So, then, stand them up, problem solved. But how? A side view would be best, you could see both of them clearly. The setting had been obvious to Vivienne: it had to be the kitchen, the very heart of the home that the soldier husband was away fighting for. But then there was another problem: what should she include to indicate a kitchen, while not crowding out the central characters? Here, Vivienne had a moment of inspiration, remembering the Rowlandson prints that hung in their bedroom – tarts and lechers pictured in graphic detail using only line and a limited range of colours. Of course Vivienne couldn't mimic the subtlety of his draughtsmanship and tone, not with the crude stuff she had to work with, but then there was to be no subtlety about her design.

Against a yellow background, strong enough to catch and hold the glare of the Greek sun, Vivienne had outlined in black a stove with bubbling saucepans and a window with flowery curtains. A cat and a crying baby in a highchair (why not go the whole way?) were sketched in to either side of the lovers. A framed portrait of Hitler hung above them. And how the pair filled the space! Drawn in heavier black, the girl had been pushed over the kitchen table, her thick pigtails swinging with the movement, with at each end a pink bow, to match the colour of her mouth in an O of surprise and of her round doll cheeks, and then carrying the eye down to his cock, in the same colour (Vivienne made a tacit acknowledgement to Rowlandson: he knew how to draw these things clearly). Her laced bodice was black, also her dirndl skirt; you took in her arched body straight away, and could see her skirt had been pulled right up over her waist. His clothes – a scumble of greenish grey – stood out against the yellow kitchen.

The light on the cinema screen shifted – a battleship was about to set sail – and Vivienne remembered where she was, sitting in the cinema, and what Charles had said. She put her arm around Sam's shoulders, to feel the reassuring heft of him close to her. They were talking again, she was telling him about the greetings card and he was laughing, when there was a thump and clatter from one side. The woman who had hushed them had slumped to the floor, where she lay, unmoving. As they watched, uncertain as to what to do –

Sam half-rising from his seat – the woman pulled herself up, sat for a few seconds, head down, and then rushed out. After that Vivienne forgot about everything for a while, absorbed by the scene onboard ship, with sailors running back and forth, the deck lurching, rain and seaspray whipping at them, enemy guns blasting. There was no way, surely, that they could survive?

Chapter Thirteen

Until she fainted and had to leave the cinema, Faith Farr had been sketching the audience and the pictures on the screen. She had been managing to work until the chatter of the couple in the blackness further down the row of seats made her tense. The man was talking loudly, laughing, as if he were not in a cinema, with some female in a silly hat. Faith had not eaten that day, she had lost her appetite; in any case there was no decent food in the shops. And the shifting light and warm, fusty air did not help. Suddenly cells, tiny sea creatures or fireflies, floated and whirred across her vision which then shut down with the leaden rush of a theatre safety curtain, and she forgot who and where she was and fell to the floor.

When Faith came to she knew only that she must get out. She scrabbled her things together; stuffed her pencils and sketchbook into her handbag, felt around for her hat – crushed even further out of shape where she had fallen on to it – and sat with her head bent forward for a time to try and settle the spinning sensation. And then, pulling her old green coat tightly around her, clutching it at the neck where it was missing a button, Faith made her way to the exit.

If she walked quickly and steadily and tried not to think, she might get back home in one piece. So upsetting to find that she wasn't ready even for the cinema – she used to go to the pictures whenever she could, three times a week sometimes, and she would draw if she was alone, sitting up in the dress circle where the rows of empty seats meant she could work without hindrance and with a sweeping view of the crowd below. She would also sketch the films themselves, you could take an entire scene in at a glance and try to note it down; this was excellent training for the hand and eye. Tonight's feature – dull as it was – had lots of useful subjects; and as she reached the door she looked back to see the London family lined up for the wedding picture, the photographer's round owl glasses echoing the circle of his camera lens. A wedge of light cut into the auditorium behind her as she hurried away.

She had been too ambitious – that was it – trying to manage a whole evening far from the safety of her room and drawing too, just because Laura Knight had suggested it, when she hadn't been able to cope with either for so long. Faith's heart banged in her chest and icy, sinewy fingers squeezing her stomach stroked up into her throat as she switched on her torch and went out into the night.

She could not afford the underground or the bus. She had indulged herself with a more expensive seat in the cinema, to try and ease herself into working again, and had no more money to spend that night, not when her position at WAAC was so precarious. Faith folded her arms across her chest, holding her handbag close to her as she walked. These days after sunset there were many dangers in the city, rubble lying around, holes yawning open in front of your feet, figures lurking, waiting. At least she knew this whole area. Her map of London had unfolded over the past few years, from her parents' terrace down by Blackfriars Bridge to Miss Roy's boarding house in Kilburn, then to the beautiful flat in Hampstead as David's bride, and recently, now that everything had changed, out to Holloway, alone.

The city was black as coke as she went along; you couldn't begin to imagine the commotion of less than two years earlier, the fires and flaring lights of the Blitz. Often now the calm and the complete darkness made it seem as if you weren't in London at all. The impression of a long space slicing out in front of you and the height of the buildings enclosing you on either side made it feel like walking in a ravine between sheer cliffs. Tonight, the fog made it sinister in a stagey kind of way, the setting for a figure wrapped in a cloak to go swirling through, like the Grimpen Mire in *The Hound of the Baskervilles*, and inching along, you felt like Sherlock Holmes in the middle of a mystery story – no, less in command, actually, more like Dr Watson. She shivered and clutched her bag more tightly, held her coat together at the neck.

Faith had seen some horrible things. Once, in Balham, she walked past a hole in a street as big as a house, and poking out of it, at an angle, like a dropped toy, was a bus. The front of the row of buildings behind it had fallen away and the private possessions of the people that had lived there were all on show: two single beds balanced on a floor which sagged like a hammock – they had both slipped in towards the middle, resting close together after years of chilly distance. She had tried to take it all in but she couldn't begin to think of how to draw it. Everything looked too absurd, too difficult to make it look believable with a pencil and paper, and then, the Ministry would not approve of the subject. Timbers were casually piled up as if they were as light as kindling, ripped curtains fluttered like party streamers, there were tangles of fabric – clothes and bedding stained black and brown with blood. Some other details: a door open to show a WC, impossible to get to now as there was no staircase up to it, a house that had become only four walls and a roof, the rooms inside all gone, apart from one at the very top – a nursery, where there was a cot with its side down. Next to the hole that had swallowed the double-decker there was still the sign 'BUSES STOP HERE'.

The memory of this scene absorbed Faith's attention. She didn't notice she was off course. Turning around in the dark to retrace her steps and scanning the pavement with her torch to search for directions – painted on the ground these days to stop lost pedestrians from shining their lights up and attracting the Luftwaffe's sights – she bumped into a couple, giggling as they grabbed hold of each other and moved forward in the blackness. It must be awful, she thought, to be in love now. That was all over for her. The pair staggered off as if they were one badly jointed body with four legs. But their noise did not disappear, it merged into another footfall, fast and steady.

As Faith quickened her pace the steps sped up, rhythmic and determined. She did not dare to turn around and confront her pursuer – there was no one else on the unlit street to shout at for help. But she could not just keep going as the man – the steps were heavy and the strides long – whoever he was, would catch up with her, and soon. As she reached a corner where she remembered the road bent and then forked, she decided without even knowing it that she would stop and hide.

Faith moved forward to where the road divided, clicking off her torch and stepping swiftly into the denser darkness to one side. She felt her way backwards, not willing to turn away as she pressed into a wall and held herself still. She peered into the night air. Across the street the drops of water that made up the fog swirled and formed into a silhouette, a man keeping to the pavement and scarcely separating himself from the dark windows and doorways behind him. Looking harder she realized, with horror, that he was familiar, lean and slightly stooped – it couldn't be . . . her husband, David? He moved along the street slowly, past her, taking great care, turning his head methodically from side to side – searching – merging with the shadows and then detaching himself again. Faith did not wait to see where he would go next.

She ran back the way she had come and then turned off again, through the backstreets: she would have to reach her flat another way. She ran and did not stop. She saw a garden square ahead, the railings gone for munitions: she could hide there and wait, among the bushes and trees. She pelted towards it and crashed at full force into the wire fence that had replaced the railings, invisible in the dark.

Seconds later, sitting on the ground, winded, Faith looked about her. She had lost her hat and torch, one stocking had fallen down, her lips and throat burned from panting in the damp, freezing air. She still had her handbag, it was lying by her side. She gingerly touched her hand to her face where it had hit the mesh, and sat, forcing her breaths to slow and steady, to be noiseless.

Could it really have been David, that apparition in the fog? She had not seen her husband since that night nearly half a year ago, her last in their flat, in his bed. She had fled in terror while he slept, had left him after only eight months of marriage. How had he appeared now? She stood up, fastened her stocking, straightened her skirt and coat, cupped her hands over her mouth to warm them.

'You've been hard to find, Faith.' Behind her, a voice, David's voice. She whirled around to see him step out of the shadows and towards her, his face spectral and then solid – too close. She felt a hand on her waist, familiar fingers touched the side of her neck, her hair, there was a smell of alcohol. She brushed his hands off, took a step away from him.

'Everybody's hard to find these days. Anyway, I didn't want you to find me.'

He spoke gently: 'You know I had to. I've come for what you stole from me. Where is it?'

'Somewhere safe,' she said, lifting her chin, defiantly. His arm had found its way back around her.

'Faith . . . look at you. Are you eating? You need someone to take care of you. I haven't only come back for what you took, I've come for you, too. We did love each other. You were right to leave me, I accept that. But I've changed, come to my senses. I've stopped it all, don't even work for the Ministry any more, don't go near it. You've no need to be scared, to hide yourself away . . .'

She was so tired of running. She wanted to cry, to lean on him, to give in. And then she remembered.

'I don't know who you are any more.'

His voice tightened to a hiss. 'Always so wilful. You have to listen, even if you no longer care for me. You have to give it back to me. They won't let you make use of what you've taken, they'll find you.'

'They never will. It's somewhere safe. You didn't think I'd keep it with me, did you? I shan't tell you where. I'll hand it in to the police, the Ministry . . .' Her voice was rising.

He let go of her, looked at her, considering. 'Ah, but you haven't yet, have you? And I know why. I told you, I've lots of friends. You don't know who to turn to, who to trust. How can you be sure that you don't approach the wrong people? How can you ever be certain? Poor, poor Faith. Just give it back to me. Let's go together, now.'

He had taken her hand as he spoke, and she allowed him to . . . the memory of their skin touching. Now he gripped it. Faith opened her mouth to scream, but no sound came. She struggled to free herself but David was much stronger.

Suddenly in the blackness to the side of them a space opened, a slit of light grew into a rectangle, there was a hallway, two soldiers leaving it, and behind them stood a woman in a dressing gown fallen open to reveal a slice of her breast. Faith yelled, not words but just noise. She pulled herself free from David's grasp. The soldiers laughed, one saying, 'She don't think much of you, mate. Come over here, love, we'll show you how it's done.'

Faith bolted along the side of the garden square and up a road. She could hear David following after a few moments; he had waited until the potential witnesses were out of sight. His delay might have given her a head start, but he was taller, fitter, and she was faint, half-starved, exhausted. The steps behind were growing closer and more rapid. He had seen her, she could not escape him.

Around a corner she flew, her heart bursting, her legs failing. There was an entryway – she threw herself into it. She rattled the handle, frantic. A miracle: the door opened.

She stepped through, into space, and tipped forward, arms spread like a sleepwalker. Then her feet hit a slope, a scree of brick dust and soil that slid under her, throwing her on to her back as it carried her down.

At the bottom she lay still, gazing up at the night sky: there was no roof. She had fallen into the cellar of a bombed-out house. They must have built a bank out of the debris to shore up the façade and the street, to prevent it from collapsing, and that had saved her life. A sheer ten-foot drop might have been the end of her.

Faith listened, heard David's footsteps go by the door, but they didn't pause, they carried along and away. Still she did not stir. She was terrified, of him, of what had happened as she fell. She waited for a time, trying to understand what surrounded her in the dim light: she could just make out the legs and arms of furniture, a child's white rabbit toy, the frame of a mirror with a single jag of glass still in place. Her hands smarted, her whole body ached, but she found that she could move – her neck, her back, her limbs. Eventually she scrambled to her feet and picked her way slowly to the top.

Faith hobbled back through the door. A sign over the street said 'ANGEL' – thank God she had been running in the right direction, she felt so sick and weary that she would have had to lie down right there if she had been on the wrong side of the city. She stood rubbing her knees, her elbows.

It would take her twenty minutes, if she walked quickly, to cut across and up the Caledonian Road. She would force herself to concentrate, to look only in front of her and not to think about David, about anything apart from getting herself home, closing the door behind her and locking it. She would recite poems to herself as she went. The pattern of the words regimented her footsteps. She half-marched, half-ran, back to her own street.

As she reached her lodgings she remembered parts of the verse she'd read that morning. She still had only bits of it by heart:

> Dangerous
> Are these approaching thunderheads and these
> Attendant lightnings, and the night that falls
> Unnoticed, terrible, in the heart.

And then there was something about windows with no light coming from them – and then the part about the bombing of the British Museum, which ended with rain falling on the city and the darkness over it. Faith rallied herself and summoned up the end of the verse, the bit about dawn returning and the earth still turning as she climbed the stairs two at a time to the top floor.

Chapter Fourteen

Casting a last look behind her to make sure there was nobody in the stairwell, Faith went into her flat – one room with a kitchenette in an alcove behind a curtain, a shared bathroom two floors below. The building had been partitioned in a hurry to capitalize on the homeless multitudes – wandering the city with whatever they had salvaged from the ruins, a pair of shoes, a lamp, a photograph – as had most of the other houses in this cramped, bedraggled Holloway street. Faith shut the door behind her and stood listening – there was snoring from somewhere else in the house, a distant wireless, but no footsteps. She secured the door, leaving the key in the lock – nobody would be able to open it from outside – and moved quickly to the window. As far as she could see the street was empty. She pulled the blackout curtain across and only then put on the light.

The bulb hung from the middle of the ceiling, the shade too small for it, like a girl wearing a dress she had grown out of. It made a puny attempt to illuminate the space, but it was probably kinder to the room's occupant that too harsh a light was not thrown on to the mottled wallpaper – baskets of cornflowers and poppies – stained here and there, and on the ratty primrose-yellow satin quilt covering the single bed. Faith took in the dusty, black cast-iron fireplace with the mean two-bar electric fire wedged in where flames would once have been, the table and single chair, and the peculiarly narrow, dark brown wardrobe. Her books were stacked on the floor. She had improvised a bedside table out of her one small suitcase, with a candle in a jar upon it. She could switch the main light off and close the space around her when she was lying there, reading. Everything was just as she had left it.

Faith placed the jar on the floor and snapped open the suitcase. Her hands were shaking. It held eight letters, piled up but not bound together with an elastic band or string – innocuous stuff from the

Ministry, from her parents, from friends. Carefully she checked through them. They were exactly as she had left them, not in date order, but arranged alphabetically according to the writer's name. Looking nervously at the door – but there was not a sound from the stairs – she felt along the pink watered-silk lining of the case at the back where there were two ruched pouches for small items. They were empty apart from the single pearl blouse button she had placed in the bottom of each so that they would fall out should anyone pick up the case and shake it. Faith pulled and worked the fabric away from the corner inside one of these pockets until she could just see the edge of what she was looking for: pushed in behind the pink silk at the back was a packet covered in brown paper and bound with tape, as small as an ordinary envelope, but thick as a paperback book. She felt around it: still tightly wrapped, untouched. She had a desperate urge to take it out of its hiding place, to tear it up, burn it, throw it out of the window, even. She had lied to David, it was not somewhere safe, she had kept it with her since she had left him, and he was right, she could not think to whom she might give it, in whom she could trust. She had no choice, she must carry it with her until she was certain. She patted the fabric down over the package and systematically put everything back in its right place.

After sitting on the bed for a time, Faith lay down, fingers pressed on her temples and eyes shut. Thank God it was a manageable walk to Holloway from the centre of town; she had chosen the room because she could not have borne being exiled away from London, in the middle of nowhere, in the suburbs, and thank heaven she had been able to return on foot tonight. After a while she sat up. Looking around she felt her shoulders relax. She was alone, the door locked. Her things were near her, her books, her remaining clothes, her paintbox.

The most cherished of her few possessions, the paintbox had been bought for her by her parents on the day she'd been accepted at art school. It was the very best they could afford: a full set of oil paints and watercolours, a palette and all the right brushes. Proud of and perplexed by their daughter, they could not understand how such talent had sprung from the union of an electrician and a waitress in an ordinary street: as if an orchid had bloomed on an aspidistra. And when Faith painted outside in the city, people would approach her sometimes, look over her shoulder at what she was doing, ask her questions, to be taken aback when they heard her voice – the accent of narrow London back-to-back terraces, where washing was strung from house to house across the street and the WCs were in the backyards.

The first time Faith ever spoke to Sir Kenneth Clark – he had called her in to the Ministry after noticing a drawing she had sold to the *Illustrated London News* – he asked her about her family: who were they, where did they live? And then how was it that she had had such a decent education, had her parents really taken her to listen to classical music concerts, to art galleries? He'd annoyed her with his probing, as if she were some kind of alien species that he had never come across before. She'd become exasperated, and when he asked her what books they kept at home and she said all of Dickens, Shakespeare, the Brontës, and he looked at her surprised, and then as if he didn't really believe her, she burst out, 'We can all read, you know! Just because we live in a small house and speak like this, doesn't mean we spend our spare time round the piano in the local pub, or gossiping over the back wall. It's money we haven't got, not brains.' He had looked at her, stunned, while his secretary – a supercilious blonde – had turned away, smirking. There was silence for a moment and then he had carried on talking.

He had employed her all the same – probably found her a bit of a character, or something awful like that. And the same week that she was taken on by the Ministry, and became sure of regular commissions, she had moved out of her parents' and rented a room of her own in a respectable boarding house for single ladies – no gentlemen visitors allowed – in Kilburn.

Faith loved her parents, in an abstract sense, but had not yet grown out of despising the fact of them: how excruciating was her father's pleasure in small comforts, her mother's habit of dozing on the sofa every evening with a copy of the *Picture Post* slipping off her lap, how pitiful was it that they had settled for so little in life, were content in their limited world; even their unvarying kindness to each other she saw as fatal evidence of a lack of passion. The boys she knew she also found wanting, too much in awe of her looks and abilities. She spent her evenings reading *Wuthering Heights* and *Jane Eyre*, dreaming of a man who would be deep and difficult – only she would be able to reach him, to recognize the treasure buried within – and plotting her escape from stagnant parental order to unpredictable independence.

Even though Miss Roy's boarding house could not have been more genteel, Mother and Dad had done everything to try and stop her, leaving newspapers lying around, open at certain pages: stories of attacks in the blackout, of robbery and other villainies on the increase, as well as the usual stuff about whole streets destroyed by bombs. There was one she remembered – so very sad, a mother and her infant son found in the rubble, but not for days, they were buried so deep. There was an appeal for information because the house where they were discovered was not theirs: it was supposed to be empty, shut up for the war. The papers printed a photograph, a studio portrait of the pair that had been found with the bodies – a child with fair wavy hair and a brunette woman. They appealed for family to come forward, for the father to make himself known, but he was probably serving overseas. A horrible story – but that wasn't the point, the thing was that one or two people being killed was so common that a report only appeared in the news if there was a problem identifying the victims; otherwise the press didn't bother any more. But her parents' plan to dissuade her did not work. And Faith could still remember the thrill of stepping into her own room at Miss Roy's that first time, shutting the door behind her, putting her books on the shelf, and setting her paintbox ready on the table.

Faith had left the paintbox behind her only the once, forgetting to take it with her during her muddled flight from David, when she had spent several blank weeks alone in an air-raid hostel; everyone else there, like her, only passing through, leaving no trace. This freezing flat in Holloway with its flimsy walls and ramshackle furnishings was not much better. But she had no choice but to remain here for the present, she could not afford anything else, and it would be impossible to join her parents who were now staying with family in the country; she would not be able to paint for the Ministry there, and her mother would question her endlessly about David. She could not even stay in their empty house in Blackfriars – David knew the address.

Lying on her bed, Faith felt so sore and heavy that she wanted to shut her eyes. But she must peel off her clothes first. She got up. Her cheek throbbed. She went over to the wardrobe door, pulling it open to look at the mirror inside. A cross marked the side of her face where she had run into the wire fence and the cheek was swollen. She was streaked with dirt, her hair matted. Her toes and fingers were numb but she felt clammy and hot under her arms, between her shoulder blades, at the base of her spine. As she undressed she could smell her body, sour and musky. She wrapped herself in her dressing gown, put on some army socks and a shawl. She longed for a deep bath, for soap and steam and clean towels, but there was hot water only once a day, in the morning, and anyway the shared bathroom was far below and she was not going to unlock her door again.

Faith arranged her old green coat on top of the bed, and climbed in. She would leave the candle burning until she was warm enough to sleep. She lay there, eyes open, in dread of the dream that kept coming to her, night after night, a dream of returning to the flat she had shared with David in Hampstead. She would see again the stone lintels of the house, the last in the row, with their carved swags of tumbling flowers and fruit that had seemed to augur well for her marriage. But she would be oppressed with unease as she went into the hall, stepping over the tiles and feeling the banister slide under her hand. On the first floor, as she floated through their door, she would see the coat stand – her own best black velvet hat sprouting its cockade of feathers, David's lichen-coloured fedora, worn so often that if you ran your hand inside you would notice the way the felt had taken the shape of his head. Everything is normal, he must be at home, she would dream, smiling in her sleep. But then, as she passed through the rooms, she would tread on torn brown paper and come across a pair of scissors lying open on the seat of the armchair. She would pull back the curtain to the kitchen to find smashed crockery and discarded food on the floor. She would search the rooms, frantic, muttering in her sleep, but she could never find what she was looking for. And then she would hear David's footsteps on the stairs outside and wake herself by trying to scream.

She must fill her mind with other thoughts, she must rest; however scared she was, she would have to try and work tomorrow, to make something that the Ministry would like. If Smith stopped her commissions, she would forfeit even the precarious safety of this grim room – she would be lost.

Chapter Fifteen

Cecily Browne woke up earlier than she had to on the day of her new mission for the Ministry, even though she had hardly slept because of nerves. She was to travel from her parents' home in Kent into London. Mr Smith had telephoned the day after their meeting to say that she would be painting a party of ladies knitting army socks in a mansion in Belgravia. Lady Somebody or Other had given over her drawing room to the Red Cross for the event, and the Ministry wanted the munificent act recorded, to show the classes pulling together across the social divide, and so on, and so forth – was how Mr Smith had put it. Totally thoughtless – Cecily's mother had complained – to call her daughter away a fortnight before Christmas, and, furthermore, she had not cared for the tone of the young man's voice.

How had Dame Laura described Mr Smith – 'patronizing'? Slightly unfair, Cecily thought; pompous, yes, but she would give him the benefit of the doubt for now – he was so very young, trying to appear in control, and, so far, a relief after Sir Kenneth, who always gazed so intently when he spoke to her, but never at her face. Very awkward that he was a family friend, she could not say anything and had to put up with it.

The servants had not lit the fires yet but Cecily could not wait and went down to the hall to see if the post had arrived – if there was something from her fiancé, Richard. But among the letters there was not one for her: another day without comfort. She accepted that he was not allowed leave over the holiday – that was hard enough to bear – but she had hoped for regular news of him, at least. The only consolation was that he had not been one of those poor boys sent off to die in Norway. She went quickly into the morning room, shutting the door behind her to sit where the others would not come across her crying.

To look at this scene – a charming, spacious room in an old house, with a long walled garden beyond the tall Georgian windows, shreds of mist over the box hedges and rose bushes – you would say it was an apt setting for the girl at its centre; gently pretty, very English. And, until the war began, Cecily's life had been as pleasantly ordered as this picture appeared to be, and she had been slower than most young people to break away from her happy childhood home. She was in no hurry to separate herself from her loving, wealthy parents, who had converted one of their spare bedrooms into a studio when it became apparent that their daughter enjoyed painting. And no disaster, tragedy or betrayal had occurred to dent her belief in an overwhelming, fundamental force for good that watched benevolently over mankind. But these days Cecily was finding it difficult to see the power of goodness: it seemed to be vanishing from the greater world, there was no sign of it in the newsreels, in the papers. It was present only in small things, and keeping her eyes firmly on where it might still be discovered required increasing amounts of willpower and vigilance; in unguarded moments Cecily heard a carping, doomy voice within, casting doubt on the certainties she had lived by, criticizing her paintings, asking her, slyly, just how likely was it that Richard would survive until their wedding day. Not long to wait in the ordinary run of things – less than ten weeks now – but in wartime, when your love was one of a bomber crew, this was an eternity.

The mixture of disillusionment with mankind, with God himself, for allowing such things as were happening daily, and of fear for her fiancé's life, was altering Cecily. But when she saw herself in the mirror there was the same round, calm face as always, with its unassertive features and mild expression – no sign of anguish. And so people continued to say of her that she was sweet, and her paintings lovely; they did not recognize the effort it took to make her work, to search for these modest acts of industriousness and stoicism among the women she painted, and to fix them for ever on canvas. And Richard – she could not possibly trouble him with her problems, it would be shameful to do so when he put himself in constant danger without question, without complaint, without a single break in his resolve.

On the piano stood the framed photograph of the two of them, arm in arm, in dinner dress. Richard looked like a figure from an

Edwardian book illustration. He was Cecily's junior by a year, but it didn't matter as he was mature and strong. Cecily picked up the photograph and kissed his black and white face. She had persuaded herself that unless she performed this ritual every morning he might come to harm. She had come to believe that she must earn her fiancé's survival. She could not imagine that she would be granted happiness randomly, for no reason, that no punishment would be forthcoming if she were to fail to be deserving. She would have to struggle on with her fears, her shaken beliefs, her work as a war artist.

Two hours later Cecily sat on the London train, barrelling through the Kent countryside. It was three times as expensive and ten times as uncomfortable travelling by railway these days. There were cancellations at the last minute. As you waited on the platform the engine that was supposed to be yours would hurtle straight past pulling a full load of soldiers or munitions instead. If you did manage to claim a seat in the packed carriages it was all so unpleasant – the smeary windows, the seats puffing out dusty exhalations as you sat down. And you didn't dare lean back – you didn't want your hair to touch the fabric headrest polished shiny brown by hundreds of passengers before you; there was no guarantee that first class meant first class any more. Cecily supposed that they would have to wait until the war ended, somewhere in the distant future – 1950 perhaps – before this decrepit rolling stock was replaced with something new, clean and comfortable. But today, a small blessing: a window seat. She watched the landscape slide by under a low sky. Richard might be flying now, or soon, this evening, high above RAF Mildenhall, heading out for Germany . . . she would not allow herself to think about it. She concentrated instead on her sketchbook; inside the cover she had inscribed the name she hoped to make her own, over and over, like an incantation: *CecilyTully, CecilyTully, CecilyTully, CecilyTully* . . . The sound in her head merged with the rhythm of the wheels on the track, and she slept.

Cecily, her head resting against the window, opened her eyes to see several faces only an inch or two away staring back at her. They had arrived at a station, a town, not London yet, she could see sky over the hats of the people pressing up to the train. Half the occupants of the carriage descended, brushing down their mackintoshes ready for rain, but then twice as many attempted to board. The station manager lumbered up and down on the edge of the platform, pushing through the would-be passengers, trying to prevent any more from climbing up, and panting. 'Patience, ladies and gentlemen, let's be civilized: we aren't Germans, are we?' Cecily reached into her bag until her hand came to rest upon Richard's last letter, a week old now. She did not need to read it – it said the same, more or less, as all the others; that he was well, that his work was hard but he liked a challenge, that he loved her.

They had agreed to write, rather than use the telephone. At Cecily's home the telephone sat on its own table in the hall: impossible to have a private conversation with people passing by. And there was the problem of timing. Cecily went out to paint during the day while Richard often flew at night. After many frustrating missed or interrupted calls they had come to rely on letters – there was less chance of one misinterpreting things than in a rushed conversation, and a letter you could hold in your hand, carry with you, kiss. But it was hard to know what to put in them. Richard's, of course, were always cheerful and optimistic. He could tell her nothing about his work.

Where was Richard at this precise moment? Sitting in the mess with the other men? Clambering around in the belly of a plane? Or, worst of all, somewhere high above her head in the rattling machine whose stubby wings did not appear nearly strong enough to hold up all of those boys? The memory came to her of the afternoon at her friend Joyce's house when the telegram came about her husband. She saw the door slammed in the face of the embarrassed boy, and Joyce herself: she tore the thing open with a look of disgust and began to scream.

Cecily forced herself to examine the scene outside the train window, the fields had become suburbs, rows of red brick, church spires and occasional factories of five, six storeys with chimneys. Here and there stood a wall like a cliff rising up out of nowhere, punctured by windows empty of glass. As the train neared its destination she saw the dome of St Paul's, and, further back, she thought she could just make out the tower of Senate House.

It took Cecily longer than she thought to get across to Belgravia on the underground. Things had never been the same since the Blitz, even the better stations were cluttered with the rubbish left by air-raid shelterers – old newspapers and empty paper bags, apple peel, spent matches and cigarette stubs, some flattened cardboard boxes used as makeshift mattresses. And there was the occasional lost soul, driven mad by the bombs, who preferred life in the tunnels, and huddled against the tiled walls day and night, wrapped in a dirty army blanket. Cecily averted her eyes and hurried along.

She had to check the address twice when she arrived – a grander house than even she was used to, gleaming stucco with wide, shallow steps, columns on either side of the door. Cecily was shown into the hallway, an impressive acreage of marble floor (though the chandelier had been tied up in a dust sheet and the pictures and carpets removed), and then into what had been a drawing room. Cleared of its customary sumptuous furnishings, it housed two lines of trestle tables covered by lumpy hillocks of khaki and blue wool and surrounded by plain wooden chairs. The lofty arched windows were disfigured by the usual web of tape. Above the fireplace there hung a painting: a lady in a spiky ruff, skirts bristling with pearls, looking down her long Elizabethan nose at the unseemly mingling of the well-born and the humble taking place below. A low buzz of conversation accompanied the clicking and sliding of needles as the ladies – all still in their hats (as they were not 'at home') – produced a river of knitting: scarves, socks, balaclavas. Cecily took a place at the end of one of the tables; she could begin there and move around until she had enough material.

Sunlight filled the vast room suddenly, as if an arc lamp had been switched on. Although its splendour was camouflaged, the atmosphere remained one of a hushed, ceremonial space where rituals of polite behaviour were expected. There was hardly any sound from outside: the windows gave out on to a garden square surrounded by other white mansions, each with its wide steps, columns and fanlights; not even the usual London traffic noises disturbed the quiet. Cecily did not join in the chat: in one day she had to draw at least eight figures with sufficient detail to build her painting around them. She had to be tactful, not revealing who exactly she was sketching, and sometimes, instead of drawing an oddity of appearance, making notes in the back of her sketchbook to record it, in order not to offend the possessor of a squint, a florid complexion, a dowager's hump, a figure too exuberant to be girdled successfully. Occasionally, when the quirk was just too peculiar, she omitted it altogether. She deliberated most over the woman whom she wanted at the centre of the painting – she had such a refined face – but from whose needles spewed forth a stream of knots and tangles instead of usable garments. A series of careful adjustments to the drawing and the rogue knitter was churning out wearable army socks with the rest of her colleagues.

Then it was lunchtime and a trolley creaked in, a stack of sandwiches balanced on the lower shelf, and on top, next to the tea urn, was an entire cake, promisingly dark, as if it might even contain dried fruit, and decorated with a sprig of holly. There was a round of applause. But just as it died down and the ladies were tidying away their knitting, stretching their arms out, flexing their fingers, talking in louder voices, the cry of a siren began, rising and then sinking back. Some did not get up from their seats immediately, refusing to be rushed, others were gathering up their things, moving towards the door, Cecily with them, when a background thrum that had been there too, only no one had really noticed it, suddenly grew very near. A tearing whistle began – wheeeeeeee – becoming louder and closer until it filled your ears, and a dreadful moment held them all motionless before the scene outside the window shattered, fracturing and rearranging itself like a kaleidoscope: turf, branches and fountains of soil flew up and sideways, span down through the air. As the ladies screamed, some frozen, others throwing themselves to the floor, the picture shifted again; a great force punched the taped-up windows, which cracked, then sagged and hung like sails suddenly emptied of wind. Cecily, face down with one arm over her head, the other bent awkwardly beneath her, kept her eyes squeezed shut, and waited.

She waited to die. She thought she might have died. This must be the moment when she would sacrifice her life in order that Richard might survive. But then her arm felt as if a burning clamp were tightening around it and she knew that she had been spared. She had been allowed to live, but this was a test, to shake her out of her introspection, her self-indulgence. She prayed: 'I understand, I will try harder to see the good and ignore the bad, not to doubt.'

As she spoke to herself Cecily heard moaning and weeping from all around; the women whispered words of comfort to each other, as if by keeping their voices low the bombers overhead might forget them. But then the whole room lurched, creaked and shifted like a wooden ship on a tall wave, and there was a brilliant flash of blue-white light, a brutal slap of air. Cecily felt a light drumming of plaster dust across her back; she did not dare move, and then, when she did, there was at once a distant noise of wailing. Although it sounded far away Cecily could see that it was coming from close by, from all around her. She coughed at the dry, scorching smell. There was the sound of gushing water. A chunk of rubble had fallen from somewhere on to one of the women and spots and smears of blood patterned the floor. Two ladies lay completely still, one on a table around which some of the others were gathered, chafing her hands. The other, on the floor, had turned on her side with her knees pulled up to her chest so you could see her drawers; someone was stroking her cheek and crying. The tea urn had crashed to the ground and rested on its side at the centre of a pool of water where another woman shrieked and tugged at her skirt, which had soaked up the boiling liquid.

Cecily stood, rubbing her knees where her stockings had ripped. Her arm hurt. There was a general commotion – people were red-faced, open-mouthed, shouting and sobbing – but what she could hear, all muffled and far away, did not match this picture. Ambulance men and women rushed in, clustering around the injured, marshalling away those who could walk. Cecily, as deliberate and slow as if she were underwater, collected her sketchbooks, oddly still lying on the table exactly where she had been sitting, and joined the line of ladies waiting to be checked over. They tied up her arm, cleaned and dressed her knees, and then she passed through the hall which appeared unaltered, no debris or even dust here, the shrouded chandelier still in its place. As Cecily picked her way down the street over the strewn branches and chunks of muddy grass, feet crunching on broken glass, she looked back over her shoulder to see a plume of black smoke rising straight up from the roof of the mansion like a charcoal line drawn in the air.

Arriving home that evening, Cecily let herself in and shut the door quietly behind her. She did not want anybody to come to take her hat and coat, to call out and greet her. How could she tell her parents? They would make such a fuss about her working for the Ministry again, insist that she stop and sit out the war at home with her mother. She had to keep painting – she had been spared today, despite her weakness, for this very purpose and she had to fulfil it. But catching sight of herself in the hall looking-glass, Cecily saw a greyish layer of plaster dust covering her hair, as if she had been got up for the part of an old lady on the stage. There were bandages on her arm and legs. And the evening paper hawked at the station and now on the hall table was full of the raids on London that day – a whole schoolroom of children had been killed along with their teacher. She would have to explain. Her hearing had come back, although there was a high-pitched whine behind everything.

'Miss, there's a letter for you . . . went to the wrong house, they brought it round after you'd left.' A maid had stopped in her duties and stood behind her. Seeing Cecily as she turned, the girl's smile disappeared and she pushed the envelope into her hand hurriedly. A brief note, posted yesterday. Richard was well, he wrote, busy, but right as rain. She wasn't to worry. He had survived another week, then. Unless he had been killed yesterday night, or today, they had been granted more time.

Cecily brushed the dust out of her hair and bathed, keeping her knees and arm clear of the water, but there were other scrapes and small cuts she had so far been unaware of that announced themselves, itching and stinging. She changed into a clean dress and redid her make-up. It was still obvious that she had been caught up in the bombings. But if she were to say that she didn't feel well enough for dinner her mother would only insist on coming up to see her. She would have to go downstairs, eat, demonstrate that she was absolutely fine, and inform them in a cool and matter-of-fact manner about the day's events. She would not tell Richard.

PART TWO

January 1943

PRIME MINISTER'S PERSONAL MINUTE

10 Downing Street,
Whitehall

<u>MINISTER OF INFORMATION, MR BRENDAN BRACKEN</u>

Pray tell me what the situation is now
regarding Powell and Pressburger? You know
that I did <u>not</u> think they should be allowed
to film THE LIFE AND DEATH OF COLONEL BLIMP
in the first place, with its bumbling British
Army officer and its kindly, sensitive
German. For God's sake! This is <u>the last </u>
<u>thing</u> the British people need to see at
this juncture, when we're about to ask our
forces to carpet-bomb the buggers. Is it
true that they secured Anton Walbrook to
play the Hun? — too bloody handsome by
half. However — I do take your point, we
can't suppress the film with the law as it
stands, and you have argued persuasively
against new powers of censorship and the
protest they would cause — we are a democ-
racy. (In any case, there's not much chance
of stopping P & P without them kicking up a
stink.) You want to create a veritable flood
of culture in which our message of British
guts and stamina will be more easily carried and spread? So be it. And, dear
Brendan, when shall I see you at Chequers
again? Soon, very soon, I hope? . . .

Chapter Sixteen

Exactly one month since Clark had given him the job, and still Smith had received only one painting from his women: Cecily Browne's girls in their gas capes, which she had brought in on his very first day. As he arrived at his desk at 9.30, he saw that one of the secretaries had placed a note and a letter there. To delay having to read them he unpacked his lunch from his briefcase, putting it on his desk to cheer himself up. His mother had managed to obtain three slices of roast beef – black market – and noticing his unhappiness at breakfast had put them all in his sandwich.

At last he took a deep breath and began to read. His apprehensiveness had been entirely justified. Smith sat, head in hands, for a while. The note read, 'Cecily Browne telephoned to say she had some trouble with the knitters, she hurt her arm, so it's not quite finished and she can't bring it in yet.' He had been expecting something of this sort, but seeing it written down brought him fresh misery. The envelope held a roughly torn page from an exercise book on which Faith Farr had scrawled, 'Impossible to come in at the moment. I will see you WHEN I HAVE SOMETHING TO SHOW YOU.'

Why had this blow fallen upon him while he was still suffering the after-effects of the evening before, spent in Clark's company? Clark had invited him for dinner at his club – a 'treat', an opportunity to 'catch up after the holiday'. Throughout, as Clark talked, he eyed Smith's hastily bought ready-made bow tie askance, and actually glared at it when Smith happened to mention that he had spent the entire festive season at home in Surbiton with his mother in their five-bedroomed house on the best road – the river road. As she had first entered through its front door as a parlourmaid to an elderly bachelor, the greatest day of his mother's life was that on which she crossed the threshold again as his bride. So pleased was she with her rise in station, and with the baby boy that followed six months after the marriage, that she barely noticed the death of her husband the same year.

She played the part of the mourning widow with enormous relish, however, taking her inspiration from Queen Victoria's legendary histrionics at the loss of Prince Albert. She preserved her husband's shaving brush; his walking sticks still filled the umbrella stand. And she kept all of his clothes – clothes that she was pressing her son to wear, now that he had grown up and rationing was so severe. That very morning she had handed him an overcoat smelling of camphor, two sizes too large – his father had been a bigger man than Smith in every way, apparently. She draped it over his shoulders. It was all Smith could do to restrain himself from throwing it violently on the floor; he could not stand the thought of wearing it. However, now that he was in his office he could see a use for it. He hung the coat on a hook over the pane of glass in the door. It could stay there for ever. He would be rid of it, plus it would appear to passers-by that he was hard at work inside, even if he was resting, or wandering elsewhere. He sat back down. His head was swimming. He had drunk too much, too quickly, trying to survive dinner with his superior.

'Surbiton,' Clark had said, irritably, as they waited between courses. 'And where is that, exactly?'

'Next to Kingston upon Thames,' Smith said. Clark frowned, nonplussed. 'South of the river? It's actually very convenient – there's a parade of shops, everything you could need, a post office . . . You can whizz up to town on the train.'

'Quite,' Clark said, sceptically. 'Now to the matter in hand. What's wrong with you, Smith? I told you to look after Cecily Browne and you damn near killed her! Had her father bending my ear about it here at the club – very trying. I understand she's finding it difficult to paint at all now. And this at a time when we're desperate for something our Minister will take seriously and want to appear in the press with. I mean oils, a decent size, too; and decent subjects. When can I expect to see results, man?'

Clark banged his hand down hard on the table. Smith started and the waiter, spooning boiled carrots out on to the plates, jumped, dropping the food on to the cloth.

'Bloody, bloody fool, clear this mess up. Not you, no, no . . . useless . . . send someone else. Away, away . . .' The man, head down, hurried off and Clark sat with a theatrical air of resignation, hands in the air, as the cloth was changed and the table relaid.

Smith did not dare to say anything further. He studied the wine in his glass, rolling the stem back and forth between his fingers, pointlessly, until he realized that Clark was glaring, now, at his hand. He took a sip, and then another and another, attempting to steady his nerves before he spoke. 'Only a little while longer, I can assure you. And then I think, I *know*, you'll be very pleased. Of course, we have some paintings ready now . . . quite a few, really, but . . . they're with the artists.'

Smith took a deep breath to buy some time to think of a plausible explanation for the statement he had just made – as untrue as it was emphatic.

'Thing is . . . they've said they need to keep hold of their work . . . to help them to develop their ideas. And then . . . you know it'll be much cheaper to transport it all to Senate House in one go, when they've finished everything. It'll save petrol and . . . we do have to be careful of expenses now.'

In fact Smith had no knowledge of any further completed paintings. His campaign of writing – twice weekly – threatening and cajoling letters to Faith Farr had not produced even so much as a drawing. Neither had Laura Knight shown him any work yet; apparently some problem with a painting of a WAAF had held her up – a single portrait, of a single girl, was that really all he'd have to show Clark when the time was up?

Clark dabbed at his wide, thin smile with a linen napkin, before crumpling it up and dropping it to one side. 'That is exactly what I wished to hear.'

Smith breathed again. Could it be that he had bought himself some more time, come through this first ordeal?

But then Clark continued, 'And, in that case, so we can be seen to be "productive" in the meantime, until the paintings are safely with us, I think we have to make a splash.'

Smith did not like the way this was going.

'We'll plan an exhibition, say mid-March? Bring all of the work together. *Women Artists at War* – we'll have it at the National Gallery, advertise it straight away, put it in all the papers, that'll appease Bracken.'

The Gallery was now empty of the last of the National Collection: the only life within its damask walls were the occasional temporary exhibitions, and daily lunchtime concerts and talks – an attempt to keep London alive, culturally speaking. The priceless works had been evacuated on a guarded train to Bangor, from where Clark had arranged for them to be distributed among the country estates of his friends. They were doing the nation a great service by sheltering its treasures, and there were added incentives. In addition to the pleasure of a bona fide Raphael or Poussin on your wall, you were automatically excused the horror of flesh-and-blood evacuees descending upon you with their muddy boots, lousy hair and empty stomachs. Smith had once overheard Clark dictating a letter to one lord, who was finding himself under intolerable pressure to house rabble from the Isle of Dogs. No, Clark said, he could not possibly send him any more masterpieces. However, if the pictures that Lord Such and Such had already received were to be spread more widely among the seventeen bedrooms, rather than hung together in the Great Hall to create a (admittedly stunning) private gallery, then it could be argued that the entire place had been given over to preserving Britain's heritage and there was, very, very regrettably, no room for evacuees. The effort that Clark had to expend coddling his art-sitters propelled him to devise an alternative. He pestered the Ministry for funds to build a shelter in a slate quarry in the Welsh mountains – 'Hitler won't bother with Wales, there's not a thing there worth bombing.' Every month, just one painting made the long train journey back from the rocky depths to be displayed to a London public starved of art.

'About time we put on a proper show again,' Clark continued. 'One painting at a time's a pretty poor effort for our National Gallery, makes it look as if we've given up the ghost. I've been racking

85

my brains about what we could do. Wasn't going to suggest such a thing to you so early in your stewardship, Smith, but as you've clearly been damned effective . . .'

At his desk, Smith groaned and put his head in his hands as he relived the events of the night before. He had just laid his head on his blotter and shut his eyes, pretending to himself that he was not actually at work at all, when, without a warning knock the door opened to reveal not, as he first feared, Clark (thank God), but a peculiar figure: very tall, with a halo of springy red curls, his face a mismatched composite of plump, boyish cheeks and a square, manly chin. The smile was black and crooked. Thick glasses in round frames obscured the newcomer's eyes, the lenses so heavy that he repeatedly pushed them back up on to the bridge of his nose with one finger, blinking at the same time, giving him a twitchy, slipshod air. The man came in, though uninvited, and sat down in the chair opposite Smith, who was just about to ask him his business in a brusque and authoritative manner when something surfaced in his memory about someone with just such distinctive hair, and at that same moment he noticed the immaculate suit.

'You don't mind? I'm at a loose end, before a meeting. God, this place: a warren, and the bloody committees! So! Saw your office was occupied. The old coat-over-the-door trick, eh; used to do that myself when I needed to work flat out without interruption, to keep people off my back. I was intrigued to see who was in here. Good for me to keep in touch with every part of the Ministry and, between you and me, means I can hide out in peace for ten minutes.'

He spoke in a singular voice – the usual boarding-school bray polished by Oxford, but with odd lilts and hints breaking through: Australia, Ireland? Smith guessed, but could not be sure – definitely somewhere cut off by the sea and totally uncivilized.

'Mr . . . Sir, I'm sorry, how do I . . . ?'

'"Minister" will do.'

'Minister, Mr Bracken . . . I'm Women – Artists; responsible for. Don't keep much of their work here, of course: very small, well, you can see that. We do have this one – ladies, you see, covering up in readiness for a gas attack. Here they all are; yes, doing a grand job. Super, don't you think? And there are others, *many* others . . .'

Bracken looked at Cecily Browne's painting without expression, at Smith, and then around at the office. He pushed his glasses back up his nose, blinked, nodded, shrugged and said, 'Tell me about them then, lad.'

Smith launched into an inventive account of the many works he had commissioned. Tens of them, according to him, had already been completed, even framed, and were only awaiting the courier – terribly unreliable – to transport them in to the Ministry. So compelling did he find his own account that he found himself jumping up from his seat in his enthusiasm, sketching out with his hands the exciting compositions and relative sizes of the many canvases. They were getting on like a house on fire, Bracken interjecting with his own anecdotes which were, actually, fascinating, colourful and affecting. Of rackety, Fenian Irish parentage, transplanted to the Australian Bush (Smith inwardly congratulated himself for his accuracy in decoding an accent) on a quest for a bigger, freer life away from the strictures of the auld country – a background which proved apparently excellent preparation for the wild brutality of British public school, where he had won a place despite his lowly origins, so impressed were the governors by his talents that the school had waived the fees. And from there to Oxford University (a great disappointment: the dons had given him a place, recognizing his budding genius, but once he was there they couldn't keep up with him). Bracken spoke of the Prime Minister as if he were a close friend, and then, confiding in Smith, lowered his voice as he told of his dear and only brother, killed recently, on a mission in Norway. Large tears followed each other in relays down his cheeks and dropped on to his cashmere lapels. Smith stood appalled, unable to move, arms held out slightly at his sides.

'Here's me going on, though, when we should be talking about the masses of work you've managed to get out of those artists, marvellous, marvellous – and we need more, more, more! You know my policy? No overt censorship. I'm not bloody Goebbels. Stuck my neck right out with the PM: I'm letting Powell and Pressburger complete a film with a *good German* in it, against his express wishes – and the boss has got a point, it's not what people need to see, not at the moment – makes them ask all sorts of awkward questions. But in order for my strategy to work, we need a flood of official art. We don't try to stop material with the wrong message – that would just draw attention to it – instead, we drown it in a sea of the right stuff. Trust in the public to make the right judgement. We can do it! And meeting you now, I'm even more certain. You don't let setbacks stop you, never mind how insurmountable they seem, do you? Good lad.'

Smith, entranced, forgot the fix he was in. If you listened to Bracken, anything was possible, even when things were at their blackest. As the door shut behind the Minister, Smith took heart: he would act on this surge of positivity. He looked at the papers and files on his desk in a new way – they would not overwhelm him, he would master them. He picked up Faith Farr's scrawled note, unfolded it, ran his finger over her handwriting. He *would* win her over, in the end. He had seen it happen time and time again in films: initial hostilities, then an exchange of cool but loaded words, a struggle and, eventually, always, her capitulation. It did not matter that this note was curt, impersonal. It only mattered that her fingers had touched the paper. He pressed it to his lips and slipped it into his inside pocket, next to his heart. It would stay there – a talisman – until she eventually acquiesced. He might show it to her then, to amuse himself and remind her of how they had begun: his wisdom, her foolishness. She would blush, look confused, apologize, kiss him, and then . . .

Thus fortified, Smith decided to swallow the biggest toad, to telephone Laura Knight, immediately. He would have to give in to her for the moment, for tactical reasons. The only way in which he had the smallest hope of producing in time anything suitable for Clark's exhibition would be to allow Knight her head. Although there was a consolation: he could pile the pressure on, tell her that she had to create something astonishing and double quick, too, in order to justify the effort he would have to put in on her behalf, and the risk he was personally taking in allowing her the unprecedented opportunity of painting servicemen.

Chapter Seventeen

That evening, at her studio in St John's Wood, Laura dressed for a dinner out with her oldest friend, the painter Dod Proctor. She had vanquished Smith! Won his agreement to paint at an airfield; he had even started to make the arrangements: a permit to work at RAF Mildenhall, and digs nearby – a great victory. As she selected her clothes for the evening she hummed to herself, and sipped at a large whisky. What had changed his mind, she wondered, as she surveyed herself in a black satin evening gown. The mirror was the one she used to reflect light on to her models sitting for portraits and nudes on the dais; it was cracked down one side, spotted with age, and did not give an entirely accurate reflection; nevertheless, she could see there was something wrong with her appearance.

Smith must have been telling the truth about the threat to WAAC, she decided: things were clearly as bad as they could possibly be. But supposing WAAC were really in trouble, her new commission could still be some kind of a test. Smith and his master, Clark, might secretly want her to fail – she would not put it past the Ministry men to seek to humiliate her, to teach her to know her place, even in this situation. She had nearly exploded when Smith told her that she must work as she never had before in all her life: blasted cheek from a mere child. He wanted to see 'a masterpiece', and in only one month! He did not know, of course, that such a challenge would not daunt her, only make her all the more determined. This dress is elegant but dull, Laura thought. Over the top of it she draped a short cape of hoops of black, silver and gold sequins that encircled her neck as if she were breaking the surface of dark water and creating ripples all around her. Along both arms she stacked African wooden bangles, and then, to finish, added jade earrings so long that they brushed her shoulders. Now she recognized herself.

Smith's defeat, and a night out, would make up for a frustrating day. A postcard had arrived in the morning, a cheap plain thing, with a message from Faith Farr of all people, inviting Laura to meet that afternoon, near the old wharves on the south bank of the Thames – 'a fascinating huddle of Tudor, Georgian and Victorian buildings, cobbled alleys and ancient inns' where they might sketch together, the note said. They could talk and Faith would show her where she had wandered as a child. Laura went to the appointed place, some steps down to the water, by Blackfriars Bridge, and waited, but no Faith. She stayed for an hour – still no sign. Luckily she had her sketchbook and so the time had not been wasted. But she worried that something untoward had befallen Faith: either she was in such a state of distraction that she had forgotten her invitation to Laura or, worse, there had been some accident, some violent event of war? She would drop the girl a line, asking her what had happened – was she all right? She would tell her about the new commission: that they must meet upon her return.

The supper club was decorated with roses that night. Coming in, you were miraculously enveloped in the smell of a warm summer day. The flowers, and the singer, were reflected in the mirrored walls many times over.

> Turn off that charm
> I'm through with love for a while
> I'm through and yet, you have a fabulous smile,
> So if I forget . . .
>
> Remind me
> Not to find you so attractive
> Remind me
> That the world is full of men
>
> When I start to miss you
> To touch your hand

To kiss you
Remind me
To count to ten . . .

'So, darling, what did he say? Don't keep me guessing, tell me the good news,' said Dod. She always reminded Laura of a French china doll from the twenties – hair pinched and looped into a row of flat kiss-curls across her forehead, white-powdered skin, cupid-bow lips, and dressed in plum satin and biscuit-coloured fur.

'Well, you know how difficult the Ministry has been. Right from the start. Sixty guineas for three portraits, that's what they offered at first. Can you imagine?' Laura said.

'I'd have thought five hundred was nearer the mark for you these days . . .'

'Oh, at least.' Laura paused. 'I've had to keep pushing back at them. It's been quite good fun. When they made such a fuss over my expenses I sent in separate receipts for everything, each rubber, individual pencils, the lot. That soon put an end to that.'

'You didn't really?'

'Certainly. And the assignments . . .' Laura groaned. 'Nice, but not at all testing, if you see what I mean, not the kind I can get stuck into. Then, lately, something's changed. Clark's employed someone as a buffer: he doesn't want to have to see me himself. This young chap is to be a whipping boy, to take the blame if there's not much to show, and he's feeling the pressure . . . I'm pretty sure that's how it's come about.'

'Tell me – what's "come about"? You must *say*.'

'Only the RAF, Dod: whole thing sorted. The boy tried to unnerve me, of course, couldn't give in gracefully. "Dame Laura," he said, "are you sure? You might find it . . . difficult, working closely with all of those men, you won't be able to share things with them, truly get under their skin. And you might find it somewhat unsavoury if you did . . ."' Laura did a fair impression of Smith's attempt at insinuation and bombast.

Dod laughed. 'And what did you say?'

'"Mr Smith, men have painted women for hundreds of years without any question that they should also have to *be* women, in order to do it properly." And that did it. He called me back to say it was fixed. Now, I think some champagne, don't you?'

Dod looked at her friend with concern. 'Darling – do forgive me: I don't suppose you have considered Harold at all? He won't like it one bit, will he?'

Laura sighed; she had expected Dod to raise the problem of Harold but did not want to think about it, not here, among the roses, with a full glass in her hand. Dear Dod, so protective of Laura, so watchful for what she saw as Harold's unreasonable demands. 'I know, I know,' said Laura. 'I'll telephone this evening. Need a few more stiffeners first, mind you.'

The hall clock chimed quarter to eleven as Laura climbed the tiled steps to the front door of the house in St John's Wood. The Regency terrace had not known such darkness since its infancy. Gas and then electric lamps had glared with increasing brashness at its graceful façade, but now a decorous veil fell again every day at dusk. Laura switched on her torch and went upstairs to the first floor, to the studio. Since she and Harold had decamped to Malvern to sit out the war – his idea – she had shut up the rest of the house and lived and worked in what had been the drawing room on her solitary, and increasingly frequent, visits to London. It took her longer than usual to arrange the blackout curtain; the mixture of whisky and champagne meant she made several attempts before she was certain that not a beam would escape from the bow window, and only then did she switch on the light.

Laura poured herself a nightcap, lit a cigarette, and sat on the camp bed in the corner, looking over at two of her paintings, still wet. Propped against the wall was *Corporal J. D. M. Pearson, WAAF*, the first woman to be awarded the Empire Gallantry Medal for bravery. A hell of a time the portrait had given her. She had shown the girl, tin helmet on, rifle at the ready – but then the gun had had to go, Clark had insisted. Although everyone knew that WAAFs carried weapons all the time, they were not officially permitted to and so could not be painted with them, and Laura had been obliged to paint out the rifle and replace it with a gas mask, which made the girl look fearful and cautious, rather than ready for a fight. Still, at least Laura had won the lesser skirmish, to show the Corporal as she actually looked: fleshy face bare of make-up, eyes screwed up in concentration, prominent teeth, despite Clark's suggestion that she make the Corporal's cheeks pinker, her mouth more even, and give her a beguiling gaze.

On the easel was the painting of Faith Farr she was making as an exercise for herself, to keep her memory sharp, and a surprise for the girl, it might buck her up. She had worked up the sketch from the Kardomah café into a simple composition, waist length, showing Faith holding a palette and brushes, about to begin painting. The characteristic tense look of hers translated well into an image of hard work. Funny, but Laura could have sworn the painting had been moved. She had held it up to the window to see how it was drying that afternoon and put it by the corner over there; she was certain it was not on the easel when she went out. And her sketchbook, too, was not where she had left it; it lay on the floor open at the drawing of Faith Farr, the girl's address scrawled above it. Laura was not usually so careless, but then her thoughts were certainly muddled by the drink; she was not quite herself.

She had one more duty to perform before she could lie down for the night; she could delay making the call no longer. She went to pick up the telephone. Harold answered it at once, he must have been waiting – and that made her feel guilty, and then annoyed.

'Laura? Laura, is everything all right?'

'Why wouldn't it be?' she said stiffly, and then relented. It was late, he missed her, he was lonely. 'Apart from . . . well, bad news, my love; they're sending me away.'

Harold stayed silent.

'I argued with them, really I did. It's the last thing I want, you know that. But they insisted; almost threatened to take away my sketching permit if I didn't agree. Said I have to be more ambitious, set an example to the other women, said we should all be prepared to make a sacrifice these days. I couldn't refuse.'

'I suppose there's no choice, then . . . but Laura, I don't think it's at all good for you – the travelling, the risks, at your age. Don't they realize you're nearly seventy?'

'I'm sixty-five, Harold.'

'Yes, yes, that's exactly what I said.' He sounded very cross. And then, plaintive: 'What about me?'

'Dearest H., I know, I know.' She changed the subject, asking about his delicate stomach, the portraits he was working on – a bishop, a headmaster – until she judged an acceptable amount of time had passed and she could say goodbye.

'So . . . I'll have to wait here until I go, get everything ready, pick up the permits; it might even be as soon as next Monday. No, no time to come back to Malvern before, but I'll let you know the address as soon as I arrive, and I'll see you again soon, as soon as I can plan a few days off. Sleep tight, H., night, night.'

Laura poured another whisky and then switched off the light and pulled the blackout curtain to one side to look out at the night sky . . . When she moved her head felt light and disconnected from her body – such relief. Her back and legs were weak from the years spent standing at an easel, her eyes ached. And there was a pain in her heart – the knowledge of the things she missed or would never have. She cared for Harold greatly, had always been fond of him, and he of her, but there had never been much passion between them; their marriage was an arrangement founded on mutual and profound desire, not for each other, but to be artists. And in that sense, it had been a success. They had been husband and wife for thirty-nine years despite the vicissitudes of their careers, her public acclaim contrasting uncomfortably with his obscurity, and despite the fact that there were no children to bind them together: Harold had never wanted them, had made excuses, citing the cost of a baby, the disruption to their painting lives when they were still young. Once Laura had made her name and could afford a large house and domestic help on her own account, she was too old. Sometimes she would imagine a child – always a son – she would build a portrait in her mind's eye of how he would look as a grown-up, his mannerisms, his voice; she longed for him. How was it possible to miss somebody who had never existed?

She had married Harold because she knew that he would look after her, never leave her, never change. He was a man of fixed opinions and unbending morals, and he offered her the security of joining his solid, middle-class family. She saw herself and her sister – eighteen and twenty – sitting by their mother as she lay dying that stifling summer of 1895, the bed draped in lace from head to foot (the last fine piece the family owned) to shade the invalid and keep insects away. There was a bottle of flat champagne on the table, to be measured out in teaspoons, the only thing the doctor could suggest to dull the suffering in that house on a patch of wasteland, the last in a series of cheap rented places. A week after the funeral the two girls had to leave their home. They sold the furniture to pay the landlord of the room they took together and their next instalment of fees at art college, and kept only a blanket chest and a vase filled with peacock feathers. By then Laura had met Harold Knight in the studio, they had become friends, he had admired her devoted care of her mother, but more so her obsession with work, her shabbiness, seeing in her an ideal match for his own ascetic nature, his disdain of material pleasures. He did not realize that, in Laura, all-consuming ambition was born of fear: if she did not succeed as an artist there was no safety net. She could not afford entertainments, hats and dresses, although she would have loved them. She had not renounced the world as he had; she had been given no choice.

There were tears on Laura's cheeks: soppy, self-pitying old woman – too much alcohol, certainly, or not enough to dilute the pain sufficiently. She concentrated on the scene beyond the window, moonlight picking out the bare branches and pooling in the empty tennis court opposite. She missed being able to paint at night with the windows uncovered when, taking a break from work, you could rest your eyes on the moon, cool and serene as if no evil took place below her. She put down her glass. She must take herself in hand and go to bed.

Chapter Eighteen

Faith Farr did not understand Laura Knight's letter – what on earth did she mean about a meeting by the Thames and Faith not turning up? Faith had requested no such thing. The old lady might look and sound sharp as a tack, but she must be slowing down, becoming confused. Along with the letter, a parcel had arrived for Faith. The landlady had carried them both up to her room, making her jump as she rapped at the door.

'Didn't like it to be left in the hall, I get some funny people now-adays. You want to keep a nice house, the right sort of guests, but it is a battle. I thought it must be important, to be delivered by hand, and done up so nicely.'

Faith took the parcel, looking at it with fear. It was not stamped: somebody had sought her out on foot, had been to her home – David? The landlady stood there, expectantly, but Faith shut the door and waited until she heard the footsteps shuffle away, the voice grumbling down the stairs, 'Might at least have said thank you . . .'

She held the packet with her fingertips, turning it over, afraid to touch, let alone open, it. But then she recognized the laboured, anti-quated handwriting with relief. She tore open the brown paper; inside, each item had been wrapped in tissue paper as if it were por-celain: one orange, one hard-boiled egg, a paper bag of broken biscuits and another containing a few tablespoons of sugar. Under-neath was a letter:

Dearest Faith,

I was thinking about you – haven't seen you for such a long time: since the summer? And then I caught sight of you from the bus the other day and

you looked so thin and pale. My dear, do take care. Rest; eat; don't work
too hard. Build up your strength with the enclosed. How is David?

Yours ever,
Jean Roy

Miss Roy was Faith's erstwhile landlady, the elderly spinster of gentle birth but low income who had run the boarding house in Kilburn, Faith's first home away from her parents. She might have escaped her father and mother at last, but to her annoyance Faith had found that the old lady took it upon herself to act as chaperone and adviser, fussing, giving unwanted advice, dropping into Faith's room uninvited. Faith heard all about her life – how hard Miss Roy struggled to keep the old house she loved from falling apart, how, years ago, she had hesitated over whether to marry her lover and then lost him for ever to the trenches of the first war. By the time she had recovered she was past marrying age: 'You don't imagine that you'll only get one chance at happiness . . . ah well. Don't let that happen to you, dear, will you? It's all very well, this art business, but a woman needs a full life.' Not that Faith had welcomed the chats, but Miss Roy felt her to be a kindred spirit. Unlike the other lodgers, Faith did not complain about the brown tap water, the rattling windows, the black mould spots on the walls, the layer of sticky dust that Miss Roy never bothered to remove: Faith thought it materialistic to mind about such things.

She had never experienced such freedom before: she could spend her time exactly as she pleased, painting and drawing all day. Although she was always short of money – the Ministry's commissions did not stretch to much after she'd paid her rent and bought groceries – she would economize on food to make sure she had enough to spend the occasional evening in a café with art-school friends, and more often at the cinema. She saw *Gone with the Wind*, *Rebecca*; they looked wonderful and the men were interesting, but the women! You had two choices: to be a doormat, happy in your domestic chains, or a slut, who might be allowed some escape, but would surely get her comeuppance, most likely die, before the end. There were also concerts to go to. The government was trying to keep spirits up as the war bit down hard on the country by putting on classical music in the public halls of London, even in the empty National Gallery; you could sit in the warm and draw as much as you wanted: everyone else there was watching the musicians and you could study them without interruption. Faith worked up several large oil paintings of orchestras and audiences which had gone down quite well with Sir Kenneth Clark.

Then, in August 1941, for the first time in two years there was a Mussorgsky concert at the Royal Albert Hall. That summer Hitler had reneged on his pact with Stalin and invaded the USSR, so the British public were listening to Russian composers in honour of their new-found ally in the East. Faith was late, and running down the curving corridor she saw a man – he was standing idly, finishing his cigarette, not hurrying, even though the orchestra was already tuning up inside. He was conservatively dressed in a dark suit and hat, much older than her – forty-five perhaps – tall and with an intelligent face, like a loftier Leslie Howard, but not as handsome. He stubbed out his cigarette and, seeing a flustered Faith come to a halt by a door into the hall, he opened it for her. The usher hurried them to the nearest empty seats, next to each other at the end of the row, so they sat down together.

'David Pascoe.' He leant over, spoke quietly and held his hand out to shake hers just as the music began. He looked at her, at the orchestra, and then back at her again – pleased with what he saw. Faith was used to having that effect upon men and usually discounted it, considered it beneath her to want to attract their attention, but as they sat there she was suddenly, unaccountably, very aware of David Pascoe's proximity, the weight of his arm resting next to hers, the line of his leg. She liked the feeling of him there, did not want to move and break the connection. She mumbled her name and took her sketchbook out to draw two small girls sitting nearby, swinging their legs as they listened, bows on the sides of their heads as if two great butterflies had landed there. He didn't interfere, didn't try to see what she was doing.

When the interval came he turned to her. 'Where do you live?' He spoke very well, all the ends of his words beautifully finished.

She felt instantly defensive. What would he think when he heard her voice?

'Kilburn.'

'Alone?' was all he said. He showed no sign of minding the class divide between them that was obvious as soon as she spoke.

'Yes, alone; I've a room in a boarding house.'

'Any good?'

'Depends what you mean. It's damp, dirty, the water's foul, the landlady's a busybody. But I love my independence. There's a difference, I've found, between being alone and being lonely.'

She had not meant to sound quite so snippy and self-important. She realized that she was being defensive, that she was assuming he was interested in her as a London type and examining her as Sir Kenneth Clark had, as if she were from quite another country, another planet.

'I'm not going to fall down even further in your estimation by asking what you do for a living – you're obviously a professional artist of some sort – too good, too confident a line to be an amateur. So perhaps I'll try to raise your curiosity by telling you that I work for a government ministry, in St James's – can't say what exactly, you know how it is these days.'

Faith did not respond.

'You really don't like to give much away, do you? Won't play the game, won't act or think as others expect you to? That's fine: I'm a fellow member of the awkward squad,' David said. He had an attractive way of smiling slowly, as if something were being held in reserve. He fell silent then, and she thought she'd put him off.

The orchestra struck up again: *Pictures at an Exhibition*; Faith had heard it several years before on the wireless as her mother napped on the sofa, and had sat, enraptured by the scenes it painted in her mind of faraway places, countries she had never been to, and would never reach now, if the Nazis won. She recognized the part about the Tuileries, rapid, playful notes describing the elegant, bustling Parisian gardens. And, later, about the Great Gate of Kiev: grand, sonorous chords followed each other, building an image of the colossal edifice with its pointed arch like an ancient Russian battle helmet. The woman sitting next to her on the other side from David shut her eyes to listen, and began to conduct along with the orchestra, one hand moving in time.

Then the music ended, and as they applauded David got up to leave. Faith realized that she did not want him to go. He said good-bye, and then paused and looked back at her.

'You're quite right about being alone, by the way. I lost my child, you see – at the beginning of the Blitz. My wife left me very soon after he died . . . I was no good to be around. She told me that she'd only put up with me anyway because of the boy, there was no reason to stay now that he . . . She had someone else. Our divorce has just come through. So, you see, I live a solitary life too. And now, being with other people doesn't make me any less lonely. In fact, funny thing, I feel closest to the child, to the past, and least lonely, when I am alone.'

Faith had never met anyone who had ended their marriage before. Such things only happened to people in the newspapers, to scintillating, fast, remote beings like Mrs Simpson, and last year there had been the scandal of Laurence Olivier's affair with Vivien Leigh: they had decided to divorce their respective spouses in February and by August were married to each other. But David's divorce was not glamorous – pitiful, rather. She decided it was a mark of his strength of character, his kindness, that he spoke evenly, without rancour.

He looked at her anxiously. 'I don't know why I've told you all this. I hope you're not too horrified . . . But there's something about you, I feel as if I can confide in you . . .'

'I'm not horrified at all, not at *your* behaviour, in any case. And I apologize . . . for being so abrupt.'

He sat back down next to her.

'No need for apologies. It's wonderful, listening to music in congenial company instead of putting up with pointless chatter. Perhaps you'd care to have a drink with me?'

They went to the bar in the concert hall. David told Faith about the house where he'd grown up: a library, a ballroom, stables, surrounded by fields.

'I don't see my parents at all now – such jingoism, can't bear it, our politics are poles apart. The thing is, if you have actually fought, as I did in the last bash, the last thing you welcome is another war. They don't understand why I won't wear my medals, why the sight of the Cenotaph makes me sick. I was gassed, and I was a lucky one. So many men lost: poets, artists like you, Faith. Killed, for what?' After the drink they went out for dinner. They spent that night together.

Faith ignored her mother's warnings about keeping yourself to yourself, about the only thing men wanted, and how they would discard you like yesterday's newspaper when they'd had it. And she was glad that she trusted her instincts and did not waste time with games of flirting and delaying. Sex was a revelation to her, consuming, moving, enthralling. She stayed with David most nights, sleeping with him in his single bed in his sparsely furnished rooms in Kensington. There was no sign of his former wife there, or of the child – only a few books, clothes and other necessities. Perhaps, she thought, he's stored his things elsewhere, because he could not bear to be reminded. 'You're my new beginning,' he said.

At the end of each day they met in town – in cafés, at small, out-of-the-way restaurants – David hurrying from work with his briefcase, Faith with her sketchbook. One afternoon she had not been able to settle to her drawing – she couldn't find the right subjects, to make the lines work on the page – and so she finished early and made her way to St James's. She stood, looking up and down the street; she did not know which building was David's, but she thought she would surprise him coming out of his office. And she saw him, leaving a Georgian house with shutters and well-tended window boxes; it was imposing but discreet, like the London home of a great family, and you would never guess it belonged to the government. But, as David recognized her, he didn't look pleased, he was angry, shocked. He grabbed her arm, turned her around roughly, pulled her away. 'Do *not* do that again. Do *not* come here,' he said. After they had eaten in silence, and sat through a film without touching or speaking, he took her hand. 'I am sorry, I didn't mean to be cross. It's just that I don't want you to have anything to do with my work – it's bloody hard and bloody dull – something I have to endure. And I don't want it to touch you. We're stuck with our duties for now, but not for ever, and when we're together it's the future I want to think about.'

And he talked about what they would do when the war was over and order restored. The places they would visit! He saw them in Paris among the artists, in Florence, Rome, Prague and Leningrad. He had been to all of these cities. He described them to her and described the pair of them on their future travels. His allowance from his parents would be enough for them to live quietly abroad. Sir Kenneth Clark and the bloody Ministry would be a bad memory, Faith would paint exactly what she pleased; she would never have to work for money again. They would sit outside cafés, talking and watching the people pass by, drinking good wine. It was always summer in David's imaginings. And when he spoke of their future he grew animated, vehement, as if it were all real. He believed in it, so you did, too.

If Faith had confided in her mother about David's plans for them both – and the fact that they were already sleeping together – she knew what she would have heard: that David was leading her a merry dance, straight up the garden path and into bed, with these fairy stories. It was only two months after their first meeting that any such doubts were set aside. Faith spent a day with David on Hampstead Heath, she wanted to make a watercolour. Boys ran whooping between the trees, play-fighting imaginary Germans. David carried her things, made sure she had water for her brushes, and tea from a flask when she tired. He had a pocket sketchbook with him, and made several careful drawings of figures in the distance, impressive in their accuracy and detail. But he protested when she admired them – he was not a professional, he said – and put the book away.

Evening came and he led her over to look at the view. When Faith had climbed up there years before with her dad, setting out from the river in the afternoon, London had spread before them, ropes of lights strung out over the space like reflections on a lake. 'Lucky buggers, living up here,' her dad had said. 'You've all of this green space, and the dear old city right at your feet.' Now, at night, there was no sign of habitation apart from barrage balloons floating like huge silver fish, and, when a raid was expected, searchlights that cast beams, widening as they spread like nets into the sky. David interrupted the silence between them to say, 'You should live here, you like it so. What I mean is, you should live here with me. I'm lonely, Faith. Can't discuss my work, don't have anyone to share my life: haven't for such a long time; couldn't take the risk again. But you . . . you're so very lovely: I can't let you go. I think your painting is the most important thing to you, isn't it? It's the centre of your life. I wouldn't interfere. We both need to be alone. But we could have each other, know each other completely in time, I hope. It might mean the end of loneliness . . .'

The register office where they were married in November 1941 had been used for some other, bigger, function just before; there were chairs stacked up around the edges. Faith had no wedding dress, no flowers. She wore a new suit that David paid for, expensive but black and unadorned except for beading at the neck and cuffs, and a hat with a spray of dark, iridescent feathers. Her looks shone in this austere setting, and the lack of fuss felt appropriate for the times, romantic, even, like the scene in *Rebecca* with Laurence Olivier marrying Joan Fontaine in Monte Carlo in a mad rush. Her only concession to tradition was that she stayed with her parents the night before. David had insisted. And on the day Mother and Dad each wore a carnation buttonhole. David was charming to them, kind and attentive, and put them at their ease. His parents did not attend – he said they had sent a small gift, but they had not recovered properly from the end of his first marriage, the death of their grandchild. Faith wondered whether her modest background had anything to do with it, but she didn't ask. And she gritted her teeth and invited Miss Roy, to give the old lady something to look forward to; she had been so delighted to hear of the wedding, and was being forced to sell her beloved home in Kilburn – she could no longer afford even the most basic repairs – and planned to move to a much smaller place in Camden Town where she would only have two rooms to let.

Afterwards, as the wedding party of five stood on the steps outside, Faith was expecting to return to her parents', to sort out the things she wanted to take with her to Kensington. David said no, he had other plans for them, and Mother and Dad and Miss Roy smiled as if they knew what he meant. Rather than setting out for West London, David took her to the Hampstead bus. And when they arrived at the village's main street they climbed up towards the Heath. Standing in front of the final house of a row bordering the trees and grass David said, 'Now we're home.'

The place was Edwardian, solid, handsome and well-kept, its stone lintels carved with fruit and flowers. David showed her in, through a hall tiled in busy patterns of cream, black and conker-brown and up a wide polished-wood staircase to the first floor. Entering the flat, she looked around her in delight. There were high ceilings, windows full of sky. The kitchen was divided from the hall by a curtain of art fabric – Liberty print, perhaps – and there was a ruffle under the sink to match. David had, in secret, moved her possessions from Miss Roy's, and arranged them with his own belongings, things she had not seen in his Kensington rooms, which he must have taken out of storage. They fitted together so well that it looked like a home that had been built by a couple over time, like a stage or cinema set of a modern, educated, bohemian household. The shelves were filled with their books, her Dickens and Brontë novels and David's own library, a mixture as broad and worn as the stock of a secondhand-book shop – everything from travel guides, to poetry, to P. G. Wodehouse. On the walls hung Faith's watercolours and some Georgian etchings of landscapes near his family home in the West Country. There were three of these: undulating hills and pretty, waving trees with here and there a tumbledown cottage or a barefoot peasant and child to add interest. David said this was the present from his parents. Her own mother and father had made them a gift of their best piece of furniture, a bureau that had always taken pride of place in their parlour, but was now the single jarring note in David's stylish, comfortable arrangements. It was hideous: cheap wood varnished dark brown, with barley-sugar legs; Victorian but pretending to be older. Faith apologized but David said that he had told her parents it was delightful; even though he agreed it was the ugliest thing he had ever seen, they would never have been able to tell he didn't like it. He was such a convincing actor.

That night Faith wandered from room to room, touching the books, the pictures, marvelling at how David had created such an impression of ease and permanence, and so quickly. Only one thing struck her as missing entirely – although she did not mention it to him then. There was not a single memento of his lost son; not a photograph, a picture book, a teddy bear. Faith understood why there was no sign of his first wife there – out of sensitivity he would be careful to remove or conceal anything of hers. But of the child? It was as if he had never existed; as if David's past had never existed.

Chapter Nineteen

The sun shone down on the Black villa in the wood, whitening the branches of the trees and the long grass furred with frost, flooding the gold-striped drawing room with its desks, its metal typewriters and piles of documents. Out at the front, Stevens the driver had started the Rolls-Royce to warm her up; the engine settled into a low hum without a second's hesitation. He ran a cloth over the glossy body, whistling to himself.

'We have to talk . . . about our project,' Charles said to Vivienne. She had not heard him come into the hall as she walked through it with her breakfast coffee in her hand to begin work. His voice was light and pleasant, polite concern was all you could see on his face. In the several weeks that had passed since their discussion in the dining room, Charles had given no indication that it had even taken place. His manner had not changed: he had not tried to speak with Vivienne, or leave cryptic notes, or make secret signals.

Vivienne had met with Frido alone three times since her conversation with Charles. The first of these occasions had taken place one afternoon soon afterwards. She made sure that nobody else was in the villa. The maid and cook were out, and Sam and the other two men had been called to Bletchley Park – new material had been intercepted that Black might use.

Vivienne and Frido were in his room, in bed. It reminded her of the places her male art student friends used to inhabit. Domestic comforts were ignored – no ornaments, flowers or cushions, only books, ashtrays and a photograph that Frido kept on the table by his bed. It was not in a frame, just propped up by a water glass, and it showed his family in a garden, mother and father, arms about each other's waist, a sister in her early teens with long plaits and Frido's brow. Frido saw Vivienne looking at it. He took his hand from her naked back and picked the photograph up.

'I'm frightened that I'll never see them again. Not because I'll be killed – I'm not scared of that. But they're in danger because of me.' He held the picture carefully at its edges. She did not respond.

'You don't mind me talking about them, do you?' he said. 'I'd like you to know about them, it matters to me . . . and it helps.'

'Actually, I'd rather you didn't, Frido. It's much better, I think, if when we're together our other lives, the past, the world outside, don't come into it.'

She had not meant to sound heartless, but she could not allow him to confide in her. What if, out of weakness, or fear, she were to pass on what he said to Charles? Surely, though, Frido was being honest, he could not counterfeit such distress, and why would he offer up information about himself with such candour if Charles' suspicions were right? Frido would avoid such a conversation, not request it, desire it. No, he must be innocent.

'Frido,' she said, 'about Charles . . .'

'I had a feeling that something was the matter.' Frido kissed her forehead, embraced her. 'You're worried about him knowing about us. But don't be. Charles hasn't even mentioned finding us together that day. I think he's embarrassed – is that the right word? No, it was awkward for a moment, but that's all. He and I, we aren't close friends in any case, it's not the kind of thing we would ever discuss. We can forget it ever happened. Don't let it come between us, Vivienne. I need you.'

This was Vivienne's cue to speak, to warn Frido about Charles and his real mission at the villa. But she did not. She told herself that Frido was innocent and therefore in no danger from Charles. That the result of telling Frido the truth would be catastrophe. Frido would react with rage, Sam would find out about their affair, Charles' report detailing it would go to his superiors. And Vivienne . . . her reputation would be destroyed, her loyalty to her country under suspicion, her marriage, too, would be threatened. Sam would not look kindly on such a humiliation, and would be livid about Black collapsing as a result of her recklessness.

Vivienne remained silent that afternoon, and after that first failure to speak, it became impossible to tell Frido about Charles. The more time passed, the more difficult it would be to explain to Frido why it was that she had waited hours, days, weeks, to tell him. She had become complicit with Charles, keeping his secret.

Thus, on the surface of things, Vivienne carried on her affair with Frido as before. And if Charles had guessed that they had spent time together, he had not sought her out afterwards to demand information. Vivienne had even tried to persuade herself that Charles might not be working for Intelligence at all, that he might only be a sad little man aggrandizing himself, satisfying some perverse desire to meddle in the lives of those more attractive and interesting than himself, to punish them for his own inadequacies, someone seedy and unpleasant but not actually dangerous. And so it shocked her, now, when he spoke. As he stood in front of her a shaft of sunlight cut through the stained-glass window, casting his open mouth into shadow, scattering red and purple over his skin. His spectacles reflected the light as two empty ovals, she could not see his eyes.

'But you see, I haven't . . . Couldn't we . . . ?' she began.

Just then Sam appeared at the top of the stairs. 'Not today, Charles. It'll have to wait. Need her with me, sorry.'

Ten minutes later – Vivienne had had to change: clothes suitable for Aspley Guise were not good enough for London – she and Sam went outside towards the shining black car. She opened the back door.

'No, darling, in the front,' said Sam. 'Stevens, we won't be wanting you today, call Bletchley, perhaps someone there could do with a driver.' When the man had disappeared inside the villa, Sam said, 'I thought we could be alone for once, I'll run through things on the way, don't need another pair of ears around. And the bloody fellow crawls along. Takes a whole morning to get up to town, doesn't seem to realize that she'll do eighty, that she needs to be let loose once in a while.'

Although Vivienne stayed quiet as they set off, turning her head towards the window, Sam did not seem to notice – he talked on, amusing himself, enjoying the drive.

'His name's Louis de Wohl, a queer fish, quite repellent, but I think you'll find him an interesting study. He's an astrologer and medium, a refugee, famous in Germany before the war. I want him for a magazine I'm planning, a horoscope rag, you know the kind. Thought I'd call it "Zenith", got the right kind of spooky ring, don't you think? Foretelling the future, but not just the "stars of the famous" nonsense that shop girls love. What I thought was, if we can get him to fake some charts for Hitler and his lot, forecasts of ruin and death, and distribute it in Germany. We'll need some drawings for it, too. Do you know the signs of the zodiac?'

'How can you bear it? It's horribly frivolous, this kind of work. I hate it, Sam: Black, the villa. I can't do it any more, I won't. What possible difference can it make, your silly magazines, cartoons, radio shows? Most of them love Hitler, or at least tolerate him. Black won't change their minds.'

Sam, taken aback, waited before he replied. 'I'll tell you this in confidence, I'm really not supposed to, under strict instructions. But you are my wife, after all. And I do trust you. Black's propaganda work *is* essential – but it's not all we've been up to . . . You know that within the Reich der Führer is not universally admired?'

'Everyone knows that' – she was shouting now, uncontrolled – 'that's no secret, and everyone knows that the ones who object, the ones he doesn't like, are dealt with.'

'I don't mean the poor bastards in the camps. No: he's hated within high circles, there are rumblings – very high up, in fact. Plans, you know, to get rid. They've been thinking of it for a while, waiting for their moment; bit of a lull lately with all the victories they had in the summer, his popularity has been so very high. But we are hoping against hope that Stalingrad might just turn the tables on him – if we can help. This is our best, our last, chance to strike, the time has come.'

'But why the astrology magazine?'

'Black's official contribution, a bit of flash. But it's not all we're involved in. No . . . we've been encouraging the dissenters to act, helping with an assassination attempt. I'm not sure that Bracken knows about this other mission. He's not much liked – too fond of a tall story – apart from by Churchill himself. I wouldn't be surprised if they kept Bracken out of it . . . of course, I can't mention it to him to try to find out. And if he doesn't know, that would explain that "productivity" memo of his last month. You can understand now why I was so furious, having the prospect of the Ministry all over us while we're trying to carry out such a difficult secret task. Right hand not knowing what the bloody left hand is doing, as usual . . . We've heard that there's to be a stupendous gift, from the Reich's new territories, an "expression of gratitude from the people of France". Adolf disdains such things, usually refuses presents – never trust a man with no interest in worldly pleasures, he likes things bland, no palate, lives on boiled vegetables and teetotal, to boot. But this . . . this he won't be able to resist.

'It's a painting – you know he's always fancied himself an artist manqué – a Millet, world famous, from a Paris museum. Not our kind of thing at all – stoical peasants in a field, seven shades of mud-brown – but right up his street. Tucked in, along with the Millet, there'll be some small things for his mistress: bespoke scent from the rue du Faubourg St-Honoré . . . and a bottle of brandy supposed to be from the cellar of the Empress Josephine. She's rather a party girl, little Miss Braun, by all accounts, and Adolf does have a soft spot for her – though probably he feels less affection for her than for that blasted dog of his. Everything will be meticulously wrapped, swaddled up for transportation – the flunkeys won't dare tamper with such a cargo. And, you see, the Millet's so precious that the gifts will be taken to Adolf's private plane, to fly from Berlin to Berchtesgaden with him. However, the brandy . . . the brandy won't be quite what it says on the label – the bottle is actually a bomb. Then, when they're thousands of feet over Bavaria . . .'

Vivienne recalled what Charles had said to her about Black being 'of the utmost importance at the moment'. She had not understood what he meant at the time, had argued that all Black did was make propaganda. She remembered how Charles had scrutinized her as she spoke. Of course – he was watching her to see if she was lying, if she knew about the other work going on at Black, about the assassination plot. And she had not known about it, not until today. Charles must have seen the incomprehension in her face, and that would help Sam, it was evidence of his loyalty: he had not told his wife, he had behaved exactly as he had been told to. Sam was true to his country, Charles had said he thought as much, but she had proved it to him without even knowing so.

'I see,' was all she said to her husband. 'You kept your secret very well. Why tell me now?'

'I'm telling you now because I don't want you to lose heart, to think that what you're doing is not important. You've not been yourself lately, Vee. But we must keep churning out our usual stuff, images, scripts, and so on. We don't want to raise suspicions, to signal that our attention's diverted elsewhere. We can't be certain that the Nazis don't know about Black, we have to behave as if they do. That's why your work's essential.'

'You said "we've" been working – who?'

'Only the most trusted. It's obvious, so there's no point in denying that Frido's invaluable – he knows them all, you see, their code names, the lot. Quite fascinating how many over there close to Adolf are actually against him. Frido's been an essential conduit, persuaded them that we're on the level. We've even supplied the explosives. If the bomb is found before it goes off, or if it fails and they get to examine it, it'll look like we British planted it, and that might save a few lives over there. Probably not, of course, as Adolf has a habit of turning on those nearest to him, regardless of their innocence . . . their wives, children. But we have to make the plotters think we're right behind them.'

Vivienne was only half-listening, trying to absorb what Sam was telling her and to work out what it all meant. Sam was under no threat from Charles now, she hoped. But, still, she could not tell him about Charles' investigation without telling him how she knew about it, and how long she had known. And if he found out there would be a tremendous row, Black would be disrupted at this most crucial time, Sam would turn against Frido, might send him away, she would never see Frido again . . . No, she would not tell her husband. She caught Sam's last sentence.

'Surely we do support them?' she said.

'We need them to believe so, we want them to take the risk, you never know, they might even be successful. Either way, it's in our interest. If they don't pull it off but there's pandemonium, paranoia, disunity at the top – perfect. And if Adolf dies, they'll make one hell of a mess battling it out between themselves afterwards, trying to take control.'

'Say they do kill him, I suppose we'd agree an armistice, step in and help them form a new government?'

'God, no! As I said, either way, the chaos that follows something like that is what we're after. Even if they do manage to kill him, what we'll do is capitalize on the confusion, invade, finish them all off.'

Chapter Twenty

The astrologer's office – Sam and Vivienne's destination – turned out to be in a street behind Piccadilly. The high backs of the buildings and the narrowness of the alley between them meant that it would be permanently gloomy here. The bell echoed down the steps to a basement office. A long candlelit room was divided into two by a bamboo curtain, swaying and clinking in the draft. From behind the curtain there came voices, and the newcomers could discern two figures seated either side of a table.

'I see . . . I see a man. A tall man, moving towards you.'

'Is he? Where? Sidney, Sidney, is it you . . . where?' The woman looked around and cast her arms out as if to catch hold of the spectre. 'How does he look? Is he all . . . in one piece again?' she whispered.

'My dear, he is smiling upon you, he has a kind, kind smile.'

'Oh, oh,' the voice sobbed. 'That's Sidney. Definitely. Such a love. How are you feeling, Siddy? Did they hurt you?'

De Wohl stayed silent for a moment. The girl spoke again. 'Did he suffer? His pals said a shell got him. I can't bear to think of it; can't sleep because of it. Will you ask him?'

'He can hear you very well, wait . . . his voice is so faint, it's often the way when they've just passed over, it takes some time for them to acclimatize.'

'Can you hear him properly yet?' She was crying again.

'Sidney? You are still there, dear fellow?' De Wohl asked, and then paused dramatically. 'Oh yes, I can understand you, yes. Yes . . . of course, of course – I shall tell her. Yes, you go and rest now. Join your friends. Do not worry . . . He has told me to tell you that he felt nothing, he woke on the other side as if from a dream, into the daylight. He is whole again; his worry for you is the only thing paining him now. But you can help with that. You have it in your power to release him, to give him peace. Your journey is not over – you must take courage, you must live, as he cannot. He told me to tell you, "chin up", is that correct?'

'Yes, that's him, exactly him, oh, definitely. To the life: oh, oh.' She wept on, and the man moved around to stand by her side until the sobbing petered out into sniffing and gulping.

After a discreet period had passed they heard the snap of a powder compact and then the chink of coins. A large white hand pulled the curtain aside in a clattering sweep and Louis de Wohl emerged, an obese figure with heavily oiled hair who had clearly modelled his attire on that of the 'Great Beast', Aleister Crowley. A short velvet tunic embroidered with arcane symbols in metallic thread covered his top half. He ushered out the young woman, who kept her red eyes averted from them as she rushed past to the door.

'Come through, come through, dear Sam . . . and this lovely lady? Oh, *this* is your wife. Well, well, well – charmed, my dear, quite charmed.'

They were waved behind the bamboo veil into a small alcove where De Wohl showed Vivienne to the chair vacated by the bereaved girl. All the normal furnishings of an office were present, desk, chair, lamp, blotter, but all carved and ornately decorated with 'primitive' designs. De Wohl obviously made money: Vivienne recognized a Chippendale escritoire; out of place among the exotica, its proportions appeared even more refined next to his paunchy body as he sat, sucking on a cigar.

'Sam, tell me, how can I help you today?'

As Sam explained, De Wohl's eyes half-closed and he appeared to enter a state of meditation; garlanded by tobacco smoke he looked like some native idol wreathed in incense.

'You see, De Wohl, we want you to make it look as if it will all be over – that they'll all be incarcerated, or dead, sometime in 1945. And they've got to meet horrible ends, degrading, pathetic, no heroics: suicide while staring at defeat, capture, execution, that kind of thing. Why I say two years from now is that it seems a credible amount of time. Nobody can realistically think that the war will be over next week; but two years is also short enough that people will be able to imagine themselves enduring it – any longer and they'll give up hope. Here are the birth dates and times, as far as we know – for all the Nazi top brass – although you probably don't need them at this stage, if at all; bit of an afterthought, aren't they.'

'I must insist that you stop, Mr Thayer. You are not giving my calling the respect it is due. And you are also perhaps not aware of how much you are asking of me: to draw up fake charts? And when, in two years' time, they are shown to be wrong, what of my reputation, and that of my discipline? Never have I been put in such a position – never have my duties to the country that has given me safe haven, and to my gift, been in such conflict. It is painful . . . most painful.' He clasped his hands to his heart.

'On the contrary, Mr de Wohl, we do realize the nature of your sacrifice. And . . . as we can't assuage your suffering altogether, we will attempt, at least, to make it more bearable.'

De Wohl pondered, visibly, for several minutes; he pressed his finger to his lips and then his palm to his brow. Finally, he shrugged.

'I am afraid and sorry, Mr Thayer, I am very afraid and very sorry, I cannot allow my gifts to be – dare I use the word – *prostituted* (forgive me, dear young lady) – in this manner.'

Sam gave a sigh of frustration and signalled to Vivienne to rise. He had already pulled aside the bead curtain when De Wohl held up a hand.

'Nevertheless, I appreciate that you have come to Louis de Wohl for assistance. You have demonstrated a certain amount of discernment in that you did not approach those charlatans of the fairground booth and the seaside pier. As you have taken the trouble to consult me, I will examine the stars of those you mention, and tell you the truth of what I see. That may, at least, be of some use, your journey not wasted?'

They waited as he rummaged around in the escritoire, fishing out scrolls of diagrams and tables of dates, and began to calculate and scribble.

'Herr Adolf Hitler, and who else?'

'His henchmen; the rat Goebbels will do, for one . . .'

They waited, and waited. De Wohl puffed and bit the end of his pen as he concentrated.

'It is astonishing, most astonishing. What you have asked me to find in the heavens – is actually there! Perhaps you yourself dabbled with the fortunes of these particular individuals before you came to me? No? Or it may be that you have a special sensitivity, raw and untutored, but a sensitivity none the less? Under these circumstances I am happy to provide material for you. The work will be finished by next week (we shall come to some arrangement for my trouble, we shall talk about that later). Now, is there anything else?'

'You can throw in La Dietrich, too,' Sam said. 'If I put a picture of her on the cover people will be bound to pick up the magazine. It's *streng verboten* to speak of her over there now Adolf's excommunicated her, so they're all wild to know how she's getting on. Who knows, if you plot her chart you might be able to predict her rise to even greater heights in Hollywood? Something along the lines of "Marlene shall dance on the graves of her enemies" will do nicely.'

'Quite so, quite so: we all wish Miss Dietrich that opportunity. Providing her stars are auspicious, I don't see why I should not be able to say something in that vein.'

Vivienne rose to leave. De Wohl took her hand in farewell, his grip surprisingly cool and dry. After he had touched her fingers to his lips he hesitated.

'Wait one moment before you go, dear lady. I sense a dark aura around you . . .'

Shut up, *shut up*, you fat fraud, thought Vivienne.

'Forgive me, my dear, but you face a dilemma,' he persisted.

Sam smiled. 'How do you do it, De Wohl? You're absolutely right; Vee has a pressing decision to make: is it to be white or red at dinner, darling?'

On the way back to Aspley Guise, Sam was tired, content to drive and smoke without making conversation. But the peace in the car gave Vivienne's frantic thoughts freedom to circle round and round. She would not tell her husband or her lover about Charles and his surveillance of them. But, she determined, nor would she try to gather information about Frido and his past, to entice him to speak to her and report what he said to Charles. It reeked of betrayal, even if she were doing it to prove his innocence.

Vivienne realized, sickened, that she would have to end things with Frido all the same. She might then persuade Charles that there was no point in pressing her, that she was not in Frido's confidence any longer. Even if Charles did not fall for that, if he grasped that she had never intended to help him, and wrote a damning report on the Black villa, the only thing she could do to limit the havoc was to distance herself from her lover straight away; then she could claim to Sam that it had merely been a brief fling, foolhardy but over even before it began. Sam would be angry with her, but she might manage to make him believe that she had come to her senses of her own accord; this would be better for Sam's ego than his wife being discovered in the midst of an affair and only then stopping it. Funny how she had never considered how she would feel when her time with Frido ended, as it inevitably had to, even without Charles and his interference. How she would miss the boy. How barren and bleak her life would be. For the first time in her dealings with men, Vivienne felt something uncalculated, unmanageable.

The night closed in as the Rolls-Royce left the London suburbs behind – it was freezing, with a fathomless sky full of stars, and Sam drove more slowly than he liked because of the treacherous roads. But still, too soon, there were only a few miles left to Aspley Guise. Vivienne closed her eyes and prayed that they would never arrive, that the car would skid and crash, that a bomb would land out of the clear sky on them, on the villa, and finish it all for good. One way or another, she knew that she was coming back to the end of everything.

Chapter Twenty-One

Laura drove out to a new beginning – real work, at last. On the morning of her arrival, RAF Mildenhall lay beneath an immense sky the pale grey of a London pigeon. The clouds pressed down upon the flat countryside, miniaturizing the gathered buildings, and the uniformed figures – stamping across the square, looping around the perimeter track in trucks, worrying at the aeroplanes – looked like puppets, without real weight or presence. The level reaches of plush, green land that stretched from Suffolk into Norfolk had been cut apart and re-joined with hard grey seams – the runways necessary since the Americans had joined the war, hugely swelling the ranks of planes and airmen. It was said that there was an airbase every eight miles throughout East Anglia. This most tranquil and archaic of landscapes had become a modern vista of concrete and machinery, of men and women in identical slate-blue or drab green.

Mildenhall had taken over Laura's mind since Smith's initial telephone call about it. In the five days since that victory, Smith had found it hard to relinquish their combat entirely. He had told Laura that she would be staying in a hotel a good few miles away from the base, a sedate sort of place, she would need tranquillity, would find the commission taxing. But she had insisted on a boarding house a short walk away. It was not of the best quality, apparently, and noisy with planes and other traffic, but it was essential that she could get there and back whenever she needed to, and cheaper, she could take two rooms, one for her work things. She had also demanded that he locate a studio for her to paint in at Mildenhall itself – a disused office or even a shed would do, if it had decent light. She needed space, she said, she intended to make a large, important oil. In truth, Laura had not decided what her work there would be. She did know, on the other hand, what Smith expected, that he secretly hoped for a series of small-scale, cosy portraits – spruced-up officers in their medals. She pictured Clark riffling through the paintings, bored, and heard Smith's voice in the background, persuasive, persistent: 'There's absolutely no point in going to the trouble of sending her out again, she can do this kind of thing just as well at home.' Laura would have to force herself into the thick of it to prove them wrong.

The first evening, she ventured into the hall where off-duty staff congregated. She had barely taken a seat when a whistle shrieked and the tannoy crackled and blared into life: 'Enemy overhead! Take cover! Take cover! To the dugouts!' Laura snatched up her sketchbook and reading glasses, heart thumping, but nobody else took any notice, the two WAAFs next to her continuing with their mending, so unperturbed that they did not even hesitate over the next stitch. She sat back down and reached for her pencil to draw them . . . and then stopped herself. How Smith would enjoy it if she settled for such a subject! 'I managed to arrange a pass to an airfield and she came back with *this*!' She could see the incredulous expression and the dismissive flourish of the arm in the direction of a picture of two women sewing. This was her best chance, perhaps her last and only chance, to make a truly great painting. First thing in the morning, she would go out to the aeroplanes.

'Is this the way? Can you show me to the Operations Room?'

At Laura's question the officer looked up, surprised. 'Ops? Are you sure? Well, if you must, then see that truck there? You need to stop him on his rounds.'

In the open space and blustery wind Laura stood exposed, suddenly feeling ridiculous in her wide-brimmed hat and trailing silk scarf, her scarlet cardigan and long embroidered skirt, as if she had just spent the day looking at pictures in the National Gallery or browsing the bookshops and was waiting for a bus on the Charing Cross Road.

The truck jolted to a halt in front of her.

'The tumbril awaits, madam.'

'Bloody hell, who gave you permission to come in here?'

All heads turned in her direction as Laura came through the

door. She began to say something about the Ministry, about Smith, but the man at the front waved her away impatiently. She stood, in front of the rows of uniforms, enduring the cold scrutiny, feeling wrong, but then a figure at the back beckoned to her and moved across to give her a seat. She could tell from the glances of the others that his offer of help would not make him popular. As she sat down, she appraised her helper: the face he would have as a man had not revealed itself fully yet, its form still covered by the unlined, close-knit skin of a boy – twenty at most – with only a light shading of stubble to emphasize the shape of the chin. He had brown eyes, black brows echoing the long curve of the eyelids, and a finely drawn nose and mouth.

He smiled and leant towards her to whisper, 'Glad to meet you, Mrs Knight. Should I call you Dame Laura? Are you here to paint? I know your stuff, I . . .' A man sitting in front turned to them angrily, so the boy fell silent.

The speaker continued his briefing, charting heights and courses, the tops and bases of the clouds. Behind him, a map spread out on the wall was decorated with a thin band of red ribbon, held in place by drawing pins, that zigzagged across Europe. The brown-eyed boy looked ahead intently with a studied blankness of expression, but his fingers were twisting tightly around each other.

As the rows of aircrew silently absorbed their orders, the man at the front consulted his list for any other business. During this hiatus Laura raised her hand.

'Yes?' came the exasperated response.

'Could I, I mean, would it be possible to fly in one of your planes?'

'Absolutely – unquestionably – not. Unlucky, for one thing; we don't let women run around out here if we can help it. And, no matter what the MOI thinks, we aren't a holiday camp for thrill-seekers.'

A general murmured assent rippled around the room, broken up by some sniggering. Laura baulked at the silly superstition; how could it be acceptable for women to build the planes, to fashion the rivets, to stamp out the sheets of metal, to construct the engines, even (she had heard) to fly them down from the factories to the airfields, but not to stand anywhere near them, or climb inside them once they were on site? Indignation did not dampen the niggling sensation that the men would prefer, desired it above all, that she left. But she had no choice but to sit it out. She might just as well give in and make a start on the painting of two WAAFs and a sewing basket if she were to retreat from the room now. Even if she were not allowed to fly, there must be a way to paint the men and their planes.

'Yes, I knew there was something else.' Consulting his paper the speaker continued, 'The retirement of the Stirlings and the arrival of the Lancasters' – a groan from the seated men – 'it's been confirmed, but they haven't given us a date yet.'

From the audience a hand rose and a voice was heard.

'I know there's no going back, but can I just say, on behalf of us all, that it's a bloody stupid time to change now that we're doing more missions than ever. When are we supposed to train? And the new ones – they may look swanky, but they can't take the punishment and keep going like our old girls.'

Shouts of 'hear, hear!' broke out. Laura recognized her moment. She stood up.

'I can do something for you, you know, be of some use. I'll paint them, your Stirlings. You'll have a proper record, something to remind you when the change happens, and later, when this is all over. And now, gentlemen, I think it would be most useful if I looked more closely at the aircraft.'

Laura took her sketchbook and pencils out of her bag with an air of efficient purpose and smiled at the men confidently, even though she felt the rows of eyes upon her, hostile, as she left the room.

The ground crew, engrossed in their tasks against the rhythmic phut-phut-phut of the bowsers, stopped, one by one, to watch Laura as she approached. She breathed deeply to calm herself, inhaling the smell of fuel, tarmac and soaked grass that gusted across the expanse of field and runway. Then she began, with slow deliberation, to walk around each of the planes, as if she were conducting an inspection. She had never been anywhere near an aeroplane before, and had always wanted to. Harold did not like the idea of flying.

After the trial of the first meeting, matters improved. The men allowed Laura to go among them while they prepared and waited for the signal to join their planes. She studied their flying clothes closely, as bulky as if the figure cocooned within was about to set off for the North Pole. The complexity of the costume meant that it took great concentration to understand and sketch it accurately: at one end giant rubber-soled suede boots, at the other a close-fitting cap of stitched leather with ear pieces and goggles. The body in between was swaddled in a padded suit with a waistcoat over it, both covered in pockets; on top of these garments webbing circled the torso and ran between the legs. Everything was held together by a system of buttons, zips and toggles, with clips and a whistle dangling at the front. And the smell of it all, worn so many times, sharp and gamy as an old mattress, heightened when they all waited together in the crew room – it was the imprint of the body's tension during the long nights in action.

On her third day of attending the briefings and preparations, when Laura had nearly completed a sketchbook full of uniform drawings and colour notes, the brown-eyed boy who had helped her on that first day approached her. He shook her hand.

'George Meredith – navigator. I know, like the writer, but not after him. I think the only people who didn't realize it were my parents. You must want to see some other things by now. I'll try to arrange it.'

The next morning, Laura found herself climbing up a ladder and into a hole in the belly of a plane, George Meredith steadying her uncertain progress. The man inside began to remonstrate when Laura's head appeared in the hatch; from behind her she heard George say, 'Jim, it's all right; I'll take the blame.' Laura moved awkwardly into the dark tube.

How did men work in this confinement, wrapped in all of that bulk? How did they cram themselves into the cockpit, bristling with levers, buttons and dials? This would be her subject – not the vast, impersonal, abstract patterns of entire squadrons in the sky, but the intimate experience, the physical reality of the bodies inside the machine.

When she had finished, and they were back on the tarmac, George said, 'There's the Flight Sergeant walking over now. You'd better go quickly. But you can come back and draw the ground crew, later this afternoon perhaps, when there's no one else around.'

'But, George, to do you all justice I need to see the men together in the plane just before take-off.'

George whistled. 'That's a tall order, Mrs Knight.'

She watched as he went towards the Sergeant who had been joined by other uniformed men. George stood respectfully, waiting his turn. He began to speak. They looked at her, and then back at George. They turned away from him. Then Laura heard his voice again, persistent. Finally he touched his hand to his forehead and came back towards her.

'Sergeant Midgley says I'm pushing it, really pushing it. But he agreed that you can have fifteen minutes before we head off if you keep it quiet . . . oh, and "never darken our cockpit again" – his words, not mine. In return, I've got to get everything spot on tonight, one mistake and I'll be for it, sent back to training.'

When Laura entered the plane again after dark it had become a different space – smaller now that it held the crew, and the atmosphere had altered, quickened. Faster than she had ever worked before, Laura tried to note the crucial things that she could not have guessed at: the dull, undersea cast of light echoing off the metal walls, the manner in which the unwieldy figures moved and communicated, George sitting over his maps, with his compass and pencil. As she lowered herself back down the ladder, Laura repeated a list to herself of those details she had not had time to record to try and hold them in her mind. 'Burnt sienna; yellow ochre; oxygen canisters; the exact expression on George's face.'

Between briefings and missions, George gave up his time to pose for the figures in the painting, sitting as the pilot, the wireless operator, the bomber-aimer, and himself. In return, she offered to decorate his crew's beloved Stirling, christened by them 'Midgley's Flying Circus'. She painted a clown, up on the side, near what she thought of as the nose of the plane. He stood, knock-kneed and perplexed, as if a prank involving a custard pie or a bucket of water had just been played on him. The scaffold by the plane was not high enough for Laura, so George carried a toolbox up for her to stand upon, and she felt his hands on the small of her back, helping her to balance. When she thought about her time at Mildenhall afterwards, Laura wondered at her confidence that he would return every day and that they would complete her painting of the airmen together. Familiar faces were vanishing and new men filling the gaps. Thanks to her patient, considerate model – George did not interrupt her concentration with talk; he remained motionless until she put down her brushes – the painting, Laura knew, was a triumph.

It took two weeks of work before she was ready to scrawl her signature across the bottom of the canvas with a brush dipped in alizarin. As she did so, George applauded. 'Mrs Knight, I'm not flying tonight, and I insist we celebrate. See you outside the rec hall at 1900 hours.'

Standing by the door that evening, as the young men and women came and went, Laura felt like a girl waiting for her sweetheart at the cinema, worked up, full of fluttering feelings of anticipation: absurd at her age. From across the tarmac she saw George appear, but her pleasure at his arrival was checked by the sight of the two bicycles he wheeled.

'I can't possibly. I'm an old woman. Haven't cycled for years.'

'You can. We'll get there much quicker.'

'No, really. Isn't there ice about? I can't possibly.'

'Yes, you can.'

'I can't.'

'Let's go.'

As George pedalled off confidently, Laura waited a moment. She did not want him to see her shaky ascent and uncertain wobble after him, while trying to avoid the frozen puddles.

Inside the pub – low-ceilinged and smelling of woodsmoke from a fireplace nearly as tall as the room – most of the clientele were from Mildenhall. She was relieved to find WAAFs among them; she had feared being the only woman there, but the girls appeared at ease among the horse brasses and advertisements for Guinness.

Laura sipped at her beer, the thick glass rubbed around the rim by all of these thirsty young mouths, with an opaque bloom on it as if it had washed up on the seashore. George told her about his – very recent – childhood.

'I want to paint more than anything, but the old folks don't like the idea – I'm to follow my father into the bank. The only vaguely modern artist they've heard of is Toulouse-Lautrec, so they think it would mean cancan dancers and absinthe – though I wouldn't mind some of that.' He fell silent.

Laura thought to tell him not to be too hard on his parents; having never known her own father, and lost her mother as a young woman, she knew the desolation of their absence to be far greater than any petty annoyance at their shortcomings. But then she thought better of it; she did not want to lecture George, to take that role, to sound pompous and old. She wanted to spend time with him, stay close to him, to listen.

As she watched, Laura saw his expression darken. 'I wish I'd had a chance to enjoy myself, just for a couple of years – to find out if I have any talent, before this.'

Then he seemed to rally, his voice brightened as he asked her to tell him about art school, studios and galleries, the painter's life. 'Do carry on. I'm not tired of your stories. More – please. You know I always look for your work in the Academy.'

That night, on her return to her digs (walking and pushing the bicycle, as they had stayed in the pub for several hours), Laura decided she could no longer ignore Harold's existence. She sat down to begin a letter: 'Missing you – it's terribly hard. You were absolutely right, my darling, I should never have come.' She couldn't think of anything else to write, not a word, and disliking the feeling of having so little to say to her own husband, she took out a blank postcard and scrawled a note to Faith Farr instead: 'Write and reassure me that all is well with you . . . at RAF Mildenhall! I am, at the age of sixty-five, having the time of my life.'

She spent a minute or so sketching a vignette on the picture side of herself brandishing her brushes, dwarfed by a Stirling. That was better, she was pleased with the comedy of the sketch, it might cheer the child up, spur her to action. But the one line to Harold still sat there, the empty paper reproaching her, and she still could not think of what on earth to put. Unease at her neglect of him rankled. She must telephone first thing in the morning.

'Laura? Laura!' Harold asked about her work, proud of her progress – but as always the anxiety, the irritating old-man querulousness, underlay his conversation.

He talked of the Worcestershire countryside that he spent his days walking through and had begun to paint. 'As important as war subjects; don't you think? To let people see that the land remains ours – for the moment.'

He told her how difficult he found it to concentrate on his work without her there. 'Come back to me, Laura; just for a week. It feels like an age. I won't hear any more excuses. I need you as much as the Ministry does.'

But Laura did not want to leave Mildenhall, to leave George. She knew, though, that if she didn't make a plan to go – perhaps when George and his crew would be on leave and she could be certain of his safety for the short time she was away – then she would find herself having to travel back to Malvern at an inconvenient time: while George was away on a mission, or when she was struggling in the middle of a painting. Harold would insist, growing increasingly fractious and upset until she gave in. There was no possibility of avoiding it; Laura would have to return to her husband soon – *for a visit*, she reassured herself.

Chapter Twenty-Two

Since the bombing of the knitting party, Cecily Browne's father had made it a condition of her continuing with the Ministry that, from now on, she work only in small towns or in the countryside, miles from any risk. His anger at the harm his daughter had come to while sketching in the Belgravia mansion had not much abated by the first week of the new year, when Smith telephoned with a new commission. Thankfully the Co-ordinator of Women Artists – as Smith introduced himself to Mr Browne – had been solicitous and apologetic, and had asked if Cecily might agree to paint land girls. Smith had telephoned again to go through the arrangements carefully, explaining that he was paying a farmer handsomely to put her up, and that she could stay for however long she needed to complete her work in peace and in the fresh air. He had also said that he thought that a painting of the young women all together in their dormitory would be best; she could show them relaxing in private, perhaps preparing for bed? And she must be certain to capture all of the tiniest details, just as she had with the knitting party. It was unusual for the Ministry to be so specific about a commission. But when she sounded uncertain, Smith said he could already see the painting in his head. That he was entirely confident that it would be a huge success; and that he was convinced that Sir Kenneth would appreciate such a subject too.

Motoring along in the winter sunshine in her mother's car (Smith had even procured a petrol allowance), Cecily saw empty fields fringed with high hedges, here and there some horses, a sheep pen, a figure on a tractor. Looking at the quiet scenery you would never guess that there was a war on. As for the land girls themselves and their billet, she imagined a kind of Eden, without the snake – a sisterhood, similar to the Girl Guides.

She reached the farmhouse in the late afternoon; it was a long building set at an angle to the road, with the wall at one end hard against it. Low barns of wood and corrugated-iron sheets surrounded the yard where she parked. The place was spartan; there had been no recent expenditure on its looks, even though the house itself, with its mullioned windows and the carved lintel over the door which read 1637, could have been extremely pretty. But the farm was obviously well-organized, with none of the clutter of broken-down equipment, old tyres, bits of rope and empty sacks heaped up outside some of the ramshackle rural places she had seen along the way.

A boy came to the door, wiping his nose on his sleeve as Cecily told him who she was. A grey-haired woman smiled at her from the kitchen range. 'We try to look after everyone here,' she said. 'Doing our bit.' She told the boy, Thomas, to show Cecily where she would be working. In a storeroom down a long passageway and up some steps, they had cleared a space, pushing a pile of junk – some broken chairs, an old sofa with the stuffing bursting out – to one side, and there was a large window looking over the fields and an electric light. But she would be sleeping with the other girls. 'No room, you see, we've four lads ourselves. None of them old enough to go, thankfully.' Thomas showed Cecily up to the bedroom, plain like the rest of the house, with bare floorboards and faded curtains, clean, though, and freshly swept. There were two sets of bunk beds, one littered with movie magazines and underwear. A bottle of expensive scent stood on the dressing table. Whorls of frost patterned the inside of the window pane. A fire had been laid – waiting for the evening when the others would be there. Cecily kept her coat on as she unpacked.

She sat and read for a while, and then, much earlier than she expected dinner to be served, Thomas reappeared bearing a tray with a bowl of soup, a baked apple and a cup of tea. 'Bathroom's second down the hall,' he said. 'Mother said you should wash as soon as you've had this before the others use all of the hot water up.' As she was eating she heard the voices of girls in the kitchen, the sound of chairs and cutlery, and then, thumping up the stairs, in they came: Ivy, Mabel and Connie. They had been told of Cecily's purpose, and she wondered whether it was because they were to be painted that Ivy and Mabel looked so glamorous for a day in the fields. Surely they did not make such efforts for farm work? Both wore lipstick. Ivy had arranged her auburn hair in a velvet snood. Mabel, who shared her pair of bunks, made up for unfortunate buck teeth with long, dark waves and a sultry fringe over one eye – at the right angle, when you couldn't quite see her mouth, she looked like a brunette Veronica Lake.

'You sound exactly like that film star, Cecily. You know the one, Ive: married to Heathcliff.'

'Vivien Leigh?' said Ivy.

'That's it: Lady Hamilton.'

'D'you think? I'd say more like Celia Johnson. Can't believe they've put you in here with us. Connie, don't you think you'd better give her the top bunk?'

'Please don't bother,' said Cecily, 'I really shouldn't like any fuss.'

'It's no trouble, miss,' said Connie, an ungainly girl, her hair, messy and uncurled, tied back with a piece of string. While Ivy and Mabel smoked and chattered, Connie swapped the bedding around.

'Thank you, Connie. And please – not miss, it's Cecily.'

The girl looked at Cecily shyly, as if she were peering out from behind her own eyes. Then she turned away and Cecily was surprised to see her dab some of the expensive scent on to each wrist, holding them up to her face to breathe it in. She had supposed that it belonged to one of the others.

The flannel nightdress Cecily's mother had insisted that she pack was as voluminous as a parachute. Cecily tugged down the long sleeves – elasticated around the wrists to trap the warmth – and clambered up on to the thin mattress, intending to write to Richard. His letters had been much more regular, one every single day over the past couple of weeks, and there had been no sorrow after the postman's visits. The others, having asked polite questions – where are you from? Do you have a boyfriend? – and having admired the photograph of Richard and Cecily together that she had taken from the piano at home, went about their routines. Cecily drifted between composing her letter and listening.

'So how *do* you stop it from happening, then? We're miles away from town. I think I'll just trust to my luck,' said Mabel.

'Don't you know anything? You've got to take care of yourself.' This was Ivy. 'You heard what happened to Dolly's brother's friend.'

'Stop. I don't want to think about it,' Mabel said, but Ivy was enjoying herself.

'She keeps it all secret, leaves it too late, and then what? Goes and decides she can't cope.' Mabel squealed and covered her ears with her hands, but Ivy continued. 'All on her own.'

No words, only shuffling, from Mabel, who had covered her head with the blanket.

'The neighbours noticed her getting fatter and fatter, never going out of the house except for after dark – and her husband a POW for the past two years. Then she turns up in the corner shop one day, stick thin and white as a ghost but no sign of baby. It was the shopkeeper that put two and two together and reported her. They found a heap of tiny bones in the stove.' Ivy finished her story with a flourish, deepening her voice and dragging out the words. Mabel giggled.

From over the top of her letter Cecily could see Ivy and Mabel, together on the bottom bunk opposite; clearly, they had not considered practical matters when choosing their nightclothes. Ivy, in filmy pink, lay with her head in her friend's mauve satin lap, smoking. Both had covered their shoulders with the farm's scratchy striped blankets and looked like squaws from a Hollywood film. Connie, Cecily noticed with amazement, didn't even own a nightdress – she had gone to bed in the same vest and knickers she had worn all day and now lay still and silent. She must already be asleep.

Cecily put down her letter, and quietly – she hoped that they wouldn't notice her – turned to face the wall. It was only about nine o'clock, but all of the driving and then having to find her feet in an unfamiliar place had tired her out, and they would be getting up at dawn.

She shut her eyes and planned her work; some evenings she would paint the bedroom scene of all the girls that Smith had requested. However, she also decided on a group at labour in the fields, and another, altogether simpler but grander, picture: a landscape with the single figure of a woman striding out in the early morning. These two paintings would mean days spent outside drawing and making watercolours, and nights in the storeroom, with oil paints and canvas. One thing was certain, she said to herself, it wouldn't be either Ivy or Mabel in the big picture, no matter how nice their hair – a 'wholesome' girl was required. Then, as Cecily tried to sleep, the insidious voice whispered, *Go home, go home; you'll never make anything out of this lot.*

Sometime in the night a scraping sound woke her briefly. Out of the blackness two figures swam into outline; there were whispers and a smell of alcohol. The next morning, by Ivy and Mabel's beds lay a jumble of clothing, among it a polka-dot frock and a lace slip threaded with ribbons. On top of the pile sat two unopened packs of silk stockings.

These things would not appear in Cecily's painting – nor would the cigarettes, Connie's scent, or Mabel's Dorothy Lamour mules, with their trimming of marabou feathers and red Louis XV heels that went clattering down the farmhouse corridors. Instead, Cecily painted spotless, demure cotton petticoats hanging from a hook, cosy sheepskin slippers side by side beneath a bunk and figures dressed in sensible nightgowns absorbed in tidying up or patting on face cream. One girl, already in bed, lay with the blanket pulled so high that she was only visible from the nose upwards. Cecily showed Connie undressing, it was true, but in the act of stretching her jumper over her head, the girl revealed only a white blouse buttoned all the way up and tucked firmly in around her waist.

Finishing the first painting against such odds was a small triumph, and Cecily wrote to Richard: 'Such a jolly team, and so hardworking. It sounds boastful, and I don't like to say it, but I feel I'm making something fine out of the time I've been given here. I hope that people will look at my paintings and see that there is still truth and beauty in the world.'

Connie was such a patient sitter, placid and reasonably pleasant to look at when you weren't distracted by the flashiness of the other two, that Cecily decided to use her for the painting of a field at sunrise. The scene came off extremely well. It showed a pasture under an imaginary mackerel sky – Cecily had replaced the grey cloud that hung above their heads each and every day with something more uplifting worked up from photographs – with the young woman in her boots and gaiters at its centre.

Finally, Cecily tackled the group picture, of fruit trees being pruned. There was the chill weather to contend with, and there were the girls themselves. Ivy and Mabel wore overalls and heavy boots and sweaters, but the concession to their work ended at the neck. They stopped regularly to touch up their lipstick ('we *are* near a road, we might be *seen*'). Through the bare branches you could often discern two blue threads of smoke unravelling upwards above the scarves they had taken to wearing elaborately knotted into turbans. They tackled only the easy branches – not those that required reaching through a tangle, risking their headgear getting caught on rogue twigs, and their efforts lasted only for short periods of time before a rest in the barn was required, out of the harsh wind that would ruin the complexion.

After a week of drawing this subject all day, and painting in the evening, Cecily had only to make certain sketches and colour notes outside in the orchard before the pruning picture could be finished. But as she often found, these final minutiae were more difficult to get exactly right than she had expected. So she spent most of a day struggling and blowing on her fingers to try to keep them agile enough for work. By mid-afternoon, even though she did not have everything she needed, Cecily decided that unlike the others, who went to huddle in the barn with a flask of tea before continuing for another hour, she would have to return to the farmhouse to sit by the kitchen range and thaw out properly. While you stood still, the cold crept up more rapidly than if you were moving about. And there was the chance that she would have some time alone, before they all came back, to write to Richard.

After the long march down the lane, she stayed in the kitchen for a while and then went up to the bedroom. As she closed the door behind her, she heard weeping. There on a bunk lay Connie, who lifted a wet, red face from the pillow.

'Can I do anything, is there anything . . . ?' As Cecily began, the girl's tears grew more passionate.

'I hoped no one would come yet.' She turned away.

'I thought you were out in the lower field today?'

'I was, but then . . . I didn't feel right.'

There was quiet for a while and Cecily settled herself on her bed with her writing paper and book. But then the crying started again, sobs punctuated by gulps and sniffing.

'You might as well know. I've had it. It's my own fault, but he's gone, he'll never come back and what'll . . . what'll happen to me . . . to us?' The sobbing took over again, and the face was pushed back into the pillow.

Cecily climbed down to sit next to the girl and, not knowing what to do, rested a hand on her shoulder. There was no response, so she took it away again.

'Have you thought . . . I mean, was there any talk of marriage?'

'I told you, he's gone.' The girl said this angrily, and there was a third crescendo of crying; Cecily waited for it to subside. 'Anyway, he'll never come back here if he comes back at all, he's American.'

'I believe there are places . . . they help in such circumstances. If you left quickly, no one here need find out.'

Connie squirmed around and bunched up on her side. Cecily sat for a few moments more, and then climbed up on to her bunk again to allow the girl some privacy in which to recover.

The crying finally ceased and there was silence, interrupted by Connie, calmer now. 'You're right, I'll have to go, sort it out and pretend it never happened. It's the only way. You won't ever tell about me – will you . . . *please*? Not a word, not to anyone.'

'Of course not – never; I promise.'

Connie lay quietly. Then, before the others returned, Cecily went to wash; when she came back from the bathroom, she found Connie sitting up on the bed flicking through a magazine. She had powdered her face to try to cover the flush and shine. She must have taken Ivy or Mabel's make-up, as she didn't own any herself, and clearly she did not know how to apply it – her cheeks were pale and chalky while her nose remained damp and pink. All of the girls and Cecily ate supper together, and though Connie was silent throughout, this was not remarked upon as she never really spoke much, and Ivy and Mabel assumed she was still feeling ill. Connie avoided looking at Cecily as they readied themselves for sleep.

The following morning, Connie did not go out to work in the fields with the rest of them, and when evening came, she and her things were gone. After supper Cecily escaped from Ivy and Mabel, who were speculating avidly about what had happened to Connie, and went down to the storeroom to look over her paintings. The pruning picture was coming out very well, after all. The girls were depicted against the rolling landscape, bending stolidly into the wind in smart brown overalls, intent on their work of humping ladders around and balancing bravely on them to tackle the highest branches. Around the edges of the picture Cecily was painting hands – dextrous, capable hands, wielding secateurs, pliers, a saw. The painting of the dormitory was all right, too, with poor Connie there right at the front, her face obscured by the sweater she was pulling over her head.

But the glorious portrait of Connie walking out into a luminous dawn, although it was the best Cecily had ever painted, could never be shown. What if the girl, having managed to cover everything up, put her time in the country behind her and make a fresh start, were to see the painting by chance in a magazine, a newspaper, or even – although this was unlikely – a gallery? All that had happened would come back to torment her; the man taken away by the war, the ill-starred, unwanted baby given up to another family – if she let it survive. Cecily had promised that she would never tell, but wasn't the painting a very public reminder of Connie's time as a land girl? Besides, the painting had been completely spoilt for Cecily; she would not be able to look at it, to enjoy it herself. There was only one thing to do. She would have to alter it. She would paint Connie out of the picture and put her own face there instead.

Chapter Twenty-Three

Faith awoke with the feeling that something was wrong. She had been deeply asleep; the first proper rest in weeks with no bad dreams, no scares in the night. For once she did not feel dragged back down by a swell of exhaustion at the thought of rising from her bed, but all the same there was a sense that something untoward had happened.

She opened her eyes and at first could not tell where she was. Then the space around her shrank and coalesced into the four walls of her room in Holloway, the mysterious, hulking forms in the granular darkness became her narrow wardrobe, the table and single chair, the black cast-iron fireplace. But even when her surroundings had become familiar the sense of menace remained, like an odour in the air.

Faith rose quickly. She stumbled against the suitcase next to her bed and the jar with the candle rolled across the floor. She went to the window to pull back the blackout curtain and let the reassuring, ordinary daylight in. A morning of crystalline winter sunshine, and it must already be quite late – the street was busy. She looked about her. The room seemed the same as ever: the suitcase had moved, of course, when she had bumped into it, but everything else remained in its place.

She switched on one bar of the electric fire and got back under the covers to wait until the warmth had spread. She had Laura Knight's autobiography by her bed. Curious about the woman who had rescued her from Smith and carried her off for tea, whose achievements eclipsed her silly 'artistic' clothes, Faith had sought out the book, finding a secondhand copy. She opened it where she had stopped reading the night before. It was fifty years ago, the old Queen was still on the throne, and Laura's childhood was ending.

Ugly threads were being woven into the material of my character. I shook hands with hate; he and morbidity were my bedfellows. I contemplated jumping out of the window, but that was no use; I should only bounce off the roof of the outside lavatories.

The troubled young woman who emerged from these pages, bedevilled by tragedy, poverty and self-doubt, seemed impossible to relate to the successful artist one saw today – forceful, canny, famous – living life entirely on her own terms. Laura Knight had triumphed; it could be possible.

Then, as Faith turned on her side to settle to her reading, she caught sight of the door and knew immediately what was amiss. As if a freezing wind had blown through the room, the flesh on her scalp, on her arms, tightened. The key – which she always left in the lock to make sure that no one could open it from outside – was now lying on the floor at the foot of the door, as if someone had managed to push it out. Swiftly she moved to test the handle: the door was locked. She might have dropped the key herself, in a hurry to secure the door and get into her bed the night before, distracted, oblivious, but still the sight of the key on the floor unnerved her. What if someone had managed to push out the key, on to a piece of paper that they then pulled back under the door, to open it and creep in while she slept? She had seen a prowler enter a house this very way in a film. It would be easy enough for them to secure the door again from the outside, push the key back, and sneak downstairs after they had finished. She unlocked the door and looked out, cautiously; there, on the landing, lay a page of newspaper.

Faith looked about the room; with so few possessions it was easy to tell that, on the surface, nothing had been disturbed. But then her eye fell upon the suitcase, where she had hidden the package. She clicked it open. Of course the letters were no longer piled as they should be – she had just knocked against the case herself and it was impossible to know if they had been tampered with before that. Faith worked at the pink silk at the back of the suitcase, peeling away a corner of fabric. Her fingertips touched the bundle with its wrapping of paper and tape; it was still in its place. But still she felt uneasy, exposed, as if she were being watched.

She had to leave this place – what if David had come here in the night, stood over her as she slept, been about to act, but then had not been able to bring himself to go through with what he had planned? And suppose he were to return and decide not to let her sleep on this time? But should she take the package with her? She hesitated: if David had looked around the room and not found it yet, it might be safer to leave it where it was, although he might come back, might change his tactics and tear the place apart. But should he catch her when she was out in the city and she was carrying it, she would be in greater danger. What should she do?

Faith pulled on some clothes, ran her fingers through her hair and put on her hat and coat. There was no time to wash or fuss. She took up her suitcase, opened it, ready to pack, and then stopped. If David should return, he must not come to the conclusion that she had left. If it were to appear that she was still living in this room he would carry on looking for her in this area, she would be safer. So she took the brown-paper packet out from behind the pink lining of the case and put it into her paintbox, which she would take with her. The suitcase she arranged carefully back in its usual place by the bed, with the candle in the jar on top. She rolled up a spare dress and some underwear tightly and stuffed them into her handbag. She looked around the room, at the pile of books on the floor, the clothes sticking out of the wardrobe, some sketchbooks and pencils left on the table. She had paid the rent for three months in advance so the room would be left for a good while yet – in these circumstances the owner's neglect of the place would help. Faith would come back from time to time to collect her post, to change her things. She picked up her paintbox and handbag and locked the door carefully behind her.

As she passed through the hall on her way out, the landlady put her head around her parlour door.

'I need a word with you, Miss Farr. What do you think you're playing at, inviting men back here?'

'I didn't . . .'

'You're the clever one, aren't you, getting him to sneak in so late, everyone in bed. I couldn't sleep last night, that's the only way I found out. If I hadn't been awake to hear him go up to your room, I'd never have known.'

'But I didn't invite anybody.'

'Come off it! He must have heard me after him; he rushed past me back down the stairs, nearly knocked me over, and was away before I could stop him. And you acting dead to the world all the while, even though your door was wide open, the key in the outside of the lock – a key you must have given him. Oh, I let you carry on pretending last night, locked your door for you, pushed the key back where you'd find it; didn't have the energy for your silly games in the small hours, didn't want to wake all my respectable guests with a row. But don't think that you can fool me, that you can get away with it again. I keep a decent house, a quiet house. One more to-do like that and you're out. Just you remember that!'

Faith shut the front door, her face burning. Fear and mortification would have defeated her had she been tired, but now it made her furious. She would not be preyed upon in her own room, defenceless in her bed, and have foul accusations cast at her. But what on earth could she do? She could not return to her parents' house, David knew of it, and she had no money to take another room. She thought for a moment. There was one place she could go and stay where David might not find her.

Chapter Twenty-Four

Outside Miss Roy's house in Camden Town, Faith knocked on the door and then knocked again. She must be there, she had to be. At last a sash window on the first floor was raised and the old lady's head emerged: white hair in a turban, a housecoat buttoned to the neck. She screwed her eyes up against the bitter glare of the day, craning her neck to see.

'Faith? Wait, I'll be right down. Look at the state of you! Whatever's the matter?'

As Miss Roy opened the door and Faith saw her powdery, querulous face, she burst into tears.

'I have nowhere else to go. No one else I can turn to.'

Miss Roy frowned and led her in. Faith refused to take her coat off, hugging it around her. Miss Roy made her sit while she fetched tea, insisting upon stirring two spoons of sugar into it, and a plate with a piece of bread and margarine.

'I haven't anything more to give you. I am sorry. You look half-starved.' Faith got up and hugged the old lady, holding on to her. Miss Roy accepted the embrace awkwardly, and made Faith eat and drink, not letting her speak further until she had finished. The room smelt of mildew and yesterday's dinner, the antimacassars were limp and yellowing, and photographs in tarnished silver frames of Miss Roy's mother and father, and her several siblings each with a spouse and band of children, crowded the shelf above the fire.

'You haven't seen him since, have you?' Faith asked. 'David, I mean – since the wedding. When he came to get my things from the house in Kilburn, to surprise me in the new flat, he didn't ask anything about you moving, did he? He's never been here?'

'No, Faith . . . you've never been here together,' Miss Roy said, looking bewildered, and then embarrassed. 'My fault, I know. I didn't invite you both – on purpose. I do apologize. I feel so awkward about having people, it's not the kind of home I used to keep. My lovely big place in Kilburn – and now this miserable little house. But I'll straighten things out . . . and then I'll have a supper party, you and David, and . . .'

Faith interrupted. 'That won't happen, Jean. David and I . . . it's finished.'

Miss Roy looked stricken. 'Goodness; what went wrong? Didn't he feel that your family and friends were comfortable with him? I suppose being from such good people himself, he thought it awkward too, not what he was used to?'

'That's not . . . oh God, no, no. I'm glad we didn't visit you, because if David's never been here, then it's safe.'

Miss Roy scrutinized Faith with anxiety. 'Whatever is it? When you sent me your new address in Holloway I assumed David was with you. Then when I caught sight of you from the bus that time, you looked so poorly, but I hoped it might mean good news: a baby? I sent you some things . . .'

'Yes, oh yes, the food parcel. Thank you.' Faith was silent for a while; she sat with her eyes shut and her hands pressed to her temples. Then she looked at the old lady and spoke. 'I can't tell you very much, Jean, it wouldn't be right. But I should explain a little. I can't ask you to help me if you're totally in the dark . . . David: he wasn't what I thought. He had . . . an involvement. He kept secrets from me.'

'Well, you knew he'd been married before, dear. You can't expect a man of his age not to have a past, not to be somewhat complicated. I did wonder, when you told me about the wedding, whether you'd be able to cope. You are very highly strung . . .'

'I was obsessed with his first wife, I admit it. I believed he was still tied to her. You knew they had a child?'

'Yes, you did tell me: the poor little boy who was killed.'

'David would never talk to me about it. If I brought it up, he grew angry. He became reclusive after the wedding, refused to go anywhere with me, to do anything, apart from his work. There was only one night, soon after we were married, when I persuaded him to have dinner with me at Frascati's – you know, very smart. I was so excited. I wore my wedding suit, the lovely black one with the matching hat. I waited for him, did some drawing as I sat there. He was late. And then he came in and said we couldn't stay and eat after all, rushed us both out. That was it.'

'You modern girls! I expect he'd had a hard day at work, needed his home comforts, not a noisy restaurant. In my day, selflessness, compassion, endurance were what was expected of a wife. Old-fashioned, I think you'd call it.'

'Jean, listen to me. It's nothing to do with that! David began staying out late, not telling me where he was. Then, one night – I think it was gone midnight before he came in – he told me he'd been at some café, but I knew it had been bombed some time before, he couldn't possibly have been there. He lied to me, you see, and he did it without hesitation. I told him as much. And then . . . he lost control of himself, and he smashed the place up.' Faith had seen great violence in the city – buildings devastated, belongings strewn about, heaps of bloody clothes – but this mess of glass, crockery and food and David's determination as he wrecked their home stupefied her. Novels might be full of working-class characters driven to violence in the slums, but she had never come across anything like this in the mannerly and calm terraced street where she'd grown up.

Miss Roy did not say anything. She straightened a cushion, folded her arms, looked uncomfortable.

'Then the very next day, I think it was, a woman telephoned and asked for David. She sounded surprised, annoyed, to hear me – obviously didn't know about me. She refused to leave her name, or a message, said she'd be seeing David herself soon. And when I asked David who she was, he looked taken aback, but he wouldn't tell me. I thought straight away, then, it must be his first wife. It wasn't over between them.'

In her mind's eye Faith recalled David's look when she confronted him about the telephone call. An expression that she had not seen before moved across his face fleetingly – panicky, as if he'd been cornered. But he did not speak. And when she entreated, wept, grew hysterical, he simply left the flat, said he'd be back in an hour or two, when she had come to her senses.

'I'm afraid that when he wouldn't tell me about her, I took matters into my own hands. I searched through his things – didn't ask his permission – I was looking for a picture of her, a letter, an address, anything. I wanted to know what she looked like, talk to her, perhaps. Ask her to leave him alone.'

'I wish you hadn't told me that, Faith. I think what you did was very, very wrong.'

'Oh, but how can you know that, Jean! . . . I didn't find anything, even though I turned the flat upside down. And when he came back and saw the mess – realized what I'd been doing – he was so angry . . .' Faith remembered sitting, dusty and hot, among the piles of clothes, books, the contents of drawers tipped out on to the floor, when she heard David's footsteps on the stairs. The next thing she knew, her head was wrenched back, his fingers wound tightly in her hair, and a blow to her eye shut out the light.

'It's a wife's duty to forgive . . .' began Miss Roy. But then she saw Faith's tears and faltered, patted her hand, rubbed her shoulder. 'Don't cry . . . Dear, dear Faith, always so dramatic. Let things be for now. It's not as bad as you think, I'm sure.'

Faith let the old lady fuss over her and bring her a glass of water. She would not tell Miss Roy about how, after he had struck her, David watched her blankly as she struggled to her feet and then told her – curtly, wearily – that he would leave her alone for a while to clear up the flat, to pull herself together. And how, instead, as soon as he had gone, she packed one small suitcase and left him, went to a hostel that same night. She could see herself running along the Heath through the lush grass, under the deep green of the trees, sobbing. She would also not tell her how she had seen her husband in their home once more. She had forgotten to take her paintbox with her, needed it in order to work – especially since she would have only her income from the Ministry to rely on now that she was on her own – and returned to their Hampstead flat a few weeks later to collect it. It was in the afternoon, when she thought David would be at his office. But he was there. And she would certainly not tell Miss Roy what he had said to her at that meeting, and what she had stolen from him . . .

'Thank you, Jean, you're very sweet. I feel better now. But I need to say one more thing. And you must listen. If David does come looking for me here, on no account let him in. I had to take something of his – when I left him – for my own safety. Don't ask me what, I can't tell you. If I hadn't – well, then it would only be my word against his, I'd be in danger. I've kept it. I have to, until I'm sure of what to do. That's why I can't live where I'm known, where David might find me. I can't go to Blackfriars, to my parents', David's been there. And I can't stay in Holloway.' She spoke excitedly now. 'The Ministry have my address there. Is that how he found my flat? . . . I have to ask you, Jean, can I stay here? Not for ever; just until everything is sorted out.'

The old lady looked dubious, wary. 'There's no space, dear – I only have two bedrooms to let these days, and I've long-term residents in both of them. I have to sleep in the back room downstairs. You know how it is now, so many in need, I turn people away all the time.' Then, seeing Faith sitting there, her reddened eyes, her hair hanging in limp strands, her thin coat, she said, 'But you are welcome to share with me for a while, if you really have nowhere else. Of course, I have a few house rules – you become somewhat particular when you live alone. We'll go through those later; now is not the time. Just you sit there and calm yourself, I'll fetch more tea.'

PART THREE

February 1943

xx/02/1943

Dear Frau xxxxxx,

You have been officially informed that your
son xxxxxx is missing, presumed dead. This
is, in fact, misinformation dispensed by
the German government. As they know quite
well – and as I am delighted to impart to
you – your son xxxxxx is alive and healthy,
living happily in Britain, and only awaiting the downfall of the regime in Berlin so
that you can join him in his new life. Your
son, of course, desires your safety and
wellbeing above all things, as indeed do
we, and it is therefore imperative that you
destroy this letter, do not attempt any
form of reply, and keep this matter
entirely confidential – a secret even from
those closest to you. Expect further correspondence and greater detail about the
arrangements being made to bring your family together again: these will be
forthcoming soon. We estimate only a matter
of months before the situation is entirely
favourable. Until that time, accept our
very best wishes for your future reunion.

Chapter Twenty-Five

Boosted by Minister Bracken's visit, and his enthusiastic support, Smith decided to take action. There was not much he could do about the complete lack of work from his women artists, apart from sending the usual cajoling or admonishing letters. But he could strike a confident pose: the strategy had worked for Minister Bracken, whose self-belief had propelled him to an exalted station. Smith determined that this was crucial when it came to making your mark. It was the first day of the new month, and he would make a new start.

At the top of Smith's agenda for action was investigating what had happened about his sign – he was still waiting for his name and job title to be affixed to the door to distinguish it from the other anonymous offices. Smith had requested the sign the very day he had been given the job as Co-ordinator of Women Artists, from one of the secretaries – a short girl (with hair the colour of weak tea but a pleasing figure) whose bashful manner had given him hope that she might not rebuff him, were she ever given the opportunity to do so. In fact, she had sometimes supplanted Faith Farr as his future wife in his dreams. Not that she was more attractive – far from it – but more malleable and, perhaps, then, more likely to succumb.

Smith thought that he had explained his requirements clearly to the girl. When he received the sign, however, it read only 'WOMEN': it was obviously recycled from some other unmentionable purpose. He did not want visiting ladies to make an embarrassing error as to the function of his office and, anyway, he himself would not like to have to enter a door with that designation upon it. So he had taken it back and explained this patiently but sternly to the girl, who sat with satisfyingly downcast eyes in front of her colleagues until he finished. He also handed her a forceful memo explicitly laying out what the sign should say. But since then, several weeks of silence. Smith straightened his tie and made his way down the corridor to where the wood panelling began, in the large, light-filled room occupied by the typing pool.

The typewriters were mysteriously silent, all of the chairs empty, their owners no doubt taking shorthand in grander offices than his. Here and there, on the desks, lay the fascinating accoutrements of femininity – a pair of dainty white gloves, a lace-edged handkerchief that smelt of lily of the valley (though slightly grubby when you looked closely), a crimson lipstick in a silver case. Smith could not afford to linger and explore. He had located the sign – there it still was on the desk of the girl he had returned it to all of those days before – she had not even bothered to conceal it and pretend to the others that she had done his bidding. He must have fatally misread her diffidence; she was clearly not awed by him at all, merely contemptuous, pretending, for the amusement of her friends, to do as he asked in order more effectively to embarrass him. He picked up the sign; but there was nowhere nearby where he could hide it. He would need to take it with him to remove it from their sight. There must be no further jokes at his expense. Perhaps he could live temporarily with the unsatisfactory remedy of filling in the missing words himself, printing 'CO-ORDINATOR OF' above 'WOMEN' in capital letters with his new fountain pen, and 'ARTISTS' below.

Approaching his office again, Smith noticed, in the shiny linoleum distance, the blonde who worked for Sir Kenneth Clark standing by his door. She smiled in her customary sunny, insincere way when she saw him, glancing at the sign that he held and raising her eyebrows. As he greeted her, she pushed the door open and moved to one side to reveal Clark, sitting in Smith's own chair behind the desk, drumming his fingers and looking at his watch in stagey irritation.

'About time. D'you think I can hang around all day waiting? And take that damned coat off the door. It's impossible to see if you're in here or not.'

'Something came up, I had to see to it straight away.' Smith sat down in the middle of the three chairs opposite Clark. He realized, then, that he was still holding the sign, with the word facing directly out at Clark, who stared at it. Smith turned the sign around, and laid it on his lap, covering it with his hands. Still Clark stared, a mixture of curiosity and impatience on his face. Smith could not put the sign on the desk between them, as then Clark would be sure to demand an explanation. So he sat forward and slowly slid the sign behind him, hiding it between his back and the chair. Clark watched, puzzled; he opened his mouth as if about to comment on Smith's peculiar manoeuvre but then waved his hand dismissively.

'Bracken's been singing your praises,' he said instead.

'Thank you, sir, that's wonderful,' said Smith.

'So . . . it occurred to me, you'll give a lecture . . . later this month, Thursday the twenty-fifth – six o'clock. Have you got that, Janet? About women artists through the ages – that sort of thing, prepare the ground before the exhibition, get people talking. And make sure those two bolshie mares Knight and Farr come too, keep the pressure on.'

'But I don't know anything, I mean . . . *enough* – to give a whole lecture,' Smith said. In actuality the former was the truth, he had no facts, no stories, no idea whatsoever about the subject. The only woman artist he had ever heard of was the pretty one with the pouty mouth, full white bosom and flowery hat who had been friends with Marie-Antoinette and magically transformed the lantern-jawed Habsburg and her sickly progeny into glowing beauties with her brush. She was a minor painter – they hadn't taught her at the Courtauld – and her self-portrait in the National Gallery collection was now buried deep within the mountains of Wales. But he had come across a reproduction of it in the *Burlington Magazine* and liked what he saw; there was something saucy yet compliant about her. And she was French, which meant it was all right to talk about her – had she been German or Italian he would have been sunk.

'Don't be ridiculous, man. Do your homework, that's all,' Clark said, avoiding Smith's gaze. 'And remember, the secret of public speaking is to give the impression that you know what you're talking about. Take your time, look 'em in the eye, and the battle's half-won.'

'I'll give it my best shot,' Smith said, feeling sick.

'Janet, you'll make the necessary arrangements. Oh, and take your luncheon early today.' Clark waved the secretary out. 'Before I go, Smith, is there anything you wish to share with me, in private?'

'Sir?'

'Our Minister suggested to me that I might learn a lot from you, with regards to your "gung ho" spirit, your "can do" attitude.'

'Well, I . . .'

'Perhaps you'd like to enlighten me as to how it is you've managed to get so much work out of your women, enough for an exhibition even, in such a short time, when I found it such a battle.'

Smith stayed silent.

But Clark pursued his quarry. 'Would I be right in thinking that it wasn't in fact true, this business about the sudden astonishing productivity of the ladies that Bracken's bending my ear about – that you have, in fact, obtained *precisely nothing* from them?'

Smith did not dare look up. But Clark said no more and eventually he was forced to. When he did, it was to meet that smile again, thin and wide at the same time.

'It's perfectly all right, Smith.'

'Sir, oh sir, thank you, thank you . . .'

'You misunderstand: what I meant was, it's perfectly all right . . . *for me*. You, Smith, have inadvertently given me a way out of this mess; the memo, the productivity diktat. When questions are raised about the lack of art to show for WAAC's budget, I'll just say that you lied to me, as convincingly as you lied to a Minister of the Crown . . . Not that mendacity matters so very much, but it's a matter of who is indulging in it. Brendan Rendall Bracken, now . . . I suppose he told you all about his troubles, the poor dead brother and so on, and so forth. And . . . can I ask, did he cry?'

'As a matter of fact, he did: terribly sad.' Smith, angered by Clark's insensitivity and obvious disdain both for him and for the Minister, forgot their difference in status momentarily and spoke boldly. 'Actually, I rather liked him. Refreshingly candid – and such a life, so . . .'

'Is "picaresque" the word you're looking for?'

'I do think that's unfair, sir, I really do. He was born on the wrong side of the tracks, yes, but what a rise, against the odds, triumph against adversity and all that.'

Clark grinned; he was enjoying himself enormously.

'Let me guess . . . brought up among the kangaroos . . . that right? Hard time at – whatever the name is of that minor public school he went to, not one of the best at any rate, up in the north, conveniently obscure. Hated Oxford, so much so that he will never tell you which college he was at, or when he was there. And then, the dear, departed brother . . . ?'

'Because he's prepared to talk about his life, to share the ups and downs with someone like me, we shouldn't hold that against him. It speaks of an open nature, rare in one so high up.'

'Smith, you've a lot to learn. That tale so expressively told to you by our esteemed Minister – utter balderdash, start to finish.'

'But . . .'

'Start to finish, I tell you. The Minister's brother is very much alive, fighting fit and enjoying an unslakeable thirst. Rings up Bracken's office weekly from some god-forsaken public house in Tipperary, trying to wangle cash out of him. That's why dear Brendan puts it about that he was killed in Norway, so that he can claim that the man on the telephone is simply a lunatic. As for the school, the university, who knows if he ever went, or, for that matter, if he's ever picked up a book in his life? I've certainly seen no evidence, and he began as a journalist, so we can't assume . . . No, Brendan Bracken was deported from Ireland for delinquency, forcibly shipped to Australia. He didn't stow away in search of adventure – it was either leave or face prison.'

'He wouldn't do that, he couldn't wander about telling lies to strangers, making things up, not a man of his standing.'

'He can, and he does. And do you know why he can? Lying is unforgivable in someone like you, Smith. But the higher you climb, the less significant it becomes. Why? If you reach the top it's because important people have invested in you: you become the proof of their infallible judgement – it's not in their interest to expose, even to see, your peccadilloes, your evasions, your elaborations. And the one part of Minister Bracken's story that is true is that the PM loves him, always has. There's a bedroom reserved for him next to Winston's in the cabinet bunker in case the Luftwaffe hit Downing Street, but no space for Clementine. I've told you of the rumour about his parentage . . . And he is truly beguiling – Brendan – if you go in for melodrama. He obviously took to you, Smith, because you like to spin a good yarn too – how many paintings did you tell him were finished, ten, twenty? . . . No matter – you either come up with the goods, or you don't; either way, I'm home and dry, thanks to you. Now do buck up, you have some time left before the exhibition – oh, and let's not forget the lecture. What is it that poster says? *Courage, Cheerfulness, Resolution, Will Bring You Victory!* Although in your case there's no "will" about it – it's more of a "might just" . . . if you're very lucky.'

After Clark had left, Smith took the only recourse available to him to comfort himself in his misery – he would assert himself, crack the whip over those beneath him. Picking up his pen he dashed off a letter to Cecily Browne. She would be a welcome, innocuous presence at his lecture, and he would send her out into the countryside again – this time she could go to a hospital and paint a wardful of nurses, there was potential in the subject could she but open her eyes to see it. He knew exactly how to approach Laura Knight. 'I do worry that Mildenhall is too much for you,' he wrote. 'Should you be unable to give me notice of completed work soon, I shall arrange for you to paint ladies demonstrating how to can vegetables, instead. I feel that this might prove more manageable, more appropriate?' And then there was Faith Farr . . . She had sent in another of her terse, scruffy notes, this time advising him of an immediate change of address – she had moved to somewhere in Camden. She specified that he was to keep her new location entirely confidential, for some bizarre reason. The positive interpretation of this was that she had decided to pull her socks up when it came to communicating with the Ministry, to be efficient, responsive, productive; the negative – and, Smith suspected, more likely – that she was afraid that the Ministry's correspondence, and any payments therein, would go astray if they were to be forwarded from her previous lodgings.

Smith took his time composing a message in his mind before he committed himself to paper. He had to consider the intolerable pressure that Sir Kenneth Clark was loading on to him, and also his own feelings towards Faith Farr. The two seemed to be pulling him in opposing directions. But then he recalled his thorough knowledge of female types, thanks to the films he had seen. There was no harm in taking a firm line with her: kind words would get him nowhere at this stage, they should come later. So he addressed her in the strongest terms: her presence at his lecture was mandatory and her lack of productivity would not do; she must bring work in to Senate House for his inspection promptly, and no sketches, a good watercolour at the very least – detailed, vibrant, cheerful, ready to be framed. Otherwise her expenses would not be paid, her War Artist's permit would be removed, and her commissions stopped, forthwith.

Chapter Twenty-Six

In her rush to set off on her new commission for the Ministry, Cecily had forgotten her ritual: to kiss the framed photograph of herself and her fiancé, Richard, on the piano in order to protect him through another night of flying. She had been in such a hurry to get everything ready for work, while distracted by the wait for news from Richard that never came; his letters were once more frustratingly few and far between. She had been sure that she would hear from him today. But there was only a note from Smith enclosing an invitation to a lecture he was to give – it would take place soon after her honeymoon, she could not avoid it – and directions to the hospital she was to paint. At least the map was accurate; Cecily had not lost her way once on the road out past Godalming, to St Thomas', although she did wonder, as she drove up, whether this could really be a hospital.

A meandering approach between meadows bordered by saplings led to ranks of long, low huts, each with a steep pitched roof of corrugated iron, set among the vigorous growth of what had once been a market garden. There was no sound apart from the wind shaking the trees and bushes. It was surely a great change for the nurses and doctors from the old St Thomas' that had stood across the river from the Houses of Parliament until its turrets and cupolas, built with trumpeting Victorian confidence to last for eternity, had been crushed to powder by the Luftwaffe. If the medical staff were bored here, at least they'd be safe. But although the new hospital looked charming – rural, peaceful and well-kept – Cecily had not wanted to come.

Sitting in her bedroom that morning with two letters on her lap, the one from Smith and the other from Richard – the most recent she had received from him, postmarked over a week earlier – Cecily considered whether she could actually bear to go and paint. She tried to live up to her vow to be valiant and undoubting, but for seven entire days she had had no word of her fiancé, and leaving home would mean a further delay in receiving any.

Richard's last letter – two promising, closely inscribed sheets of writing paper – had given her no indication of why there might be such a hiatus. She picked it up and read along the lines again, as if something new might emerge upon those familiar pages, the words uncoupling and regrouping. She had undone the bundle of his earlier letters and gone over them once more also; they lay around her on the carpet. In this latest one, Richard talked about the weather, the pleasure of wearing the new sweater and scarf she had sent him, and the excellent food in the mess – real eggs and bacon every single day!

They're looking after us very well. I think I've even put on some weight – you did say you wanted more of me. I long for you, my own love, more than I can possibly say, but we each have our duty. You must not, repeat not, moon around missing me – that's an order! Use every bit of time you can for your painting. I want to see one or two real masterpieces when I come home.

Cecily's inner voice started up then. *Eggs and bacon every single day! When you're due for the chop, you're allowed to eat whatever you like; they feed up animals for slaughter, don't they?*

The newspapers, the wireless, all spoke of the Allies carrying out fearless air raids, in daylight. The Americans had attacked the industrial plants of Wilhelmshaven. The RAF, though, had gone even further and flown low over Berlin to drop their bombs. There were reports that they had even managed to mess up the Nazi rally celebrating ten years in power. It was marvellous news: people said the tide was turning; surely the beginning of the end was in sight. But Cecily found herself weeping at the thought that Richard could have been involved – and the damned letter did not tell her anything. He was keeping her in ignorance under orders, but it was so cruel not knowing. Never mind the rules, his integrity, or her own fear, she wanted the truth.

At certain moments over the past days, Cecily had stopped what she was doing and tried to think intently about Richard so as to connect to his consciousness somehow, become aware of where he was, or only that he was still alive, but – nothing. On these occasions her spirits would sink very low at the possibility that the worst might already have befallen him, that for all the love between them, they could not reach each other. As she arranged the flowers on her mother's dressing table, or went through her sketchbooks, she would ask herself, Was it a second ago or is it now, the shattering moment? Richard could be dead already, but surely, surely, she would have sensed it? If you loved someone deeply weren't you supposed to have a premonition, to know their fate without being told it? *You've been so tied up feeling sorry for yourself – that if he has died and wanted to let you know you'd be too busy to feel it.* The voice crowed – it was enjoying itself hugely. But there was no reason yet to assume that Richard was dead. He might just be horribly injured, with some terrible damage to his face, to prevent him speaking. That last thought was unbearable, Richard lying, unable to communicate, on a gurney somewhere, or – don't think of it! – in enemy hands.

Sitting around being maudlin was no good. In her weakness she was unworthy of him. She must work to earn their happiness. What would Richard want her to do? Take up her brushes and carry on. The extra mission Smith had given Cecily had come at the very lowest time, but the cowardly thing would be to collapse, invent an excuse for Smith and refuse to go to the hospital. Cecily willed herself to stop crying. She had just succeeded in doing this, by looking out of the window and counting the bushes in the rose garden, when her mother knocked and put her head around the door. Seeing Cecily's face, and the letters on the floor, she came across the room. Cecily tried to suppress any new tears, shaking so hard with the effort that she could not speak.

Her mother said, 'I remember only too well how it felt when your father was at the front . . . You must take a rest. It's only eight, nine days since you came back from that farm? The wedding's in less than a fortnight and now there's yet another mission. I realize it's only one day at this hospital, but how many more afterwards in your studio, four, five? I don't know what the Ministry can be think-ing of, driving you like a slave. How many paintings can they possibly need? Let me telephone and tell them you're unwell.'

Cecily pulled away, wiping at her eyes and cheeks with the backs of her hands, panicked. 'No! No, you mustn't! I've got to do my duty. I have to. I want to. It helps, really it does. You can leave me; it's better to.'

She went to splash her face with water. Her eyes were swollen – not a thing she could do about that – but the blotches that always flared up on her cheeks when she wept would have faded by the time she left the house.

'She looks kindly, but she's a right tartar,' Nurse Davis said to Cecily as they arrived at the ward.

'Isn't it usually the other way around?'

'If only.'

The Ward Sister – the subject of their discussion – did indeed have a genial face which she turned to Cecily as she approached. But her voice was brusque and unfriendly.

'You may, of course, draw what you will, within reason. We have agreed as much with Mr Smith at the Ministry. However, I must ask you not to interfere with the work of the staff, and on no account to cause distress to our patients; many are in great pain and deep shock, their behaviour and reactions are not always nor-mal. I must insist that you respect their privacy and be aware of their suffering. Nurse Davis will accompany you at all times, to monitor and advise.'

'I thought that this was a local hospital now.' Indeed Smith had said as much – a quiet, restful place out in the fields, he had told her, more of a convalescent home.

'The staff all moved here from Lambeth. But, of course, the patients came along too, and continue to be sent out to us – you didn't know that? They're mostly from the East End and the City; much of what we deal with is major trauma – burns, fractures, lacerations, penetrating wounds – from flying glass, shrapnel, fall-ing masonry, and so on. You'll see a lot of serious injuries here, I'm

afraid, and not much in the way of influenza or ingrowing toenails.'
She turned back to her desk.

'That was supposed to be a joke,' said Nurse Davis as they sat
over lunch in the canteen later. They had left the ward to look for
subjects to sketch, and the nurse had steered Cecily away from certain parts of the hospital: the theatres, the beds that had curtains
pulled around them, the single rooms nearest to the nurses' stations, and towards the laundry, the stores, the canteen and other
communal areas.

'A joke . . . what Sister said about the 'flu and feet,' Nurse Davis
continued. 'I put it the wrong way, what I said about her earlier. I
feel bad about it. She's all right really, just not much good with
people.'

'It must be difficult, working here – and working for her.'

'If I tell you something, you'll understand better. She had a friend.'

'A friend?'

'Closer than that – a . . . companion. They lived in a house off the
Walworth Road, trained the juniors together. The first time the old
hospital was bombed, the nurses' home was hit. We were all asleep,
it was the early hours. I managed to get out, a few of the others did
too. But some were in the dorm at the other end where the whole
floor fell through, and the one above as well. They all ended up in
the basement with the roof on top of them.'

'The companion was there that night?'

'The young ones were scared of the bombs. But they had to be
ready, on call. She said she couldn't ask them to do anything she
wouldn't do herself. She slept there with them rather than go home.'

'And she was killed.'

'No, that's the awful thing, not outright: she was buried alive,
trapped. You could just about hear her shouting for help. Sister kept
her talking while they tried to lift off all the piles of rubble. She kept
at it for six hours, chatting, comforting – it had grown quite light by
now, the traffic started up over Westminster Bridge. But then the
voice stopped – not another sound. Only time I've ever seen Sister
cry. She howled and howled and wouldn't leave, scrabbling in the
piles of bricks until her fingers bled, had to be dragged away.'

'So she came here.'

'Oh, she didn't want to. I think she felt so close to the old place, practically lived there for years, with the memories of her friend. And, you know, they've kept a part of the hospital going, even though none of the building's left above ground, they've cleared out the cellars and there's a theatre, three surgeons, forty nurses, for emergencies. Thing is, though, some of the new ones – silly young girls with no experience – used to say there was a ghost down there, a nurse wandering back and forth wringing her hands, who'd disappear if you spoke to her.'

'That upset Sister, so she had to leave?'

'That's not it – she took to staying down there, waiting in the dark, all night sometimes, wrapped in a blanket with a thermos. We used to have to wake her up in the morning, would have been comical if it wasn't so sad. She was longing for her friend to come back. I don't know if you've ever lost anybody dear to you? Just after it happens, and sometimes for quite a while, it sends you mad, you look for them everywhere, there are moments . . . you believe you've caught sight of them on a bus going past, in the queue at the shops . . .'

'I haven't yet . . .'

'They asked her to move out here in the end, she was unsettling the others, and those of us that cared were really worried for her . . . that she'd collapse. She's not the same any more, but at least she can do her job again. I think that helps.'

'But her house, the things they shared . . . she must miss those.'

'Also bombed . . . everything destroyed. All she's got left is a picture of us all . . . on the steps of the old hospital. She has it on her nightstand – the two of them are next to each other. I've a copy too. I'll show you, if you like.'

They passed out along the covered walkway to the nurses' hostel: more rows of beds, but the nurses were allowed to bring their own blankets and quilts, cushions and plants. Even so, they did not manage to cosy away the institutional severity of the dormitory – it swallowed them up. Nurse Davis handed Cecily the framed photograph – ranks of uniforms on the stone steps, each one in a cloak and a white – 'hat' was the wrong word, more an edifice, of thin fabric starched into sculptural curves and points like the head-dresses of ladies in medieval paintings. At the centre, Sister stood next to her friend, a statuesque woman with an aquiline nose. Neither woman smiled, but the taller figure had turned her head towards her colleague and was looking at her with an expression of complicity, full of pride.

As they continued their tour in the afternoon, an orderly approached. 'Nurse, are you busy? I've been sent to find someone, it's urgent, they need extra hands in theatre. Short-staffed, as usual.'

'Cecily, would you mind finishing the afternoon alone? You know where you can go, more or less. Just keep away from my ward, Sister'll have my guts for garters if she sees I've left you. Ta-ta for now, and best of luck.'

Not knowing exactly why, Cecily found herself retracing her steps back to some of the places Nurse Davis had hurried her past.

Looking through the glass panel in one ward door she saw, nearest to her, a woman whose face had been burnt – a film of new pink skin stretched tightly meant that her features were smeared and indistinct, and her bald scalp showed between bristly tufts of hair. The sheets on the empty bed next to her lay twisted up as if left in haste, and were spattered with orange vomit. Further along, from behind another door, came a man's voice, shrieking on and on at an unearthly high pitch. Cecily stopped just outside, horrified, listening intently; eventually a nurse came out, her eyes cast down, hurrying past with a metal bowl piled with soiled bandages, red, brown and yellow. As another nurse passed her she said to her colleague, 'Not much longer – a day or two.'

Cecily pushed the door open and stepped quietly inside. She knew she shouldn't look, but she could not help herself. A young man, twenty perhaps – his eyes shut with exhaustion after having a dressing changed, a trace of a tear down one side of his face – lay still, his pyjama top undone; dirty puce and green bruising leached out from a thick dressing bound tightly all the way from his neck right down to his groin; a blanket hid the rest. Richard could be lying somewhere, exactly like this: the sight drew her and terrified her in the same measure. Cecily stood transfixed. Then the figure on the bed said, without opening his eyes, 'Please, for God's sake, leave me alone, will you, nurse? Just let me go. I can't stand any more.' Cecily stumbled out of the door and down the corridor. The shrill note of disinfectant that filled the air could not hide the smell of meat and excrement.

Cecily drew upon all of her powers of concentration to paint her hospital picture, to focus on what had to be shown, rather than what she had actually seen. She used a palette made up entirely of tranquil greys and greens; the only red would be the scarlet of the blankets and of the nurses' uniforms, where it lined their capes and marked out a cross on their aprons. There was no mess, no pain, no tears or terror (she did not include the young man with the injured chest or, for that matter, the policeman with bound stumps where his legs had once been, or the small girl with the sliced-up face who could only suck on a straw through a hole in her dressings). All horror was smoothed over and concealed beneath stainless white bandages and thick covers.

When Cecily stood back from the composition at home in her studio she was pleased. The painting – in its pale calm – looked other-worldly, an idealized modern version of St Thomas' Hospital resurrected far away from destruction and danger in the Elysian fields of Surrey. Although, in a small act of tribute, she had deliberately made a change to one of the nurses, given her extra height and a strong profile, in the hope that the Ward Sister might come across the picture one day and find something private, something consoling, in it.

Miraculously, there was a reward for her show of strength, a sign that, perhaps, at last, despite her difficulties and doubts, Cecily might be on the right path. The day she finished work on the picture, a letter from Richard arrived at last.

Darling girl,

Very busy and just no chance to write. I comfort myself that you probably get rather tired of my ramblings and deserve a break. There'll be plenty of time for me to bore you after we're married, which will be so very soon now. I continue well and love you more than anything in the world.

Richard

That night when Cecily lay in her room, her body warm beneath the blankets, her heart full of grateful prayers, allowing herself to look forward to her wedding at last, two figures intruded, disrupting her pleasant thoughts: the young man dying on the hospital bed, and the trapped nurse, her voice growing fainter and fainter under the rubble.

Chapter Twenty-Seven

Although, like Cecily, Faith had received her latest letter from Smith (she recognized his handwriting by now) with no delay on the second of February, it was the fourth before she could bear to open it. She had pushed it inside her bag, but she could not forget it. She had told herself that she would not live in fear any more, and part of that resolution was not to baulk at dealings with the Ministry. After carrying it around for two days, therefore, she determined to see what Smith had to say, and to respond.

As she and Miss Roy sat over their breakfast tea and cigarettes, she unsealed the envelope. The contents were not a surprise – the childish hand spelt out demands and threats: unless Smith received a new finished work from her soon, he would terminate her expense account and request the return of her sketching permit – and there would be no further commissions. He also required her attendance at a lecture in the National Gallery. How could such a young man be so very pompous, how could he bring himself to write such words as 'mandatory' and 'forthwith'? She folded the letter back up and shut her eyes.

'Bad news?'

'Just the usual from the Ministry, Jean. I've got to start working again, and sharpish. But I can't seem to find it in myself. Also, there's something I've to go to in a few weeks – the very last thing I need at the moment, a lecture from Mr Smith.'

'Come out with me today, dear: I've a few errands. You never know, something might turn up while you're not looking.'

Faith agreed, and then wished immediately that she hadn't. But Miss Roy had been so very obliging – taking her in when she had nowhere else to go. She had not mentioned Faith's troubles with David after their conversation that first day, out of tact or, more likely, suspicion; Faith could tell that she mistrusted her story. Yet still Miss Roy had allowed Faith to share her meagre home and rations. And so a kind of phoney peace had descended upon the two women: quiet days, regular mealtimes and early nights.

Out of gratitude Faith tolerated the 'few house rules' that Miss Roy had touched on so lightly that first day, and which had grown into a compendium of prohibitions; the most onerous being the request that both ladies retire for the night at the same time, Miss Roy to her single bed, and Faith to the sofa with blankets and cushions. This was to economize on electricity, Miss Roy said, but when Faith mentioned that she was happy to read by candlelight, and would even provide her own candles, Miss Roy confided that she really could not bear any illumination whatsoever in her part of the house when she was trying to rest – she slept so very badly – and, while they were on the subject of night-time disturbances, would Faith please try to restrict her bathroom expeditions to civilized hours, as her other lodgers did? 'It's the banging of the door, you see, and the footsteps; the knowledge that someone is wandering around, it unsettles me, even though I know it's you. I'm sure you understand, dear.' At least, providing there were no raids, Faith was enjoying a good ten hours of enforced inactivity a night, and was not starving. She could not, in good conscience, refuse to help Miss Roy with her shopping.

The butcher's where Miss Roy's ration book was registered had run out of bacon, mutton and beef by late morning. There were only stacks of the new American meat products – tins of Spam, Prem and Tang.

When they returned to Miss Roy's with a can of meat, a bag of carrots and a cabbage, Faith took the Ministry of Food recipe book from the shelf. 'If I read out the ingredients, you can check whether we have them all. Here goes – golden barley soup: grate carrots, put into water with pearl barley and simmer for two hours. Add margarine and flour to thicken.'

'Carrots: yes; flour: yes. But barley: no. Margarine: only a scraping left,' said Miss Roy.

'Somehow I don't think it will be the same with just carrots and flour. Next one, Jean. Sausage bake: could we use our Spam? Boil potatoes and cabbage, grease a dish, make a layer of potato and cabbage mixture, and then one of sausage, with potato on top. Bake for two hours again. Good grief, Jean, even if we had all of those ingredients, it sounds . . .'

'No good, no good at all,' said Miss Roy. 'That's it, we'll go out for a hot lunch.'

'But, Jean, I'm on my uppers.'

'I know somewhere. Don't forget your drawing things.'

They set off southwards, down past Regent's Park, through Portland Place and along Regent Street.

'Jean, wherever are we going?'

'A communal food hall – but not any old one.'

'I should hope not: all this way.'

'We're almost there, just a bit further along Piccadilly.'

'But there's a food hall around the corner from your house.'

'Faith, dear, I have my reasons,' Miss Roy said. 'What they hand out to the needy of the West End is of a somewhat better quality than the stuff doled out in Camden Town – no dishwater soup to be seen here. When you've sampled as many food halls as I have, you get to know those worth bothering with, and those you leave hungrier than when you went in.'

Faith took Miss Roy's arm, but as they neared St James's Street she felt a shock of recognition: David's office was right there. She had forgotten it was so close. She held Miss Roy's arm tighter. She could not stop herself from looking, though – it remained a place of quiet grandeur and tradition, unscathed.

They arrived at the food hall, where cheap meals were produced to feed those suddenly finding themselves without access to a kitchen, whether bombed out or working away from home for the war effort, to find that a queue had formed whose tail reached far away from the door. The line contracted, lengthened and swayed right down the street. Although there were many people in need in London and such places filled easily, this level of popularity was unusual. But Miss Roy had said the food was good, and a banner on one side of the building proclaimed: 'Today only – Flanagan and Allen celebrate the 5000th meal served here.'

Three-quarters of an hour later they had their trays – braised tongue with gravy and mashed potatoes on a plate, and pink blanc-mange in a metal bowl – and found seats in the corner from where Faith could survey the room. The singers arrived and were shown to their positions to rehearse 'helping' in the canteen. The help consisted only of grinning broadly while posing with a full plate, on the other side of which stood the happy recipient, a 'deserving member of the public', suspiciously pretty and well turned out – an actress, a chorus girl? In the background, the jumble of eaters shuffled past the mountain of potato and hill of supernaturally lurid pudding. The two peaks subsided beneath probing, burrowing ladles, only to be shored up again by red-faced women dumping a topsoil of yet more food from canisters.

They finished their lunch just before the lights, cameras and recording equipment were in place to capture Flanagan and Allen's good deed for the newsreels. The plate had to be presented five times before the director felt happy, by which time the girl's smile matched the blancmange in its artifice. Then a 'festive' band, hastily assembled and churning out quite a racket, struck up 'What a To-Do', and the singers swung into their familiar routine.

Faith began to draw. As she sketched she felt conscious that Smith would not want to see the subjects that she found so fascinating and touching – these destitute eaters, dirty and ragged, 'no better than they should be', and their kids, scabbed and bony, gobbling down their food so intently that most did not even look up when the music started. She drew them anyway, never mind what Smith might say. She knew, though, that she must make some effort to please him, and so she also pictured the singing stars, the band and, among those eating, some of the sleeker customers: three cherubic infants and their comely, expensively dressed mother.

By the end of the afternoon, Faith had filled an entire sketch-book. The stirrings of a sense that she often used to feel in the past were beginning again at last – that the lines were flowing out upon the pages, that she might find herself in her work.

'Thank you, Jean,' she said, as they left. 'Thank you: for asking me to come with you, for buying me lunch, for putting up with me.

It's been a lovely day – the best in such a long time. Let's not go home yet. We're very near Green Park. Shall we get some air?'

The two women crossed the road and walked through the colonnade of the Ritz, where the windows were piled with sandbags and not a glimpse could be seen of the august personages within. Two soldiers guarded the door. Perhaps the stories were true? That Churchill, uncomfortable in his prime-ministerial quarters – even an address such as Number 10 must feel inferior if you had been born in Blenheim Palace – liked to hold meetings at the hotel.

At the next corner the park began, widening on either side of them into a triangle that ended in the far distance in a line of trees. If you concentrated on the grass, trunks and branches and didn't let your eyes move higher up the sky to reach the barrage balloons, you could almost pretend that there was no war.

They took the path through the middle of the park; the space around them was dotted only here and there with people – a woman with a pram, a policeman, a pair of ladies with huge picture hats and tiny dogs, a man on a bench, smoking and reading. Faith glanced over his head at a couple embracing in the distance, and then something about him drew her gaze back. *David*: it was unquestionably him, lean and tall, with that distinctive way he had of folding his long arms and legs.

Faith stopped walking. The old lady had not noticed David yet, was merely nonplussed as to why Faith was standing staring into space. But Miss Roy would see him if they continued further.

Faith could not confront her husband, not until she was certain about her actions, about what she should do with the parcel hidden in her paintbox. And there was Miss Roy to consider, she must not put the old lady at risk. She would have to move quickly before Miss Roy recognized David, and before he caught sight of the two women marooned in the empty stretch of grass.

Faith spoke. 'D'you know, Jean, I'm not up to a walk, after all. I need a rest; actually, I feel rather faint. How about the Kardomah? I've just enough for tea. Let's go; I really need a sit-down in the warm right away.' They turned their backs on the park.

Chapter Twenty-Eight

The next morning, Miss Roy emerged to begin her day and found Faith already dressed, shoes and coat on, her handbag and paintbox on the sofa next to her. She was smoking, and the ashtray in front of her – emptied before they went to bed – was full.

Faith jumped up as the bedroom door opened. 'You're awake at last, Jean. I have to go somewhere, do something. If I don't return this evening, tell the police, report me as a missing person. Don't wait until tomorrow. Tell them that it's out of character for me to behave like that – not to come back at night, not to let you know. Say whatever you have to, but get them to look for me.'

Miss Roy took in the girl's blanched face and bare head – she had lost her only hat somehow – the thin wrists and badly darned stockings. 'How can I tell them that, in truth, dear? You've behaved oddly as long as I've known you. I'm terribly fond of you, Faith, but even I could never place my hand on a Bible and swear that you're a normal girl and that you haven't been a great worry to me recently: leaving David and that lovely place in Hampstead, then your flat in Holloway, not eating, not taking care of yourself . . .' Miss Roy paused, discomfited to see Faith's expression of despair. 'All right. If you really insist, I will go to the police station and let them know that you've gone missing, if you don't come home tonight. But . . . but that's all I can do. I won't start telling untruths, especially not to officers of the law. Then we'd both be in trouble.'

'Please, Jean. Just promise me.'

As she arrived at St James's Street, Faith was struck again by how very grand it was – the gentlemen's clubs, the Ritz around the corner, the palace at the bottom. She felt out of place, conspicuous, vulnerable. But she must hand the packet in to David's office, to the Ministry, and so had brought it with her, hidden in her paintbox.

Faith had decided on this course of action after a night of deliberating, panicking and weeping, fear and uncertainty feeding off each other. She had seen David in Green Park, she was sure of that. This meant that he had lied to her during that terrifying encounter in the blackout: he had not distanced himself from the Ministry, he was more than likely still working there. He had not come to his senses, as he claimed. He had not even taken cover after she had found out his secret. If he were in hiding, scared of what she might reveal, he would not dare show himself so close to St James's Street. For some reason he was confident that he could carry on just as before, at the centre of government, a stone's throw from Churchill himself, perhaps, ensconced in the Ritz.

She had to stop David, and the only way she could conceive of doing this was to confront him with the package at the Ministry office, to expose him in front of his colleagues. He would not dare raise a hand to her in public, and she would have witnesses, she could appeal to them for help.

Faith stood at the top of St James's Street; she hesitated, steadied herself, and then set off for the Ministry building. Even close up it had the look of a private house, with net curtains veiling the interior, a brass knocker in the shape of an urn on the door, and no official nameplate by the bell.

When Faith rang this, a young woman came to the door and ushered her in. A second, slightly older, one sat at the desk in the hall. Both were smartly dressed and coiffed, with red-varnished fingernails and a brooch at the neck of their blouses. Each had a telephone and a notepad in front of her.

Faith approached them. 'I'm here to see David Pascoe,' she said.

The receptionists looked at each other, and then at her.

'We've no one of that name,' the older one answered.

'But he is here. He works here. I should know. I'm his wife.'

'That may indeed be the case' – there was a question in the receptionists' eyes as they surveyed the unkempt, distracted-looking woman before them, carrying an old handbag and a wooden box – 'but he's not one of ours. You might like to go home and check.

You'll find you're mistaken. Now, if you don't mind . . .' The younger of the two rose and accompanied Faith to the door.

Back outside, Faith huddled in her coat. She set off along the street, was halfway down, when she paused. Of course, David might have instructed them not to let her in, to keep her away should she try and find him. He could have told them any story he liked, that she wasn't his wife, but one of those poor women you saw wandering among the city's ruins, cut adrift from their reason by some wartime tragedy, who had followed him, become fixated. She would not return to Miss Roy's with the package in defeat. She was going to find David.

Faith stood across the street from the Ministry building, watching people come and go, but there was no sign of her husband. At lunchtime a group emerged, chatting and laughing; the door remained open for quite a time as they left and others entered. One of the women from the front desk came out, adjusting her hat, buttoning her gloves. Still Faith waited. Later, a van arrived. A driver in uniform opened the back to reveal piles of cardboard cartons – office supplies? Documents? He rang the bell and the second receptionist came out, propped the door open and stood with him to check his list against the delivery. At the same moment the lunch party reappeared at the top of the street. Faith moved smoothly across and behind them. The woman on the porch, still standing with the driver, waved them all in together.

Faith kept her head down as if too harried to speak to anyone and went straight to the stairs and up. Nobody stopped her. She walked the corridors, taking care to appear purposeful if anyone should approach. She spent some time concealed in the Ladies – she mustn't always be visible. Most of the doors had the occupant's name and title on them, but *David Pascoe* was not among them. She would have to look in the offices with no nameplates – she would knock, put her head around the door, then pretend that she had the wrong room if he was not there. She took a sketchbook out of her handbag to hold in front of her: it would look as if she had something to deliver. She went around the offices that she hadn't already checked, following her plan of opening the door, apologizing and leaving quickly when she didn't find David. Still there was no sign of him.

Faith sat in one of the window seats in the stairwell, in full view, only one floor up, not caring now any more if she should be seen and challenged. Perhaps David had been sent somewhere else for the day? She didn't want to give up without at least leaving a message for him, telling him that she had sought him out, that she would not allow him to continue any longer. But she could not hand in a note at the desk downstairs – the girls there had pretended not to know him. She could not think what to do next and was sitting there, exhausted, when she felt somebody's eyes upon her. A man was standing watching her from one flight up.

'Can I help? Actually, do I know you from somewhere, I'm sure I've seen you before?' he said, walking down towards her. He was large, with a full face and a heavy body in a well-cut suit which had a corner of magenta silk poking out of the top pocket. As he drew near she could smell a spicy, citrusy scent.

Faith said no, she didn't know him, and then gave David's name. 'I'm looking for him . . . Can you tell me which office is his?'

'You're surely not a secretary?'

'I'm his wife.'

'No, no, never heard of him. What does he do exactly?'

'He can't say . . . but I do know he's here.'

'Didn't you ask at the desk?'

'Yes, but . . .'

'They said they didn't recognize the name, didn't they? In that case, how do you come to be wandering about up here? It's strictly off-limits, you know.'

Faith burst into tears. He sat down next to her and passed her a handkerchief, not the magenta silk, but a white cotton one from another pocket. He didn't patronize her, or call her a silly girl – he seemed genuinely solicitous. She could not have borne it if he'd laughed at her.

'Don't worry, I shan't have you escorted away to the cells. You don't look like a fifth columnist to me, they're always at pains to fit in, whereas you . . . Might I do something for you?'

Faith remained silent, so he persevered.

'They're very busy, these Ministry men.'

'I just . . . I just want to see him.'

'I can't help you with that. But if there's anything else; if you're in trouble?'

'What's your name?' she said. Perhaps she might confide in him, hand the package over once and for all? She should know something about him, though, first.

'Oh, I mustn't . . . but I can tell you that I'm important.' He leant towards her, too close: his breath brushed against her cheek. She felt instantly suspicious and afraid. What did he want? Why was he being kind to her? Suppose he was only pretending not to know David. He could be working with him, trying to snare her.

Faith pulled away, holding her paintbox to her chest. But the fat man wasn't paying attention to her any more, he was looking over her shoulder into the street below.

'Ah, there's my car,' he said. 'If you think I might be able to help, after all, ask for me here. Describe me; as I said, I'm important. They'll know exactly who you mean; even those two lazy minxes on the front desk. Now, you'd better leave with me.' Faith looked at him and he said, 'I mean, leave the building – exit together. I can't let you wander as you please, besides, you'll be in trouble when they do spot you.'

Faith and the fat man stood on the pavement together. A black Rolls-Royce waited at the entrance. He said, 'Remember, if I can be of help . . .' and then turned to watch his driver get out and open the passenger door. When the fat man had climbed into the car, a table was pulled down from the back of the seat; a glass was filled with amber liquid and handed to him with a napkin. The fat man sipped as they moved away. Faith had never seen anything like it before in her life.

She waited across the street from the Ministry building for the rest of the day. The fat man was long gone but still she stayed. She stayed until it was quite dark and it looked as if everyone had left the building; but no David.

Chapter Twenty-Nine

Like the art galleries, the museums and the cinemas, the London theatres stood empty for a time when war broke out, ordered to shut for the public's safety, but they were quickly allowed to reopen. The government needed all the help it could get in keeping up the general mood; it hoped that the stage would distract the people from their privations, raise morale. And it did. At the Windmill, which specialized in *tableaux vivants* with titles such as 'June Morn' featuring young ladies in 'artistic' poses clad only in bodystockings, a soubrette, shivering in flesh-coloured net, waiting her turn, peeked around the curtain. She saw a full house entirely made up of men with mackintoshes arranged strategically over their laps.

Even at Bletchley Park the various committees that filled the former drawing rooms, bedrooms and library of the mock-Tudor mansion agreed that theatre, in the form of the Bletchley Park Drama Group, fulfilled a valuable role, giving the different ranks and occupations the opportunity to unite with a common purpose, thus 'encouraging teamwork'. At large events such as these performances, the Black team were allowed to be present – among the throng passing through the checkpoints, mingling in the makeshift bar, they would go unnoticed. Tonight it was to be Shakespeare – *Twelfth Night*.

'Appropriate – from what I remember . . . all about forged letters and people not being who you thought they were,' Sam said. 'And I think I might have found our Lotte Leckerbissen; you know we have the voice, but I've been looking for a face . . . a body. She's on stage this evening, playing a lead, thought I'd take a closer look. Anyone else fancy it?'

Neville nodded vigorously, pipe between his teeth. 'Count me in: I'd love to see my greatest creation made flesh. And it'd be good to get away from the villa.'

'How about you, Vivienne?' said Frido.

'I think I'll have an early night. I'm utterly worn out.' As she spoke, Vivienne could see Frido's disappointment and feel Charles' eyes upon her.

'I don't really get on with Shakespeare,' Charles said. 'You won't mind if I stay here too, will you, Mrs Thayer? I shan't disturb you.'

Vivienne cast her gaze back down upon the papers in front of her to conceal her panic. She had wanted to avoid spending time with Frido in public, to appear to be separating herself from him, had hoped that Charles might read into this a cooling of the affair, that he might take the pressure off her just for a while. But if she stayed at home with Charles, he would pursue her for information as soon as the others had left. He would, perhaps, even feel entitled to seek her out in her bedroom should she not appear downstairs, if he were sure they were alone. She would have to think quickly . . . the only way out would be to ready herself at the last minute and slip out to the car just as the others were about to leave, without telling them beforehand or alerting Charles. He must not have the opportunity to decide to come with them, to lie in wait all evening at Bletchley, watching her, looking for an opportunity to sidle up to her.

Vivienne looked at her work and tried to concentrate. The aim of the project was to demoralize; its desired outcome, to inspire an invaluable blend of pity and terror. Leaflets would be dropped over those major German cities that had, so far, escaped the attentions of the Allied bombers. They were to feature rows of photographs of the heads and shoulders of individuals lined up like in a beauty pageant, although here the similarity ended, for these were corpses, the fatalities of an air raid. Vivienne had to sort through the pictures, to select the most 'eye-catching' and to create a composition of them.

It was not true that the dead looked as if they slumbered peacefully. 'Your father has fallen asleep,' Vivienne's mother had said to her. But when Vivienne approached the bed on which her father's body lay she found him transformed. He seemed smaller, thinner – yes, he had been ill for weeks – but also not as tall, and so still without even the hum of blood in his veins that he looked like only an approximation, a poor likeness of the man she had known. The globes of his eyes dropped back, flattened under the lids. His face fell away from the dark oval of his mouth, which stretched open and upwards, as if he were straining to let something huge out, or in; the face's expression an abandoned blank.

Despite the grainy quality of the photographs Vivienne held, she could see they had absorbed that same look. She thought about the poor parents, children, sisters, brothers, lovers of the victims in this frozen parade; and about the poor recipients of the leaflets who were likely to have already lost a dear one, and for several years would have believed in, hoped for, any other fate for their beloved but this. They probably dreamt at night that it was all a mistake, they would surely hear again the lost footfall, the voice over the telephone, they would receive a letter in that cherished hand. And, thanks to Black, some would find the fantasy come true – their dead would write to them.

As Vivienne arranged the images in rows (placing a child in the centre looked most effective) Frido tapped out another of his 'dead letters'. Next to his German typewriter sat a stack of mail intercepted by Prisoner of War Postal Censorship. Written by the relatives of missing German soldiers who, in their grief, could not accept that their dearest boy had been killed, these messages were sent to Britain in the vain hope that he was, secretly, a prisoner there. The freight of emotion was carried along lines of banal family news, their chattiness at odds with the anguish driving the hands that composed them.

> *Your sister Inge has married. They have a baby named Josef after you –*
> *imagine, you are an uncle! Your father says that we should stay a while*
> *with Tante Else in Bavaria, but I think that now the bombing has started*
> *there as well there is no point. Besides, there would be Else and her little*
> *ways – and her cats – to put up with. We think of you, dear Josef, all*
> *the time . . .*

In response to such letters Frido composed different permutations on the same theme. The family had been deliberately hoodwinked by the German authorities because the truth was that their boy was in good health and happy – he had built a new life in Britain. Of course, Berlin did not want the relatives to know this, to hear that their loved one was waiting for the fall of the Nazis, when the family could be reunited with him. The letters were to be transported to Germany and distributed to special agents there, who would post them out, Sam's idea being that the recipients, swept up in a turmoil of joy, would be unable to resist telling someone close to them about their great luck. That was where the dead letters were psychologically cunning. By insisting that the relatives keep the secret of their missing boy's survival to themselves, they made it more likely that they would be tempted to ignore the instruction, and so news of German soldiers being kept safe and well treated in Britain would spread.

Vivienne spent the afternoon finishing the layouts; earlier than usual, she would disappear to her room, claiming a headache. She could bathe and prepare for Bletchley without anyone knowing. She had spent long enough that day in the company of the dead; as she pushed the photographs into a separate pile for each leaflet, she flipped them over like a pack of cards so that the faces were not staring up at her.

When Sam opened the door to their bedroom at seven o'clock, after an early dinner, to dress for the evening out, he was surprised to see Vivienne sitting on the bed in her silver Vionnet evening gown and a velvet cape.

'So you've changed your mind. I'm glad.' But he didn't look it.

They descended to the car at the last minute, Frido and Neville already inside it, and she caught the way that her lover's face lit up as she approached; she imagined, with some satisfaction, Charles sitting alone in the drawing room, waiting for her to appear.

Half an hour later they sat among a rowdy audience who had spent the time between the end of their working day and the rise of the curtain drinking. The noise from the seats drowned out the actors' lines, which were gabbled, shouted or whispered, and the figures on the stage were in any case unprepossessing in their everyday uniforms or civilian clothes. The director had decided that to make

Shakespeare accessible to a crowd more used to *ITMA* and 'The White Cliffs of Dover', the whole thing would have to be in modern dress. The costumes, therefore, did not hold the attention, and as the acting was so very bad, the players looked as if they had mistakenly wandered on to the stage from the stalls – until Viola made her first entrance in disguise as a young man. Vivienne had not recognized the be-frocked Viola at the very start of the play, but now she sat up in her seat and looked more closely.

It was the motorcycle dispatch rider – the girl who had come into their room at dawn to deliver Minister Bracken's memo to Sam a couple of months earlier. She sauntered on to the stage just as she had appeared at Sam's bedside, in full uniform, with her lovely blonde hair and rosy complexion (she can't be more than nineteen, thought Vivienne), her long slender legs in tight jodhpurs, the glint of buckles all the way up her knee-length leather boots. The audience fell under a spell. A chorus of whistling and clapping greeted her every appearance, the male characters were bombarded with boos for treating Viola badly (or for standing too close to her). The girl could not help but begin to blush, her mouth working hard to keep to the text and not break into a self-conscious, delighted grin. At one point, spurred on by a frenetic spell of applause, she stepped out of the scene and bowed with a flourish, like a principal boy in a pantomime. Only once did the audience notice anything apart from Viola. The Clown had been an undistinguished presence, mumbling and stumbling about the stage. Then he began to sing mournfully. A pure, clear voice cut through the makeshift theatre.

> Not a flower, not a flower sweet
> On my black coffin let there be strown:
> Not a friend, not a friend greet
> My poor corpse, where my bones shall be thrown:
> A thousand thousand sighs to save,
> Lay me, O, where
> Sad true lover never find my grave,
> To weep there!

There was silence at the end, broken only by sniffling among the Wrens.

Disconcerted that the Clown's song had thrown the rest of the shambles into stark relief, the cast stepped up the tempo of the remainder of the play and raced to the final exit – lovers parcelled off into orderly married couples, uppity servants pushed back into their lowly positions – at a gallop. The final applause was for sheer relief and for Viola (resplendent in flowered silk and suede heels), who received an ovation a West End actress could have pined for her whole career, albeit interspersed with catcalls and lewd suggestions. And then Vivienne noticed Sam. He was gazing, entranced, at the girl centre stage, as he had once looked at Vivienne in the Café Royal, and, as Viola coloured up, giggled and curtseyed coquettishly once again, he raised a hand. Vivienne watched as the girl flashed a glance at him in return.

Afterwards, Vivienne sat at the bar, looking over the heads – alternately oiled or waved – to see Sam laughing with the girl in the middle of a circle of the other actors. She felt a pressure on her arm, and turned to see Frido.

'You look very charming tonight, Mrs Thayer.'

'Frido – that's lovely, but you know . . .' Someone bumped into her then. Her drink splashed on to the floor, but missed her gown.

'What a mess, it's all over your dress, look,' Frido said, dabbing at nothing with his handkerchief. 'Here, you must come with me, no, come with me now, and we'll find something to clean you up properly.'

He pushed with her through the crowd and out into the corridor. Around the corner they went and along the dark passageway until he stopped at a door, opening it to find an empty meeting room, blackout blinds down. Frido switched on a lamp, and shut the door, turning the key in the lock. He came over and took her face in his hands, looking hard at her, and then glided one hand along her side, smoothing down the silver fabric, to hold her; he made her sway into a slow dance in time to the distant music coming from the bar.

'It's not right, Frido, this can't go on. We have to end it.'

'What . . . why?'

'Sam, you see. I don't think he knows about us yet, I hope not . . . but I shouldn't like to hurt his feelings.'

Frido gently put his hands back on either side of her face.

'Vivienne, wonderful, wonderful Vivienne. I need you. You're the only thing that matters. I have my work. But, Christ – those letters, the pictures, the dead: every day surrounded by them. I often think that there is no point, we are fooling ourselves if we don't admit that we've lost already. And then . . . there's you. Think about it, admit to yourself how hard it is to find someone that you can like every part of, every single part of. And you realize, you know what's between us, I can tell. No, don't you dare turn away, look at me. This might have happened to you many times, but never in my life. And I will not give it up. Not now, especially not now.'

'I'm afraid you'll have to. Sam . . .'

'Damn your husband!' Frido said. 'I am sorry . . . I like Sam. It's difficult not to. But he doesn't give even this much for you.' Frido snapped his fingers. 'I've come to wonder if he knows about us already, but is pretending he doesn't, because you don't matter to him, and because it suits him. If he were to admit he knows, he'd have to act, he'd have to put a stop to it as a matter of pride, and he'd have to send me away, which isn't what he wants. He needs me in Black at the moment, and the more preoccupied you are, the more he can be with that girl – that child. No doubt he's pretending to you that he's just come across her again tonight. But I've seen her before, she's been to the villa several times, never when you are there. Next thing you know, he'll have you sketch her as Lotte, he'll drive her back and forth in his big car. But it won't end with her, there'll be another after her, and another. You might be blind to it, but everyone else knows. It's a big joke.'

Vivienne turned away. Of course it might all be true, everything he said, but she mustn't give in.

'Frido, you're not married, you don't know how it works, you don't understand about Sam, about me. No, my mind is made up, quite decided,' she declared. But the tenor of her voice said the opposite. He put his arms around her again. She could only murmur, 'Frido, my own love. It's the last time, the last time.'

They drove back to the villa at two in the morning – Sam at the wheel of the Rolls, going faster even than usual, enjoying himself, hurtling through the lanes, cutting up the sodden verges. Neville, also in the front, sang his own adapted version of the Clown's song. Vivienne, sitting on the back seat in the dark, felt Frido's hand grasp hers.

They piled out of the car and into the hall, hushing each other in stage whispers. 'Another drink?' said Sam, and they all agreed, following him into the drawing room. Vivienne went off to the kitchen, bumping around drunkenly, collecting ice from the American fridge into a bowl, looking for the silver tongs. She had a sensation, then, of being watched, and thought she heard footsteps in the passageway: there was no one there. But as she passed through the hall to join the others, there on the stairs was Charles. He turned towards her briefly before he made his way silently up; he looked at her, and then shook his head.

Chapter Thirty

Despite the best efforts of the Nazis, despite her own thoughtlessness – how could she have ever forgotten to kiss his photograph? – the heavens smiled upon Cecily Browne and Richard Tully: their wedding day had come and he was still alive.

Cecily's hair had been taken out of the rollers and brushed into full waves, her nose powdered, her lips painted red, but not too red (there was a lot of pink in the shade). The flowers were brought in: a bouquet of white carnations and ferns. And then the dress slid in a chilly rush over her, settling into slippery folds that clung and then flared.

The dressmaker had transformed her mother's late-Edwardian wedding costume into a modern gown. 'Of course,' her mother had said, 'we can find a way to get all the fabric you need – there's always a way. But I think it's better like this, there's so much good silk in this skirt, and we won't offend the make-do-and-menders.'

Cecily had marvelled at the slender waist of the original garment; however, when it had been unpicked and restyled she realized that her own measurements were not much bigger, and nowadays you had to maintain a fashionably thin figure without the help of corsets. Gone were the puffed sleeves, ribbons and draperies of the original in favour of simplicity and clean lines. The only extravagant touch was the 'Tudor' collar which stood up before curling away into two points, emphasizing the line of Cecily's neck. She had shown the dressmaker a portrait of Katherine Parr, Henry VIII's last wife, the one Miss Handley had lingered over during those long lessons on the history of the British Empire. 'The best of Henry's queens, girls, because, unlike Catherine of Aragon (a foreigner), and Anne Boleyn (only concerned with her own pleasure), Katherine was a true Englishwoman. She always put her husband's needs before her own and gave him a happy home life. One has to conclude that Henry would have been a better man had he met this Katherine first.'

Early that afternoon, the train carrying Richard and Cecily to their short honeymoon rolled and jolted towards their destination, a farmhouse in fields outside St Margaret's Bay, a village by the sea near Dover. Richard had always said he would take his new bride to the bay, having spent so many holidays there as a child, but it had been taken over by defence operations, so they had to settle for the countryside nearby. It was typical of his strength of mind: he had always planned to go to the bay, and despite the war would get as close as he could.

As the newlyweds boarded the carriage at Canterbury station, Cecily expected it to be as crowded as usual – more so, perhaps packed with troops – if the rumours were right that it would soon be time for a great push into Europe. There were air raids day and night now over the German cities. Hitler had not been heard on German radio or seen in the newsreels for weeks. But although the platform at Canterbury bristled with the usual amount of rifles and backpacks, the train to Dover and then onwards was only comfortably full. Cecily, able to sit next to her new husband, thought that perhaps the invasion of France was not imminent after all. She removed her gloves and they held hands and looked out at the fields and hedges reaching out towards the coast. From time to time they kissed, oblivious to the other passengers.

At the country station – a single ticket booth with a small waiting room attached – a pony and cart waited for them. Again, Cecily was struck by the soldiers: their presence was obvious, as it had been along the coast throughout the war, but there did not appear to be greater numbers than usual, and they certainly did not give the impression of an army marshalling for an attack. Cecily would wait for the right moment and ask Richard what he knew: he must have some idea when it would all begin. And Cecily had decided that now that they were man and wife Richard would have to tell her more. She already felt closer to him, after this heavenly day, and as he helped her up into the cart with such care.

They trotted up a lane, down into a dip and then on up to the crown of a hill where in the distance they could see the flint-clad village houses. The farmhouse where they were to spend their honeymoon looked like something out of a jigsaw puzzle or the cover of a biscuit tin: a real survivor of Ye Olde England, seventeenth-century, with casement windows and purplish bricks, irregular in shape and shade. The gateposts were each topped with a fruit carved in stone, a pineapple, probably easier to get in the days when you waited for the tall ships than now, when U-boats sent all the merchantmen to the bottom of the sea.

At last, up in their room, they pulled back the heavy curtain and the lace one behind it; though the cold made them shiver, they pushed the window wide open to smell the air and glimpse a strip of sea. They could have gone down, as they had been invited to, for some tea. But Richard opened his case decisively, took out his pyjamas, and said that he would go to the bathroom to allow Cecily privacy in which to prepare. She sprayed scent around her neck and then, self-conscious in the daylight, undressed and put on her new nightgown – peach rayon with a white-daisy print. She waited on the edge of the bed. Sitting upright, with her feet flat on the floor and her hands lying awkwardly in her lap, seemed too formal, as if she were waiting at the dentist. She plumped up the pillows, kicked off her slippers and lay back. At which the voice, thankfully silent during the wedding, piped up: *Just like Jean Harlow*. She put her slippers on again, but leant backwards on one arm – this would, she hoped, appear natural, but not too forward (although she could not hold the position indefinitely – where *was* he?).

She had gathered her knowledge of what was about to happen from *The Guide*. The day before the wedding, Cecily had found, mysteriously left on her pillow, this volume embossed with gold letters, subtitled 'Instructions for the Bride-to-Be'. 'Your caring nature, united with complete trust in the guidance of your husband, will lead to the supreme communion of the marriage,' it explained, obscurely. The supreme communion, it continued, would transport the bride to 'the summit of rapture'. But there were no further directions, not even an indication of how to set out for the summit. Cecily would have to do as the book said and rely upon Richard's knowledge.

When he came back into the room, Richard sat on the bed next to Cecily. Now they were together in their nightclothes for the first time, they looked at each other uncertainly. He began to kiss her again: a breathless, dizzy sensation. The embrace continued. Cecily opened her eyes once to see Richard's shut tight in concentration. And she was pressed so very close to him, closer than she had ever been. She desired more of this, for it never to stop, but also for it to build up into something else, for the next stage – whatever it might be – to begin. She had relaxed and was thinking how odd it was that she did not feel shy at all, when Richard pulled himself from her and turned away. He sat up, hunched and still. He would not look at her when she said his name, and then, when she moved around to the other side of the bed, she saw his unhappy face.

'It's no good. I'm no good. I've been waiting too long for this, worrying about it and wanting it to be wonderful. I'm so terrified of messing it up that I've gone and let you down anyway. I'm not the ideal man, the hero you believe me to be. I'm a fraud,' he said miserably.

'Whatever you think about yourself, I love you.'

'But you don't know the truth about me. I try to appear strong, but it's all pretend, Cecily. You've no idea what I'm really like, the awful things I've done, the bombing raids. And I can't tell you! But after the war, after the war – then, I swear, there'll be no more secrets.'

Cecily surprised herself by pulling back the covers and gesturing to him to climb under the sheet with her.

Richard and Cecily lay on their backs, side by side in the double bed, in silence. Cecily had placed one arm under Richard's neck. Even when her hand began to prickle with pins and needles she was unwilling to move and break this connection between them. Then, after a while, she turned to face Richard and the kissing started again, this time with its own momentum. When the unknown culmination Cecily had waited for happened, it was not at all the sublime encounter she expected, and quite unlike her own cautious, private experiments with her body; it was an ungainly, repetitive, shoving motion, crassly physical and painful at first. But – and this was the odd thing – the idealized visions of mountain peaks that

The Guide had placed in her mind vanished. Even the photograph of the two of them smiling politely for the camera, which she had treasured, which she had kissed each day, would now be inadequate. This new, most intimate proximity, awkward as it may be, was not a beautiful picture, but it gave her an impression – overwhelming while it lasted – that they were no longer entirely separated from each other by the borders of their own skin.

Before the sun had set, Cecily and Richard left their room and took a path that cut between the fields. They would venture as near as they could to the bay. The beach was out of bounds, littered with defences, and used for army training. But Richard had told her about the rockpools, the caves in the chalk cliffs, and had shown her photographs of summer days in the nineteen-twenties, of rows of sunloungers, each displaying a lady with a cigarette holder in her hand, of men in striped costumes, children splashing in the shallows. There had been buildings hard by the edge of the shore, a group of modern houses, plain, white and flat-roofed, with balconies and metal windows. You would have looked out from them across the Channel and not seen menace and a lost civilization; instead, you would have spent days watching, dreaming of the City of Light over the water.

Their walk was halted by a barricade of wood and barbed wire, they could go no further. They could taste salt in the air but were cut off from the sea, roiling and unravelling – green, grey, purple, white, brown, ochre – every colour apart from the cerulean blue it was usually painted. Cecily desired more than anything to break through the barrier, to run down to the shore and into the waves until she lost her footing, to be lifted, rocked and pulled, dipping and rising, to be taken out of herself, to be taken over.

They spent their three-day honeymoon walking as near to the bay as they were allowed, or lying together in their room, talking, reading to each other and kissing, holding each other with greater ease and pleasure. On the final morning, Cecily woke first and looked at her husband, sleeping on his side, hands tucked together under his cheek and knees pulled up – so very young. They had kept the window open and, as she lay there, spreading her fingers out between sheets warmed by the new heat of two bodies together, she heard a low humming sound. She tensed to listen, but it was not a plane far off, it was a bee which circled over the bed twice and then flew out again with an impression of great deliberation.

Later that day, Cecily took the train back to her parents' house alone while Richard returned to RAF Mildenhall. Time, which had extended out before her only a few days earlier, had abruptly telescoped shut and disappeared. Her old bedroom was inadequate for the woman who had returned as a wife, a place suitable only for a girl; its neat certainties – the china ornaments, the matching cushions and curtains – did not fit with the commotion inside. Richard would fly over and over before they could be together again. She would have to be so very deserving, and he so very lucky, for him to survive. And then the voice, which had been quiet for much of the honeymoon, began to whisper again, to insist: *He'll never come back, you know, never.*

At night Cecily lay awake in her single bed, which stretched out cold and empty around her but at the same time felt mean and narrow. She cried hard, but covered her mouth with her hands. She did not want to be heard.

Chapter Thirty-One

Husbands leaving wives for the airfield, the barracks, the front, for who knows where: the image we have of the war is of the moment of departure. The convention in film is a shot of a train about to shoulder its way out of the station amid a stream of hats, upturned faces and hands held fast across the gap between the platform and the already moving carriages; he leans down out of the window while she balances on the tips of her brogues to reach up to him just this one last time. But here, in a Worcestershire hotel, early in 1943, a wife takes leave of her husband.

Laura Knight had spent five days with Harold. She had held out before making this visit for as long as she could – had been at Mildenhall an entire month – but the more she waited, the more difficult the telephone calls became. When George spoke of his crew having a week's leave imminent, and there was a greater chance than usual that no harm would come to him while she was away, Laura had made the arrangements to travel to Malvern.

Harold's delight at her presence made her feel guilty about her restlessness as well as uncomfortable. The only point at which she roused herself and felt pleasure in his company was during their last evening together. And even then she was conscious that she was not happy because of his efforts, but because she was about to leave, that he was miserably aware of this too, but would not mention it, unwilling to risk spoiling the one companionable period of the visit. He had saved his coupons to conjure up a memorable farewell dinner. The fire – he would invoke the wrath of the manageress for using too much coal to stoke up such a blaze – threw a warm autumnal light on to the pair as they sat in the hotel's best room among the brass ornaments – a pair of candlesticks, a matchbox cover with *Llandudno* engraved upon it, a Scotty dog. Soon it would be time to shut her suitcase and return to the station, and Laura was thinking of this when Harold said, 'Is there something you want to tell me? Because you can, you know, Laura; anything that troubles you, whatever it is. I'll try to understand.'

As he spoke she looked past his profile, emphatic as a classical bust; it had not much altered over the years, only been dragged down and softened slightly as if a hand had brushed over a drawing. Behind him, out of the window, she could see the Malvern Hills, a stripe of viridian beneath a thicker band of pure ultramarine.

'I'm just tired – preoccupied with work. It's not easy, this commission.'

In their bedroom – Harold's, in truth, as she lived there so infrequently – Laura finished packing. A pattern of brown flowers on vines clambered fussily up and across the wallpaper; the twin counterpanes in sepia and curtains in a darker shade gave the room the colouring of the past. As she refolded a scarf Laura saw, tucked to one side, something fluffy, in baby pink, a colour she never wore: bedsocks! Harold must have bought them and put them there. Laura saw the thoughtfulness of the act, but she took the socks out all the same. She might be past her prime, but not yet so old that she would wear such things, which would signal the beginning of the end, surely; only a short step from bedsocks to a walking stick and a bath chair; she might as well knit herself a shawl, park herself by the fire and have done with it. Laura did, however, want to take an evening frock and heels back with her to Mildenhall. She would have to search in her trunk, stowed in the depths of the hotel with the property of the other long-stay visitors, refugees from the cities. She did not want to have to go back to London first to pick up some things from the house there. She had not told Harold, but she felt uneasy in the studio in St John's Wood; the sense that someone had been there uninvited had not left her.

When she returned from the cellar, Harold was sitting on the bed. He observed her folding the dress carefully. As she laid it upon the top layer in the suitcase, she noticed that not only had the socks returned to their previous position, they had been joined by a bed-jacket in the same colour.

'For heaven's sake, H., I don't need those, I'm not so decrepit. Do leave it alone!' She rooted out the pink garments, throwing them down on her bed, and then, wanting to make clear that she would never think of wearing them, opened the bottom drawer of the dressing table and shoved them in roughly.

'Oh, and Harold . . . please stop worrying.'

He did not respond. Instead, moving to her bedside, he picked up the water jug and glass and said, 'I'll take these back to the kitchen: they're so short of staff now.'

The worry lines had still not gone from his forehead by the time she boarded the train.

The sun had set when Laura arrived at the boarding house close to RAF Mildenhall. Tomorrow she would see George; he was due back from leave in the morning. It would be the right thing now to unpack, to ready herself for the next day's work, to have an early night, but in her rooms she could not rest. She put on her coat and lit a cigarette. She would walk and think – no, she would go to the airfield, to catch up with events. She felt awake for the first time in a week, and picked up her sketchbook – if the right subject appeared she was not too tired to work.

A yellow moon looked down upon the base: it was clear and still, perfect flying weather. In the distance, the sharp-edged box of the control tower rose over a spread of such breadth and flatness – with a silver shimmer upon it – that it could have been sea rather than grass. The windowed turret at the top had a decadent appearance, like the bridge of an ocean liner, as if it were a place for scanning the horizon, sunning yourself and taking in the view. Around the turret ran a balcony with iron railings, and tonight this was full of people: the staff meant to be there had been joined by off-duty flyers and ground crew. Perhaps they felt closer to the men in battle, less helpless, standing out there watching for them.

In the control room, so many crowded around the radio operators and the two young WAAFs chalking hieroglyphs on to a blackboard that no one remarked upon Laura as she sat in the corner drawing the scene. For a long time there was no great activity, only talk between the radio operators and the girls, and the officers consulting over charts and lists. And then there began to be shouts from the balcony as a returning plane was sighted and bumped down the runway. At first these landings were spaced far apart, and then they came rapidly. Laura tried to push her way on to the balcony to see more closely, but the wall of backs held tight. Bursts of cheering followed hard on one another, and every time the WAAFs added to the tally of survivors, two of the officers ritually shook hands and slapped each other on the back. Then came a lull; after a while, the group on the balcony turned away from the scene outside and stood about in silence for an interval before coming back into the tower. The quiet lasted while the radio operators listened on. At a certain time, near dawn, the cry went out: 'No hope . . . put out the lights, put out the lights.'

Laura did not wake until nearly lunchtime, and even then her muzzy head felt too great a burden for her neck, her body inflexible. 'There is no extra reserve to be drawn upon,' she thought, 'when you're old.' She had lost the morning already so did not wait for breakfast. She made her way to the gates and flagged down the tumbril running its slow circuit, and as they drew up closer to the airfield, she saw the signs of last night's battle stretched out before her. The planes, incontestably machines when intact, took on, when damaged, a forlorn animal appearance, as if they had felt the mutilation. Writhing innards – metal, glass and wire – erupted from the flank of one, spilling on to the tarmac. The ground crew were trying to patch up the wounded and to estimate the number of hopeless cases. Some way off stood a group of still pristine planes, among them *Midgley's Flying Circus*.

The broken bodies of the machines would give Laura a new painting: an image of the price of the conflict and the heroism of the men. Surely Smith must see that not all of the artists' work need have 'happy' subject matter in order to transmit the right message? Laura planned compositions in her head as she made her way back to the recreation hall to hear the details of last night's events, to see if her crew had returned yet from their leave, to find George again. And she felt slightly guilty about her pleasure in working at the centre of things at last, that her desire to defeat Smith, to advance her art, had overtaken feeling compassion for the violent havoc that her crew – that George – had thrown themselves into. Her brief return to Harold made her admit to herself how much she loved, needed, the young navigator's company.

The recreation hall held an odd hush: not enough noise came from the crowd within. Even though Laura knew that her boys were safe – she had seen *Circus* unscathed on the airfield – she still felt a rush of recognition and relief when she caught sight of them all there, beneath a ledge of cigarette smoke, playing cards – but then she looked again. Their unwillingness to return her greeting as she approached gave her a quick presentiment of what they would tell her.

'We weren't flying last night, but George was – gone for a Burton, I'm afraid. Skipped the last part of his leave: stood in for another chap – Richard Tully – off getting married.'

Only one thing tied her, however slightly, to him; she would send a photograph of her painting to his mother. It took Laura some time to decide what to say on the back; just to sign it would appear grandiose. Unable to tell what she truly felt, she could summon up only platitudes: 'My dear Mrs Meredith, I don't presume to understand your suffering. I had the pleasure of knowing George. Such a very fine young man.' And that was all she could write. Laura contemplated the young face in her painting: his characteristic expression, bent over his maps and compasses, absorbed, as if he were sketching for pleasure. She stroked his smooth cheek with her finger before covering the painting gently with a blanket, ready to be transported to Smith.

Chapter Thirty-Two

By 5.30 p.m. on the day of his lecture, Aubrey Smith could clearly be seen huddled at the end of a bench in the corner of one of the empty and unlit rooms of the National Gallery. In his imagination, however, he had already mounted the stage, cleared his throat, and surveyed the audience with a commanding yet serene expression, the expression of a man who knew what he was talking about. A shiver of anticipation and a ripple of premature applause ran through the audience. As he spoke, purposefully, but with lightness and humour, row upon row of beaming faces turned towards him like sunflowers. Even Clark's habitual testy or impervious air was replaced by a look of fascination – he could not help himself – and then pride. And, afterwards, Clark bounded on to the platform, eager to claim Smith as his protégé, gave him a proprietorial slap on the back and steered him through the crowd to mingle with his own exalted circle. 'Minister, Brigadier, Your Grace, may I introduce . . .' As the vision evaporated, Smith saw that it would soon be time to make the final preparations; he should go to the lecture room. Accompanying a resurgence of his terror, the thought came that perhaps some rain – or even, with luck, a tiny air raid – might deter the invitees from attending something so trivial as an art-history lecture. There was still the faint hope that the whole thing would be called off.

The octagonal room in the National Gallery, where Smith's talk was to take place, had proved a great success as a temporary home for concerts of classical music; an hour could be snatched away from the filing cabinet, the works canteen, the mop or the factory floor and spent instead in the company of a performer as renowned as Myra Hess, and the music of Mozart or Benjamin Britten. Against one wall stood a music stand, where Smith would have to rest his lecture notes; next to it was propped a blackboard upon which was chalked: *'The Gentler Brush: Women Artists Through the Ages': Aubrey Smith*, BA *(Lond.)*. Directly behind this, Smith saw that month's masterpiece brought from storage in the Welsh quarry – it would hang above his head as he spoke. A painting by Bronzino: two lustrous figures, a boy Cupid and a Venus, totally, ravishingly, naked. Other characters romped less importantly in the background and around the edges. With one hand, Cupid held the goddess by the hair, guiding her mouth towards his. The other cupped her breast, squeezing the nipple. Smith tried to divert his mind towards the real significance of the painting – as he had been taught to at the Courtauld. According to the tutor there, this Bronzino was not erotic at all, but allegorical. Nevertheless, Smith still found it difficult to see past fingers and lips: how good must that feel, and how much she seemed to enjoy it, too, pushing her tongue out playfully. He pulled himself up short again. The putto scattering rose petals symbolized the pleasure enjoyed by the intertwined couple; the figure clutching his hair and howling, despair at the brevity of such delights. Smith thought that if he were offered only five minutes of such activity with a girl like that he would not howl when his time was up, but would be so very, very grateful. At the back of the painting an old man with an hourglass resting upon his back represented time, how it weighed upon you. Smith saw that it was 5.45, only fifteen minutes left. It would be hard to concentrate with that pearly body showing itself off over his shoulder.

The guests began to arrive. The crowd – at least there was a crowd – two hundred at a guess, began to take their seats. The critics were easy to distinguish, of a uniform, calculated shabbiness, here and there sporting important scarves in abstract designs. There was a large number of young women artists, a new breed Smith found off-putting, frightening even, with their loud voices and trousers. Several of their older lady colleagues wore dark velvets in mossy tones of green and brown, grey hair stacked untidily or bobbed brutally. Smith sighed to himself: none of the big guns had bothered to attend, no Moore, no Sutherland.

Smith spotted Laura Knight – it was impossible not to notice her even among this eccentric group. Tonight she appeared to have come as a flamenco dancer, complete with a lace mantilla and fan. Knight rattled her bracelets at him and sat down next to an equally dreadful-looking friend – quite sinister, in Smith's opinion, with eyes like shiny beads and dark-painted lips, like an old French doll. A shake of Knight's bangles again and he watched as Faith Farr moved along the row, in her tatty green coat, towards the astonishing figure in ruffles and lace beckoning to her. And there, on the other side, was Cecily Browne, back from honeymoon, he presumed, in grey-brown again – someone must have told her that it matched her eyes.

Kenneth Clark, meanwhile, had taken up position to one side of the music stand. As if the Bronzino weren't enough of a distraction, everyone would notice Clark there, resplendent in one of his Savile Row suits, and Smith would be as constantly, uncomfortably, aware of his presence, as he was of his own stiff, ill-fitting Utility trousers and jacket.

He didn't hear what Clark said to introduce him, intent as he was on clearing his throat, swallowing several times and arranging his papers. Only after a moment or two of silence did he glance up to see Clark looking at him expectantly. Smith began, and found that by focusing hard on the black and white lines in front of him (his own handwriting; the secretaries had been too hard pressed to type the thing up, or so they said) he could mentally blur the faces of his audience until they almost disintegrated. Pace was crucial, Clark had instructed him; 'you must speak more slowly than you would normally', in order to sound like a man who knows what he is talking about. The material for the lecture Smith had cribbed, piecemeal. Trying to find things to say about women artists had been difficult. He had decided to talk very generally about how hard it had been for ladies in the past before inventions such as the vacuum cleaner, the electric cooker and the elasticated girdle (his habit of perusing his mother's magazines had given him useful intelligence on the life of the modern female) and then he added in some colourful details about coal-fired kitchen ranges, whalebone corsets, voluminous petticoats and crinolines. He planned to end on an entirely positive note: now free of such domestic and bodily restrictions, he would say, and supported in every possible way by the latest technology, women were making a very special contribution to the contemporary art world, even in this difficult time of conflict.

He was about halfway through his script – talking about the corsets – when he saw that Clark was scribbling on and then holding up a piece of paper, which he flapped to attract Smith's attention. Smith glanced across. 'Stop talking about underwear. Do get to the point!' it said, vigorously underlined twice. Recovering himself, Smith looked down at his page again, but not before he caught sight of the amused expression upon Laura Knight's face, and saw her whisper to Faith Farr behind her hand. Smith rallied himself – look for something about stays, about skirts – he found the line, cleared his throat and began again.

His voice, which he had carefully modulated to sound, he thought, measured and authoritative, now, for some reason, leapt up an octave. He stopped again, coughed, and tried to wrestle it down to what he hoped was a more natural pitch, but when he had managed that, the voice began to speed up, uncontrollably. Much sooner than he had anticipated Smith reached the final page. There was silence from the audience – some looked at their watches, unsure if there was more yet to come – broken by a cry of bravo, enthusiastic clapping and a percussion of jewellery from Laura Knight.

Chapter Thirty-Three

'Wonderful to see you both again!' said Laura Knight to Faith and Cecily, as Smith hurried away from the music stand at the front of the gallery, the restrained applause died away and the audience began to shuffle in their seats, to turn to their neighbours and talk. 'I hope that congratulations are now in order, Cecily? Good! But you, Faith, have not been following my advice. Still awfully peaky. Did you get my card from RAF Mildenhall?'

'I did,' said Faith, taking in the full, overwhelming effect of the mantilla and fan, the cascades of ruffles at neck and hem.

'Finally, finally! I'm doing the work I was born for, eh, Dod?'

Laura's friend pursed her burgundy-coloured lips in agreement.

'I know it might sound a terribly long wait to you girls,' Laura continued. 'But I can tell you, it's worth it: all the pain, the struggle to carry on painting down the years. And at least I am more than ready for my big moment – ravenous for the chance – there's something to be said for it happening at my great age . . . By the way, Faith, I meant to tell you, I do understand that you made a genuine mistake that day back in January when you asked me to meet you by the river, and then didn't come. You're distracted, not yourself still, I can see that.'

'But I didn't – I didn't ask you to meet me.'

Laura smiled at Faith tolerantly, but Dod gave the younger woman a disapproving look.

'It's quite all right, you know,' Laura said. 'I do understand. I have my moments. I've been unsettled recently, been working too hard, I think. I began to imagine that things were moving around my studio. One of my pictures, I was sure I left it on the floor by the window before I went out one day; but when I came back I found it on the easel, I began to think that someone must have broken in, gave myself quite a fright.'

Faith immediately suspected what had happened. David had sent a note, pretending to be her, to entice Laura away in order to search her studio. Perhaps he had seen them together, maybe that time at the Kardomah, or, because Laura was so famous and easy to find, had sought out her studio in the hope that she might well be in contact with other women working for WAAC, Faith among them. And yes, she had written her address in Laura's sketchbook. Suppose David had seen it, it would explain him finding her flat in Holloway. She had been right to leave immediately, to take refuge at Miss Roy's. As Faith thought this, Dod said, 'We have to go. Dame Laura's so in demand. Her time is precious and not to be wasted.' This last sentence was aimed at Faith.

'Dod's right, we've a dinner reservation. Also: want to avoid Smith, can't have him raining on my parade; he'll feel like it, too, after that ludicrous lecture – Hoovers and girdles indeed! But you'll be at the private view, of course? Both of you? All of us together! We'll show Smith what we're made of. We'll talk then.'

Cecily and Faith were left alone in the row of seats, two empty chairs between them. Faith hoped that the girl might rise, say goodbye, but she showed no sign of wanting to go. Instead, she smiled at Faith, nervously.

'She's marvellous, isn't she, Dame Laura?' said Cecily, tentatively.
'But?'

'She's so entirely sure of herself . . . and I'm not, you see. I'd hate her to realize how weak I am, how feeble and full of doubt . . . I can't tell anyone, but I don't love working for the Ministry at all.'

Faith looked at Cecily with interest for the first time.

'What I said that time the three of us went to the Kardomah wasn't true. And since then, it's been terrible, actually. First, I got injured: my arm, pretty badly. Smith sent me to paint a knitting party; a house in Belgravia, sunshine, tea and sandwiches. And then, out of the blue, an air raid. I think two of the women died. Then, when I went to paint the land girls, something happened, I can't say what, but it upsets me still. And my last mission was at a hospital, and that was, that was . . . I can tell you how hard it's been because I don't know you – I can't admit it to anyone close, especially not my parents, they'd make me give up. Certainly not to Smith or Sir Kenneth, and not even to my husband – my concerns seem so trivial next to the danger he faces every day. But you, I thought . . . you don't look to me as if you've found things easy, either? I don't mean that you look awful – you've a lovely face – but you do seem . . . uncared for, I mean, unhappy . . . I can't find the right words. I'm making a hash of this, I should just shut up.' Cecily stopped, embarrassed.

Faith had a choice, to stamp on Cecily's desire to talk, or to respond. She moved along to sit next to the girl.

'You mean to say I'm not at my best?' Faith said with mock horror, touching her hand to her old green coat, her lank hair.

'Are you quite alone, is that it?'

'No, I have parents. They survived the Blitz, now they're in the country, they're all right. And . . . I did have a husband.'

'I didn't know – you don't wear a ring. I'm so sorry.'

'He isn't dead, we just aren't together.'

'I see,' said Cecily, confused.

'We married in a rush, I was in love with him. But quickly, very quickly, it became clear that I'd made a dreadful mistake. Things haven't been right ever since. And then, there's what to do about Smith . . .'

'I know, I thought at the beginning that he was better than Sir Kenneth, more approachable. Only after a while did I realize how low Smith's opinion of me is. He's one of those where the less he rates you, the nicer he is. I'm sure he's only kind to me because he pities me, thinks I'm a mouse, that my work's trivial, pretty – safe.'

Faith did not disagree.

'But, you see, I don't want to paint men with guns, people suffering, hunger and dirt, blood and ruins. The newsreels are full of that, the papers too. I want to show that there is goodness still in the world, that the women I paint are carrying on despite everything, trying their best in whatever area they're allowed to work in. Insignificant, everyday activities, far away from the front, small acts of kindness, of endurance. It's grand gestures that got us into this mess in the first place. That was what my painting of women putting on those ridiculous, enormous gas capes was really about: we don't fit the world that men have created, the situation isn't of our making, but we struggle on and cope just the same. And if civilization does survive, it will be because of that – however unimportant Smith and Sir Kenneth consider such efforts to be.'

'Now it's my turn to say sorry. I thought . . . rather, I didn't think, when I first met you . . .' said Faith.

Cecily wasn't listening. She continued talking, her voice growing in confidence.

'Do you understand, Faith? I'm trying to paint what I think is important, but in a way that will pass muster with Smith and the Ministry. They don't admire what I do, but they don't object because I never challenge them directly; being thought a mouse actually helps. I used to hate the way I look – gentle and sweet – but now I've realized it's very useful. It's a good disguise. When they look at me they can't imagine that I'd ever have ideas of my own, and when they look at my work they're so blinkered by their assumptions about me they don't see what it's actually about. Have you thought, perhaps you could do the same? Find a way to mollify them while carrying on in your own direction. That's not compromising your talent, it's preserving it. These are tough times, and artists have to eat, too. Fighting with them only works if you're a Dame Laura, a – what does Sir Kenneth call the famous ones? – a *big gun*.' They both laughed.

'Anyway, I do hope I'll see you at the private view. You've still time to finish something for the exhibition, not an oil painting, but a watercolour, definitely. Will you try, will you do it?'

PART FOUR

March 1943

'Men haven't changed much in the last two
thousand years; and, in consequence, we must still
try to learn from history, history is ourselves.'

Sir Kenneth Clark, *Civilisation*, 1969

Chapter Thirty-Four

Smith's day of reckoning had come: it was time for the private view of the exhibition he had cobbled together from the submissions of the women. It had been advertised in the newspapers with a reproduction of Laura Knight's picture of Faith Farr, captioned 'One of the talented lady artists on show'. The portrait now hung on the wall of the gallery along with Knight's painting of the RAF men at Mildenhall. There was Farr's watercolour of a communal food hall – surprisingly jolly, a band, singers, all sorts of Londoners gathered in harmony together – along with some of her sketches. She had handed in an entire book full of these, which meant that Smith had had a choice, and among all the depressing scenes, he'd been able to root out a few of pretty children and an attractive mother, their plates piled high with food. On the opposite wall hung Cecily Browne's knitters, enjoying the sunshine in the grand drawing room (before the bomb landed on them, Smith thought guiltily); her happy hospital, full of calm nurses and contented patients; and the land girls going to bed (how had she managed to make such a promising subject so very tedious, all you could see were blankets and sheepskin slippers?). There were also bits of work by less troublesome women, grateful, conscientious types Smith hadn't even had to bother to meet with or write to, who had, unexpectedly, sent in drawings or canvases just in time.

Smith had spread the pieces about the walls as thinly as he could to try and fill the space, but still it looked to him as if half the exhibition were missing. And Clark would soon be there, frowning, grimacing, making his disappointment clear, humiliating him in front of Minister Bracken, and in broad daylight. They were holding the private view much earlier than was usual: it would begin at three o'clock in the afternoon. Events involving free alcohol always went on far longer than expected and there were qualms about hordes of lady artists – never the most practical of types – struggling home in the blackout after several drinks. The press would be there in force too, Smith knew, because despite the unprepossessing theme of the show they would not miss the opportunity for a sherry at the Ministry's expense – and would be fully prepared to sip and smile, sip and smile, only sharpening their pencils later to inquire indignantly how much this indulgence was costing the government, and hence the Great British Tax Payer, surviving as he was on stoicism and starvation rations . . .

Smith hurried along the side of Trafalgar Square towards the National Gallery. Even Nelson's column had been altered by the war. From his vantage point, with his one good eye, the Admiral surveyed the extent of the destruction. In the East End, the burnt and shattered docks spread out blackly, as if that part of the city had been drawn in Indian ink. Big Ben looked sorry for himself – his round cheeks pitted and crazed. Out at leafy Chelsea, the modest Old Church where St Thomas More once prayed and itched in his hair shirt had been flattened, the bones of ancient Christians blasted out of their quiet tombs, skulls gaping in shock at the fresh air. Nelson himself had escaped unscathed so far, but at the base of his memorial the bronze reliefs depicting his triumphs were now obscured by a gaudy hoarding. 'Dig for Victory,' it read, beneath a cartoon of a parade of jaunty root vegetables, marching along with stick arms and legs and grinning faces.

Under normal circumstances, Smith would have been delighted to see the first exhibition that he had organized so very well attended. Scarcely had the double doors at the front of the National Gallery been opened than a crowd – they had been queuing outside – pushed through. Thirsting equally for culture and free alcohol they filled the foyer and moved up the stairs quickly, four and five abreast. Smith knew just how underwhelmed they would be by what they found at the top.

There was nowhere for Smith to hide, but there was at least the chance of passing largely unnoticed for a while among so many people, camouflaged amid the smart clothes of the others in his Utility jacket and trousers. Smith could not hope to avoid Sir Kenneth Clark, of course. And there he was – Smith spotted the domed head and quick, small eyes – accompanied by Henry Moore and Graham Sutherland, no less. Smith recognized them immediately from their newspaper photographs, and momentarily forgot his discomfiture at the sight of the two 'big guns' of the art world. Sutherland, dressed in baggy flannels and a garish tie, looked as louche as a jazz musician. But he appeared to be wearing his hair the wrong way round: luxuriant eyebrows sprouted from the front of his head, a bald patch shone behind. And what a typically Yorkshire face Henry Moore had, thought Smith – dour, rough-hewn and weather-blasted. Neither man, Smith was pleased to note, had any physical gifts whatsoever, yet as they toured the room with Clark, it was clear they shared with him that magical confidence . . . Minister Bracken's red curls floated over the hubbub – he was at least a foot taller than most of the guests. He smiled and waved at Smith over the heads around him and, looking down to continue a conversation, he pushed his glasses back up his nose.

When Laura Knight entered the room there was a lull in conversation as the crowd stopped to look at her. The sight was astounding indeed. She was dressed as a Chinese empress, in a yellow silk-brocade robe, floor-length, with deep, embroidered sleeves and scarlet frogging; the two grey coils of her hair were pinned up with clusters of hanging beads that shook and shimmered as she spoke. The ensemble was garlanded with a fur stole – a white fox with jewelled eyes biting its own tail – and the smoke from her cigarette.

Knight took the arm of Faith Farr. Was it Smith's imagination, or had Farr tidied herself up considerably: he saw the effects of a touch of lipstick, a trip to the hairdresser's and clothes that did not appear dirty, cobbled together, or too big. She had removed the ugly green coat and her striking looks were set off by a deep-blue gown and a modish Juliet cap in the same colour, which brought to Smith's mind his first impression of her as a Pre-Raphaelite heroine – before all of the difficulties between them had altered this picture of her. He wondered, given the improvement in her appearance, if this afternoon would also be an auspicious time to broach an altogether more personal subject. Could he make his true feelings known to her? How long would it take her to get over whatever it was that had happened to her husband? After a moment's thought, he decided against it. Given that his lecture had been mortifying, the exhibition was bound to be a disaster, too, and he would surely be moved out of Clark's department after today; he should postpone approaching her for a month or two.

Cecily Browne circled the gallery on the arm of a young man in RAF blues; he must be her husband, thought Smith. He did not appear a day older than Smith himself, but he carried himself confidently, shoulders back and chin high, aware of the deference the wings on his chest inspired in the other guests. Although under normal circumstances Cecily Browne's company would have provided a safe haven at the private view – no matter how poor the exhibition, she could be relied on to be meek and polite to him – Smith could not possibly bring himself to speak to her when she was with her airman, the dashing uniform such a contrast to his own shameful civvies.

And then Smith saw an absolute stunner wandering through the room alone, but cool and unperturbed; her pink dress skimmed her body so closely that it might have grown upon her, and it clung to her prominent curves as she moved from picture to picture, carrying a drink. A halo of raven hair and red lips, although arranged in a rather sardonic expression, completed the image.

Clark had noticed the same woman, and the sight of her stirred up a debate within him. It was true that he had not had a chance, yet, to have a good look at what else had turned up in the Gallery that day – there might be other avenues to investigate. It was also true that, in the ordinary run of things, she was a trifle too ripe for his taste, a regular full-blown peony. These dark-haired, voluptuous types went off quite quickly, he had found; he preferred them just coming into flower. However, it might pep him up to try something different. The stress of trying to keep WAAC afloat had taken its toll. It would be only a brief diversion – perhaps a quick trip to the air-raid shelter below the Gallery – nothing time-consuming or involving. On reflection, Clark decided to move in closer to the woman with the black hair and pink dress. She would be bound to recognize him soon: that would be his chance.

Chapter Thirty-Five

'A surprise for you, my dear.' Laura Knight brandished a page of yesterday's evening paper and on it Faith saw a painting of herself, standing in the pose of an old-master self-portrait, one hand on her hip, brushes and palette in the other; it filled an entire quarter-page and was entitled 'A Woman in Wartime'. The figure was built of sombre tones, plainly dressed, no pointless details or fuss, and had been caught in deep thought, unsmiling, absorbed in her work.

'But how did you do it? I didn't sit for you . . .' Faith tried to look pleased, but she was horrified. David was bound to see the article, he might even come to the museum, or lie in wait for her outside. She tasted acid at the back of her throat – he could be close to her at this very moment. She looked about, but she couldn't see him among the crowd immediately around her. Waitresses moved between the various groups, carrying trays of drinks. She followed them with her eyes.

However, right at the back of the gallery, through a doorway, were clusters of figures that she could not make out properly, and as she watched them, she thought she caught a glimpse of a man with a newspaper under his arm. He was the right height, had the right sort of bearing, but was half-hidden by others, so she wasn't sure that it was David and, in any case, what could she do? Safer, surely, to remain surrounded by people for the moment, and to stay with Laura, who held the attention of all of the visitors in her yellow silk.

As they moved together through the exhibition, Faith scanned the room for the man with the newspaper, but he was nowhere to be seen. Laura was constantly surrounded by new admirers, and as she accepted their praise, Dod, the friend who had been sitting next to her at Smith's lecture, the woman who today sported the precise, dramatic make-up of a Pierrot, lowered her voice to say to Faith, 'You know, Dame Laura is extremely busy, it's rather an honour to be painted by her, especially for free; you might at least make an effort to look happier about it, she did it to please you.'

The gallery walls were sparely hung, but Laura's painting of the airmen needed the space and a large crowd had gathered around it. You could almost hear the drone of the engine and feel the tension in the figures, swaddled up and crammed together. Standing in front of the painting to study the face of the young navigator at its centre, you felt proud and moved, but so very sad, willing him to survive the mission, to be granted another day, another year, against the odds. Faith started to say as much, but Laura hurried her past the painting, not even glancing at it, and on to where the portrait of Faith looked down from the wall, a clever counterpoint, the woman lost in reflection while the men readied themselves for action.

Along another side of the gallery Faith's own drawings and watercolour were arranged, their smaller scale suggesting a vital, unceremonious, first-hand response to everyday life continuing in the beleaguered city. Laura, holding Faith by the arm, insisted she took a glass of sherry (she herself had finished two in quick succession) and stay with her; they could pretend, she said, to be deep in conversation but listen instead to the talk around them, try to divine what the general critical opinion of the exhibition was. They circled the room, the crowd, in awe of Laura's grandeur and astonishing appearance, moving out of her way as she made her stately progress. Faith could see Smith, keeping to one corner of the room, clutching a glass with both hands for dear life. There was no sign of David, thank God, but she clung to Laura's arm all the same.

'My dear Dame Laura!' Sir Kenneth Clark had approached and was now leaning back on his heels, head to one side and arms outstretched, as if he were acting out greeting an old and very dear friend on the stage of a small-town repertory company.

Laura ignored his hands, surged forward, grabbed him by the shoulders and planted a vigorous kiss full on his mouth. '*My* dear Sir Ken! You know Dod, of course. And I'm sure you remember my gifted young colleague, Faith Farr?'

Sir Kenneth's discomfiture at the unorthodox embrace melted away as he looked Faith up and down. Her appearance momentarily captured his attention (he had seemed to her to be trailing after a voluptuous black-haired lady in deep pink who affected to ignore him). He launched into a paean: 'The Times say we've got it just right, I brought them to see the hang before we opened, in case some damage limitation was needed. Never heard anything like it; bloody difficult to please, usually. What was it their man said about our little show? I want to tell you exactly . . . "modern, confident, no Victorian clutter, reflecting the urgency of experience", and so on. He liked your watercolour very much, Faith. Wonderfully modest, he said, none of the bombast of fascist art. Reflects our national subtlety and humour, apparently – our British values. As for you, Dame Laura, a *masterpiece*, that's all it is! The scene before battle captured with the sensitivity of the female eye, never been done before, not in the entire history of art. WAAC's earnt its money today – I would be surprised if we can't make great capital from this. Ah yes, there he is, there's the Minister now. Do excuse me, I must make sure he talks to the papers, want him to hear for himself, straight from the horse's mouth, and it'll give him a chance to show off, have his picture taken. You know how keen these government types are on being photographed. By the way, have either of you seen Smith? Where is the boy?'

Laura reached for another drink as a tray moved past, her face flushed, eyes shining, voice loud.

'D'you hear that? What did I tell you? I said things would get better. And I must say, I'm very glad to see you looking so much improved, my dear. Remember what I told you, make yourself work, but don't allow it to drag you down. You are an independent woman, enjoy your freedom, there is nobody to stop you.'

'I will; I mean, I am.'

As Faith said this, out of the corner of her eye she saw at the back of the gallery a folded newspaper, a tall figure, a familiar calm and inquiring countenance turned in her direction. This time she knew it was David. She grasped Laura's arm as yet another circle of admirers, emboldened by the free sherry, gathered around. As the people laughed, talked, moved, she lost him among the crowd. What was it he was planning? Surely he would not approach her in public? Perhaps he was waiting for the private view to end, and then he would follow her. There was only one thing that she could do: she must gather her courage and take the opportunity to slip away while the party was at its busiest. She let go of Laura, saying, 'I'll write to you soon,' but not waiting for a response.

Against the flow of people into the room, Faith moved quickly, head down. On the front steps she would be too visible, leading as they did down to the exposed stretch of Trafalgar Square and the wide avenues leading off it. So instead of turning towards the entrance, she went to her right, further into the building. She walked purposefully, heart racing and, as she went, glanced repeatedly over her shoulder, to see if he was following her.

She was looking back towards the crowded entrance to the exhibition for the last time before losing sight of it when she saw David walking out of the gallery. He also turned to the right and though clearly he saw her, he did not acknowledge her. But then he squared his shoulders and directed his body as if he were about to run at her. Faith froze – he would surely reach her in seconds. But almost as soon as he had begun to move he suddenly stopped in his tracks, turned quickly around and rushed back into the exhibition. Faith could not think what had prevented him from following her, what had made him change his mind. All she could see now was the black-haired woman in pink, the woman Sir Kenneth Clark had been pursuing. A moment after David's disappearance, she wandered out of the shadows, up from the ladies' cloakroom, past the entrance of the exhibition, taking her time, enjoying the peace away from the crowd looking at the pictures. She sat down on one of the wooden benches outside the gallery and lit a cigarette.

Faith cut through the deserted galleries, empty of paintings, the marks on the damask walls showing where they had hung. It was freezing and gloomy, skylights providing the only illumination. The sound of her steps echoed off the polished floors and around the high, tunnelling walls, so she took off her shoes to run. She could hear no one else but she could not be sure she was alone, and she would not stop for long enough to listen properly. Out of the back door on to Orange Street she went. She would go to Miss Roy's house. She now knew exactly what she must do.

Luckily Miss Roy seemed not to be at home. All the same, Faith nervously checked the rooms to make absolutely sure that she was alone before she picked up the paintbox, opened it and removed the brown-paper packet in its bandage of tape. She had kept it long enough. She had wrapped it up tightly to protect it and carried it with her for months, not knowing how or when she could act. But having seen David in Green Park – no doubt still wandering in and out of the Ministry, privy to all its secrets – and this afternoon at the Gallery, daring to come after her in public, she had to stop him, she must free herself of the fear that had stymied her.

She would have to take the risk of handing the package in, no matter how much she was distrustful of the Ministry – David had worked there unimpeded for so long, he could well be part of a gang of conspirators and might be protected from within. Although . . . there was the fat man. Faith had been suspicious of him, but surely if he were protecting David, he would have tried harder to win her confidence when he came across her that day in the St James's Street building. He could easily have said that he knew her husband, that he would take her to him, only to spirit her off and draw her into the web. Or pressed her to tell him where she was staying, and given the information to David. But he had let her go, and said to get in touch if he could help her. The fat man was her only hope. No matter what the danger – even if she herself were to be suspected – she would try and get the documents to him. She must be able to live again, to work.

Perhaps David assumed that she was too afraid to act? He under-estimated her, then. She had been bereft, terrorized, starving, but she was also determined and resourceful; once she had made a decision she would carry it through. David had read her mistakenly from the beginning, his idea of her as wrong as her understanding of him.

Faith had one hand on the front door, about to open it and leave, clutching her handbag containing the brown-paper packet in the other, when she stopped to think for a second. She should take some precautions to protect Miss Roy, in case David had found out that she was living there.

She wrote quickly:

Jean,

If David comes here looking for me remember what I said, and
<u>*on no account*</u> *let him in. Keep the door locked and tell him to go away.*
Tell him that I don't have what I took from him. It's too late, I've handed
it over. Nothing he can do will make any difference now. Tell him he
should leave London immediately, they'll be looking for him. Tell him to
leave and never come back.

Faith arrived at the Ministry office in St James's Street with the package in her bag; she'd scrawled URGENT across it in black-ink capitals. She rang the bell. A girl answered, different from last time, she thought, but couldn't be sure.

'How can we help you?' the girl asked, bringing Faith over to the desk, where a second receptionist waited.

'I've got something for . . . for the fat man,' Faith said.

'Is that so?' But they hadn't asked, '*Who?*' – they must know who she meant. They smiled at each other.

'Yes, he wouldn't tell me his name – but he works here. I think he might be in charge? He told me he was important, that you would know of him. He said to describe him: a fat man in a good suit, with a silk pocket handkerchief. He has a Rolls-Royce. He said if I ever needed his help . . .'

'Oh, I know who you mean all right – we all do.' A look passed between the two.

'You will make sure that he gets this? He must. A lot depends on it.'

Noticing Faith's expression, the girl said, with greater patience, 'He won't be about for the next day or two, he's in the country, but as soon as he arrives, I'll make sure it's the first thing he sees.'

'No, that won't do! He needs to have it right away, it mustn't be left lying around. If he's not here you must send it to him now, make sure it's put directly into his hands. Call somebody, please.'

'Look here, we can't order up a courier for no reason, just on your say-so; we've to avoid unnecessary expenses, and you aren't the only one to come wandering in off the street, crying wolf. There's no end of cranks. And, anyway, we're just about to finish for the day . . .'

Faith was relieved, then, that she had made an effort for the private view, had spent the last of her money on new clothes, had had her hair washed and set. If she had been wearing her old green coat no doubt they would have thrown her out.

'I must insist, do it straight away, and you should know that I will wait here, I won't move an inch until the messenger arrives. Do as I ask, do it now, or I shan't leave and I'll kick up such a stink, you'll have to call the police.' She raised her voice even further, as if giving them a taste of what she was capable of. 'And I'll tell them about it all as soon as they arrive – they'll have to go and find the fat man, and he'll be forced to come up to town himself immediately to talk to me. He doesn't seem to me to be the kind of person who'd like being made to run about at short notice, just because you made an error of judgement.'

The girl glared at her and then picked up the telephone.

Chapter Thirty-Six

Vivienne made her way down the steps of the National Gallery, and set off towards Claridge's Hotel. She could not stand the private view another minute. The exhibition at least had been better than usual – Laura Knight had painted something interesting at long last, although she'd ruined the impressive effect of her work with that ridiculous get-up. What on earth had she come as, Widow Twankey? Vivienne had stayed at the exhibition only for half an hour, soon growing weary of trying to evade Sir Kenneth Clark – of course she recognized his famous face from the papers, but she would not give him the satisfaction of showing it, not when he had stalked her all around the gallery. Then there was the moony, importunate gaze of a wretched boy in a cheap suit; although, as part of her plan, perhaps taking up with one or other of them just for the night would have been the right thing to do. But her heart was not in it, not at all. She needed another drink – a proper drink – the private-view sherry had surely been watered down.

When she'd woken up that morning, Vivienne had admitted to herself that she could not resist Frido, not possibly. She resolved, instead, to make him want to resist her. She had seen Greta Garbo carry off something similar in a film once. She would dress in her finery, making it clear to Frido – and to Charles – that she was looking for a new diversion, that she was fickle, superficial, not worthy of true love.

As she came into the dining room at breakfast, the men looked up appreciatively. Vivienne was wearing a frock of silk crêpe made for her by Molyneux and, at her request, not in his usual muted palette but in a strong, dark pink. And although the dress covered her from collarbone to wrist and to knee it was so artfully, so closely cut, that every curve was revealed at the same time as it was concealed. She carried a kidskin vanity case. Despite feeling like some shrinking creature, dying inside its shell, she smiled brightly.

'You know, darling, you're right. It's no good for me, being down here all the time. I'm terribly bored. A trip to London's what I need. Thought I'd go up today, catch a gallery, see who I can see. I might be away a night . . . or two, haven't decided.'

Sam did not mind – he would grab the opportunity to dally with his little girl. As Vivienne took out a cigarette and accepted coffee from the maid, she could not bear to look at Frido.

'Long as you like, Vivienne,' said Sam, attempting not to seem too delighted.

She got up, then, and kissed her husband on the mouth. 'You see how I've cheered up already: just the thought of escaping.'

She sat for a further five minutes, pretending to read the newspaper and to give an impression of unhurried calm. Out of the corner of her eye she could see Frido; he stared at her and then, when she kept her gaze resolutely on the newsprint, turned away. Charles, watching Frido intently, did not look at Vivienne. She lifted the coffee cup to her lips once more, then made a show of touching up her lipstick and powdering her face. She stood up to leave.

'Wait just a sec, I'll see you off,' Sam said. In the hallway, he continued in a low voice, 'Good you're entertaining yourself. I'm going to be busy for quite a while, in and out at odd hours. That special event we talked about, you remember, that day in the car on the way to see De Wohl, didn't come off. We don't know why yet. A technical problem with the explosives – we hope. But I think the worst-case scenario is more likely: that there was an informant on our side, that they're on to our friends.'

Vivienne leant against the hall table for a second. She felt as if she had been hit.

If there was an informant, as Sam suspected, surely it couldn't be Frido? She had not helped Charles to prove Frido's trustworthiness as he had asked her to, and had she thus let down her husband, her country, all of those poor resistance fighters in Germany?

Sam looked at her with concern. 'Don't take it to heart so. The good news is, they did go ahead, they made a genuine attempt, so we know they're being straight with us, and if any of them survive, we can try again.'

'God, have they caught them?'

'Not yet, no. They packed the explosives to look like a brandy bottle, all wrapped up like I said, to be carried on to Adolf's plane. When the bomb didn't go off, one of our men managed to steal it back before they opened it; apparently, it sat there in the Führer's eyrie for three days before he had a chance to nab it . . . they hadn't even bothered to open the parcel. Which makes me think – they've obviously got so much good brandy over there that there was no urgency about having a snifter! My contacts in Paris must be spinning me a story, telling me how scarce it is, charging me the earth. I'll have to have words with them. We're almost running out over here.'

'But they're safe, for now?'

'Yes, but if you ask me, there must have been a leak somewhere, and the Nazis themselves tampered with the explosives to make sure they wouldn't go off; they're playing along with the plotters, watching and biding their time till they can round 'em all up.'

'So we'll get them out – save them?'

'Don't be silly, darling, wouldn't do at all – jeopardize our side? They know the game; anyway, they'll want to start again immediately – there'll be another plan in due course, and we have to be primed to help as soon as . . . Oh, and when you get back from London, there'll be new projects for you. Word is, the next big push is Italy – we should have some fun with that. Now off you go, enjoy yourself. Don't think of me for a single minute.'

Along Piccadilly and into Mayfair Vivienne walked on. Despite herself, she felt a lightening as she saw Claridge's standing still intact; above the revolving door, even the geometric leaded glass – modern and old-fashioned at the same time – was whole. But Vivienne did not go through the main entrance; she did not need to check in immediately, she had sent her vanity case on from the station when she arrived in London. She made her way down Davies Street to find the Causerie.

At the Causerie, the hotel tried to stifle some of London's rationing pangs, and garner extra customers by putting out a daily spread of sandwiches and pickles – you could eat as much as you liked for free, paying only for the drinks. Vivienne did not want food, but she knew that men liked the Causerie – Sam would often meet his journalist cronies there. The arrangement suited them: why waste time and money on lunch or dinner when you could spend the lot on booze? Vivienne planned to settle in a corner, with a small plate and a large Old Fashioned, anaesthetize her heart – she would attempt to forget Frido; whether he was innocent or guilty he could no longer be hers – and make a selection from among the clientele.

After her second drink, as she ate the cherry from the cocktail stick to slow herself down, Vivienne felt the danger period dawning – she would start to picture Frido, would begin to miss him terribly, unless she found distraction quickly. She had seen no promising candidates so far, and was about to go and find her room, lie down for half an hour before coming back down, refreshed, for more cocktails, when a hand brushed along her wrist and a mouth with even white teeth said, 'Do you mind?' Blond hair, blue eyes – so at least he looked something like her love – a good height, dressed in naval uniform. How appropriate, given the goings-on in the Atlantic, for her to be doing her bit for those in peril on the sea.

Two more cocktails down, and Vivienne went to collect her key. The boy at reception displayed his excellent training: the shadow of a knowing expression stayed on his face only a second at the sight of Vivienne in the lobby with the officer who – she did not try to hide it – would soon be joining her upstairs.

It was worth the extra guineas for this bigger, more luxurious room. Vivienne rang down for another drink and took off her shoes. She pulled back the covers, piled up the pillows behind her head, and sat on the bed. She waited, legs curled underneath her, sipping at her glass, steadily. She could not bear to be sober, she had to obliterate everything in her life. How could she ever return to Black, to the villa?

When the knock came, she called out to the officer to come in, that the door was unlocked, that she was ready. But the door did not open. Put out – she did not want to do this anyway, and if she was going to, she certainly would not put up with any games – she got up and went over to open it.

A blond man stood there, but not the naval officer – it was her own blond boy, awkwardly shifting his weight from one foot to the other, his face a mixture of anger and ardency.

'Frido, what the hell are you doing here?'

'You stupid, stupid woman, you are not going to discard me!' He moved towards her, grabbed her arm, held her tight. 'How could you? I told you I need you. And you need me, too. Stop lying to yourself, stop pretending. Don't think that I'll let you abandon me. Not now, *not ever*, Vivienne. I've lost my country, I'll never see my family again, many of my friends are dead. You do realize that Hitler and his kind will win; they've released a current of evil that'll never be stopped. And I can't fight them any more. I have one thing left, I have you. All I want is to live out the rest of my days with you. I am serious, I am a serious man. Why won't you believe me? Think – we could make a new life together.'

She was sure, then, that he was not a traitor, her own boy.

'But how could we? Leave the villa? You want to start again with me, alone with me?'

'Exactly that: never go back to Aspley Guise. Sam will be happy, as soon as you're out of the way.'

It could be possible, couldn't it? Vivienne thought. If they never went back, took a room somewhere, worked in whatever way they could until the war ended – in victory or defeat. Perhaps Sam would arrange a suitable, safe position for Frido if she divorced him with no fuss and moved far away; he would be saved any embarrassment and could have his little dispatch rider. And then there would be no point in Charles putting together his damning report. Even if he did, he would no longer have the power to hurt her.

Impossible, she knew, to resist Frido; Vivienne allowed him to unzip her dress and push her back on to the bed, looking down at her, enjoying her waiting and watching him, before he began to take off his own clothes. When he stood before her, naked, Vivienne thought she had never seen a finer body; the languid lines and exquisite proportions of classical sculpture come to life. But his cock – a tone darker than the rest of him and clumsily erect – was not the tender, reticent member that Michelangelo had sculpted on his David, lying softly below marble pubic hair carved into orderly loops like a provincial permanent wave. So much the better, she thought, as she reached out towards him.

Later, they slept for an hour. Vivienne dreamt of swimming among the wreckage of a merchant ship; bananas and oranges as big as mines jostled and bumped against her as she basked in warm salty water.

They woke together.

'You should not keep trying to put me off. It won't work.'

'I know, I know,' Vivienne said.

'I love you, every part of you – body, mind. Particularly body, actually.'

An hour later, they called for more drinks. They would bathe, dress, go down for dinner, and then back up for the night.

Vivienne, sitting on the bed, in the act of pulling on her stockings, straightening the seams, stopped. She turned to Frido, took his hands in hers. 'It's a miracle. *You* are a miracle. Where did you come from? How on earth did you find me, in all of this mess?'

Frido looked abashed then. 'If I tell you, you won't mind? It is important that we're honest with each other. I didn't know where you had gone today, why you were going. I was desperate, you saw it in my face at breakfast. I hated you for seeing it and leaving anyway. But I also knew that you did care, that was why you wouldn't look at me. When you'd gone, I couldn't work, I had to be alone, to go up to my room, I shouted, I think. I punched something.'

'Oh love, love – I'm sorry.'

'Charles heard me.'

'Charles? What's he got to do with it? With us?' Vivienne freed herself and got up from the bed.

'Don't mind too much. I know that I said that he and I weren't friends. I didn't tell you because I thought you might be upset, might think that I was talking about you in the wrong way. But he's been so kind, he listened to me, that's all. He knows how much I love you. He told me where you were today; he'd heard you on the telephone booking a room, I think. He gave me directions, even wrote a letter in case I was stopped, saying I was on official business, Ministry business. He's so very skilful.' Frido pulled an envelope out of his pocket and unfolded a piece of paper. 'He wrote the letter as Sam, even signed it with Sam's signature – but you have to forgive him, he did it for us.'

Vivienne had walked over and put her hands on the mantelpiece, to steady herself as he explained. She did not look at him but said, 'I have to ask you, Frido. Did you ever discuss anything else with Charles, apart from me?'

'The usual – work, you know.'

'Work?'

'What's the matter? We can't carry such a burden in silence, isolated even from each other. We talk, me and the others – it's the only way to survive. You know that. Charles has been helping me when I found it difficult. I've been talking to him quite a lot. He understands.'

'Yes, but what, what exactly, did you talk about?'

'What we were doing together.'

'So then, recently – did you discuss with him that plan . . . that plan that went wrong?'

'Do you mean the assassination plot? You know about it! Sam should not have told you, put you in danger, I never would have. Yes, we collaborated on that. Sam wasn't going to involve Charles at first, but I knew how trustworthy he was, how discreet. Do you know, he didn't breathe a word about you and me to anyone, never gave a hint of it? I persuaded Sam to use him. So they got Charles to make the documents the courier used to smuggle the explosives over, and I was right to recommend him, they were flawless . . . Of course, you probably heard, it didn't blow up, in the end. After such effort, the risks we took. And they're bound to be on to my friends in Berlin, they'll be massacred. That's why I can't be part of it any more . . . why I've come to find you, and take you away.'

Frido went towards Vivienne, tried to turn her towards him, but she stood as if petrified, eyes shut.

'Charles knew about the whole thing, he made the papers?'

'We couldn't have done it without him.'

The image of Charles in her mind warped, darkened, took on a new malign aspect. If Charles were a British Intelligence officer – as he had made her believe – and he had really doubted Frido's loyalty, he would never have allowed Frido to carry on at the centre of such a crucial task. It was Charles who was the traitor. He had worked on the men in the villa to win their confidence, to let him in at the heart of the plan in order to destroy it. He had tried to terrify Vivienne into passing on useful information about Frido's contacts to him. Although he had not succeeded in that, he had kept her usefully distant from her lover and her husband, unable to speak to them honestly, under his control. He had made her doubt Frido. And she . . . she had not warned Frido that he was being watched, she had thought of her own position first, had not trusted him with the information. Her silence had meant that Charles was able to continue. Perhaps there was something in the documents he had made for the plot that gave some signal to his Nazi friends? In any case, he had alerted them, and this had caused the failure of the attempt to kill Hitler, and would lead instead to the deaths of Frido's brave comrades, perhaps even of his family.

'Frido,' she said. 'Frido, it's over . . . No, don't touch me. You have to go.'

'Vivienne! For Christ's sake! Why? How will I . . . ?'

'Please. I want you to go. Go far away . . . from me, from the villa, from all of us. Don't look at me. *Go!*'

Chapter Thirty-Seven

At just after seven in the morning, Jean Roy heard tapping on the front door of her house in Camden and ignored it. It was too early for visitors, and although she was already out of bed and boiling the kettle for tea, she had not dressed and the front of her hair was still done up in curlers. Not that she had slept a wink – Faith Farr had not returned all night. Miss Roy had held back from bolting the door for as long as possible, but then felt she had to, there was the security of her other guests to consider; only, then, she could not sleep for fear she had locked the girl out. And Faith had sent no message to explain her absence, only leaving her a strange note instructing her on how to behave and what to say in case her husband, David, came calling. And almost as soon as Miss Roy had read it, David had appeared at the door. Faith was really most inconsiderate, involving her in her dramas – terribly hard to have to speak to David like that, and then Faith herself didn't even bother to come back, unless, of course, something bad had happened . . . The knocking did not stop, and now she could hear the key being tried in the lock. Jean sighed with irritation, buttoned up her dressing gown and hurried to the window. Pulling back the lace curtain, she saw Faith there on the step, her new blue dress crumpled as if she had slept in it, her face white, her hair unbrushed. What on earth had the girl been doing?

'Hold on, Faith, it's still bolted. I'm coming now,' she called out.

'Jean, thank God, you're alone? You're quite all right?' Faith said, as she rushed through the door, looking about her.

'Of course. Why wouldn't I be? Worried about you, though, you might have told me of your plans, you really shouldn't stay out without letting me know. Especially after you said that other time that I should inform the police if you didn't come home. I'm glad I didn't take you at your word. Where were you?'

'I slept in a shelter. I didn't like to come back here.'

'Why ever not? I sat up for hours listening for you, and: nothing.'

'Then he didn't turn up?'

'David? Oh yes, yes he did.'

'And what did you do?'

'I behaved as you told me to. Spoke to him from behind the door. He did ask to be let in, quite a few times, asked to be allowed to wait for you. I found it all most embarrassing. You really shouldn't have . . .'

'But what did he say, Jean, what did he say?'

'I told him it wasn't convenient. Very awkward: he didn't get angry, he's not the type, is he? I always liked him: very well brought up. But he did keep on so, said he was chilly, thirsty, could he have a cup of tea? That he needed to find you, was worried about you. Could he at least sit down for a moment?'

'You didn't say yes? You didn't let him in!'

'No, no, I remembered what you put in the note. When he finally gave up trying to persuade me to open the door, I passed on your message. I said that you'd handed over the things you'd taken, that he was being looked for, that he must leave immediately and never return.'

'*And?*'

'He was gone, just like that: didn't even say goodbye. What can have come over him? Faith, Faith, dear girl, whatever's wrong? Oh lord!'

Cells, tiny sea creatures and fireflies, everything swimming slowly past . . . and, then, a smell of Parma violets carried on a wave of ammonia. Faith came round to find herself lying on Jean Roy's sofa, under a shawl, with the old lady standing over her with a bottle of smelling salts.

'You must lie still, Faith. I'll make tea with lots of sugar, that's best for shock.'

But Faith was already getting up. 'I know what I need to do. I'm going. I've imposed on you for long enough. You've been very kind.'

Jean Roy looked worried. 'But where will you go?'

'My parents' house. Blackfriars.'

'You said that was impossible?'

'It was, but it's all right now. David won't dare to come back. I'm safe. And Mother and Dad will be in the country until the war is over. There are good things about being alone, aren't there: no family, no responsibilities, freedom? I'll be able to sleep downstairs and turn my old bedroom into a studio . . .'

'If you're sure there's no danger . . .'

'Danger is never quite where you expect it, Jean. Women artists aren't allowed to go to the front, are they? Supposed to keep us safe, yet I know a girl, sent to paint a knitting party – nice ladies sitting in a big house on a peaceful day – bomb lands right on top of them all! Dame Laura's right, you have to persevere no matter what.'

Chapter Thirty-Eight

The morning after she had sent Frido away from her room in Claridge's, Vivienne made her way back alone, along the quiet lane from Aspley Guise, through the dense laurels, up the driveway towards the Black villa. After a solitary, wretched, sleepless night in the warm hotel room with its smooth sheets and soft pillows, she had caught the train and then decided to walk from the village station, not wanting to telephone for Sam's driver, needing to stretch the journey out as much as possible. She passed along the gravel bordered with drenched grass as if her legs were carrying her of their own volition, as if she were floating apart from her body.

Sam's car was parked outside, Stevens sitting inside with his newspaper, waiting and smoking. The house presented its usual façade, its blank windows, to the daylight. She opened the front door and put down her vanity case. She could hear the maid in the dining room piling up the dirty lunch things, ready to carry them through to the kitchen. The wireless was playing in there, with Cook humming along. The door to the workroom was shut, but there was no sign of any disturbance within. She would go and face the others, find out what had happened, after she had washed and changed, and steeled herself.

When Vivienne reached the top of the stairs all still seemed normal; the soiled laundry had been collected, as every morning, and heaped on the landing. She opened her bedroom door.

Sam stood at the mirror, arranging his silk handkerchief in his breast pocket. He turned and looked at her, frowning. 'Come in, close that and sit down,' he said.

'What is it? You said I might stay up in town.'

'Don't be silly. I don't mind that at all. But . . . problems . . . there've been some changes. Had to let two of our small band go.'

'What? Who?'

'Frido. Came down to work this morning in a hell of a state, demanding to be sent on a mission to Germany, insisting he leave here right away. Bloody fool, he must know he can't go back – he's famous over there, all the Gestapo shits have a picture of him pinned up on their office walls, he's public enemy number one.'

'Where . . . where is he now?'

'Oh, I made a few phone calls, we have to look after him, keep him safe. An exceptional man: medals galore for him when it's over. If we win – of course. No – found him a new job *tout de suite*, another secure place to stay. Best you don't know where.'

'I see,' she said. She sat down on the bed and was quiet for a minute. 'And?'

'And, well, this part you won't like at all. It's Charles.'

'*Charles?*'

'I've been watching him for a while, frankly creepy the way he followed you around with his eyes. And then, when you were away last night, I caught him in our room, rifling through your things. Couldn't keep him on here after that.'

'You didn't . . . you didn't find him more work, I hope.'

'God, no. I made some arrangements. They took him away.' Sam finished dressing, knotted his silk tie, and, preoccupied, kissed her on the cheek. 'London now: meetings to discuss what's happened, find substitutes, and so on. It'll be rather quiet here. I'll try and get back tonight, but if I don't, have an early one, darling, it will be peaceful at least – and you look done in.'

Sitting in the Rolls-Royce later, on his way to St James's Street, Sam downed his third whisky – it was only just after lunch but it had already been a bloody nightmare of a day. He felt a short-lived pang of guilt for not telling Vivienne the truth about Charles and Frido. But it wouldn't do to upset her, to scare her, to explain that Charles had, in fact, never revealed any sinister interest in her, and that Sam had not caught him in the act of spying. Charles had played his role as a member of Black impeccably. No one at the villa, at Bletchley Park, or in London for that matter, had picked up on him: there had not been the slightest suspicion that he was working for the other side, until Sam was given the package which had been handed in to the Ministry by, apparently, the same rather beautiful woman he had come across in the window seat at St James's Street that day, with her odd green coat and even odder manner.

As the car slid towards the city, Sam had the package open on his lap. He looked through the contents again. They were fascinating, masterly. A girl dispatch rider had brought the parcel to the villa in the middle of the night. Not his own little motorcyclist – ironically, she was the one in bed with him on this occasion, in Vivienne's absence. A slender figure with an urgent delivery had materialized for a second time.

Sam had wrestled with the web of tape, using Vivienne's nail scissors to pick away at the packaging. What he found inside dumbfounded him. Three different identity cards: for the man they knew at Black as Charles, somebody called David Pascoe, and a third name. Sam guessed what was next: three passports in these three names, but all with 'Charles'' face. They were so cleverly done – not too pristine. The official stamps – slightly smudged but still legible – suggested the hand of a bored but efficient functionary. There were also papers listing details of three lives – dates, places, events, people – and even some photographs: a woman with a baby, the girl in the green coat holding a sketchbook and smiling at the camera.

In the bedroom of the Black villa, in the middle of the night, with his new lover in bed by his side, and the messenger standing and waiting, Sam had had to react quickly. Pulling on his dressing gown, he instructed the dispatch rider to wait in the room; neither woman was to open the door and try to leave until he returned, no matter what they heard. He took his pistol out of its hiding place behind the false back of the dressing-table drawer – the first time he had ever had cause to do so – and, locking the door behind him, slipped along the landing to Charles' room. He stood outside. There was not a sound. Slowly he turned the handle.

Moonlight shone through open curtains on to an empty bed, the covers neatly folded. But the man's personal effects were all still there, his suitcase and even his glasses. Sam picked them up. Without them 'Charles' surely could not be very far away. He might return at any moment. What should he do? And then Sam held the glasses up to his eyes. The room was still in focus, there was no distortion or blurring. Charles had only been pretending to be short-sighted. He had perfect vision. And he was long gone.

Waiting in the bedroom of the strange isolated villa in the small hours, the dispatch rider had gazed at the chaotic splendour around her. She thought she recognized the naked blonde wrapped in the velvet eiderdown but she returned her look impassively. It was eerily quiet: there were no raised voices, no shots were fired.

Sam came back in and sat on the bed, turning the passports and papers over in his hands. The dispatch rider broke the silence to deliver the second part of her message: she told him that Frido had just been found in London, dead, hanging from the rafters of a bombed building somewhere off Davies Street in Mayfair. He must have climbed up the ruined staircase – the four floors had mostly fallen away – right to the top, and tied a noose for himself.

Sam spent the rest of the night and the following morning on the telephone, explaining, warning, instructing, shouting. The Ministry were anxious to reassure him that none of it was his fault. They were keen to make the whole business disappear. They had employed 'Charles' after all, given him access to the Ministry, access he had used to plant doubts about Black, about Frido and Sam, subtly building a case for Intelligence to send him out to the villa to 'investigate'. And Intelligence's suspicions – once roused – meant that they did not talk to Sam directly: fools! They would have to now, though. Sam would make sure of it, rub their fucking noses in it. He owed it to himself, to Frido.

The Nazis must have traced Frido to the villa, and ordered their agent 'Charles' to inveigle his way into Black. Once there, Charles had worked out that Frido was at the centre of a plot to assassinate Hitler, and determined to stop it. And he had succeeded. Even now Charles was out there somewhere, wrapped in a thick cocoon of lies, busily metamorphosing into someone else. He was totally convincing: you could live at close quarters with him and never guess what he was capable of. Sam had never quite liked him – bloodless, brainy type, he'd thought. But, nevertheless, he had somehow managed to snare himself that beautiful girl. It never ceased to amaze Sam, the dreadful men that women were prepared to put up with.

They were only beginning to uncover Charles' past. It seemed there'd been at least one earlier wife, and a child. They'd disappeared one day, to be found dead, weeks later, far from home in a bombed building. It had been assumed that they'd been the victims of an air raid, but now it seemed more likely that Charles had disposed of them himself, or his friends had. Perhaps she'd been on to him, so that was her number up, and then he couldn't be left holding a baby . . .

Sam's immediate thought was that Charles had murdered Frido, too. But it would have been extremely difficult to string him up from the roof beams like that. Had Charles wanted to fake a suicide, he could have more easily shot Frido and wrapped his dead fingers around the gun. Stabbing and strangling were also efficient methods, and a body could easily be hidden in the rubble, as Charles was likely to know. Frido must have taken his own life.

A terrible embarrassment for the Ministry, of course, for the British government, to have a resistance hero kill himself on their patch when he was supposed to be safe, having narrowly, famously, escaped death at the hands of the Gestapo. Sam had known exactly how to proceed. He had instructed them to cut Frido down and dress him in somebody else's clothes, to record him as a vagrant, identity unknown, and bury him quickly in an unmarked grave. Any papers found on the body were to be brought straight to Sam for destruction.

Funny thing: Frido had been carrying a letter saying that he was on official business in London that night. Sam could not remember signing it – this didn't mean he hadn't, though, during one of those frantic days around the time of the assassination attempt. And there was a suicide note, the usual maudlin stuff about losing everything that mattered to him – but touching, all the same – and a request addressed to Sam himself: on his honour he was to ensure that no 'dead letters' were sent from Black to Frido's family in Germany, there must be no creative pretence that he was still alive. Sam could agree to this – to some extent. No letters would be sent. But neither could it ever be revealed that the boy had died, or when and how it had happened. He would not even confide in Vivienne. His husbandly sensitivity had picked up on her fondness for Frido – really, he knew her better than she realized. No, Sam agreed with himself. It wouldn't do at all to tell Vivienne the whole story.

Chapter Thirty-Nine

Faith went about Miss Roy's collecting her few things. She picked up her paintbox and opened it. There were the two bundles of brushes, sable for fine work and hog's hair for the oils. The pans of watercolour were dry, as was the wooden palette – unused for such a while that it was no longer sticky to the touch. The tubes of oil paint were in order, their tops tightly screwed on. Faith picked up the cadmium red, undid it: she took in the dense purity of the shade, the rich, heavy smell. She ran her fingers over the row of oil colours with pleasure.

It was the paintbox that had led her to her final night with David eight months earlier. She had fled their home in Hampstead after he'd hit her, had stayed in an air-raid hostel, for two, three weeks. June 1942 passed into July and she did not notice, she was barely eating or sleeping. Then . . . then she realized she had to work. Now that she had left David she had no other source of income but the WAAC commissions. She could not stay in the hostel for ever, so had found a room in Holloway and needed to pay her rent before she could move in. But in the trauma of leaving her marriage she had forgotten her paintbox. It was too expensive to replace, and of sentimental value, she had to get it back, so one afternoon she took courage and made her way back up to Hampstead, to the flat where she had lived with her husband. David was never home that early.

The lock hadn't been changed. She crept in, across the tiled hall, not letting her heels hit the floor to make sure that no one would hear her, and then upstairs. A turn and a click, and she was in their flat. Her feathered hat and best shoes were waiting in the hall as if she still lived there. She paused for a while by the kitchen curtain before pulling it back; everything was neat and ordered. She let the curtain fall again, moved into the drawing room and went quickly to the window, carefully standing to one side of it, to check that David was not making his way up the street.

'*You?*' A voice, David's voice.

She jumped and whirled around. She saw David; he had come in behind her so quietly that she shivered, unnerved. He was standing in the doorway, a bottle of vodka, two-thirds empty, in one hand. With a silly, drunken smile he gestured for her to sit. She took her old armchair, still in her coat. He came over to her, treating her like a child, making her stand up again while he helped her to take it off, tugging at the sleeves.

'I came back to collect my paints, I need them . . . didn't think you'd be here . . .' she said.

'I suppose you hate me,' he said, sitting opposite her, refilling the glass on the lamp table.

'I don't, that's not how I feel at all. But I can't live with you. No, I've decided: it's finished.'

He turned his head away. She had to move in her seat to follow his face, and then she saw that he looked devastated.

He said something she couldn't hear and when she asked him to repeat it, he said, 'Please don't go. I love you, Faith – beautiful Faith. I've taken a risk, to be with you I've risked everything.'

'Such a come-down, is it, from your country house to a girl from a Blackfriars terrace?'

'That's not what I mean . . . I mean, letting myself fall in love with you, in spite of everything, letting myself take that risk again. My boy was killed, you know . . .' He wept.

The sight shocked her. It was the first time she had seen David in tears, the only time he had shown his feelings about his son. Faith felt such sadness for her husband: despite his behaviour, she imagined how the child's death might have changed him. And the gas in the trenches, what he had seen there, must have poisoned his mind as well as his body. He had suffered so much in his life, and that was why he was so wrapped up in himself, so distant, why he had hurt her. She embraced him as he cried, at first to reassure and comfort, and then simply loving him. They went to the bedroom together. They were there as dusk fell.

Then, as they lay there naked, David began to talk.

'I should not have had to sacrifice my son. Britain's losing the war now, all those deaths, none of them necessary. There never should have been a war. What were we thinking, picking a fight over places and people that don't mean a thing to us? The Germans didn't want war with us, not for a minute, and they will win, it's only a matter of time. I'm just trying to make sure that it happens soon, that as few are killed as possible. I'm not alone, far from it. There's a group of us working for the same end – we haven't all been interned, don't believe Churchill's lies. There are many of us, intelligent, prepared to think for ourselves, who know that the right thing to do is to help Hitler. And you, you can help me – help us. Think of the future, Faith. I fell in love with you because you've a mind of your own, you don't care if people agree with you or not, whether they like you. You never follow blindly.'

Then he began to get much angrier. 'I gave this country my youth. Took me years to get over it, creeping around like a cripple, jumping every time a door slammed. What did I get in return? Pitying looks and a fucking pension . . . What do I feel when I see the parents, the wives, snivelling at the Cenotaph? *Disgust*. They've all been blown to pieces, those boys; artists, Faith, poets too; the best of their gener-ation. What a pointless waste . . . They aren't all sitting up there in heaven, there is no heaven. Life is all there is, and theirs was taken away from them for no reason. No, we can't say that we won the last war – not when we left a whole generation rotting in the mud – and it's right to be angry at what was lost, and to make sure it never, *never*, happens again. We need a new order in Europe . . . strong and unified. No more squabbles between puny little countries, degener-ate kings, inferior races. That's what we're working for. That's why I sacrificed everything – even my personal life – until I met you. I've been so lonely! But from the moment I saw you, I thought you could help me. I knew you'd be strong enough.'

He pressed his lips down hard upon the top of her head. 'You'll stay here with me, now, won't you? You won't leave me ever again. Come here . . . here. That's the risk I'm talking about – being with you, when I wasn't supposed to have anyone else until all was resolved, far too dangerous being involved with someone. Believe me, I know it to my cost. They forbade it, and I didn't intend to fall in love with you. But I couldn't help myself. I hid your existence from them. I'd have liked to take you out, to show you off, but I couldn't. They found out about you anyway, in the end. Must have followed me back here, I imagine, and seen you. They telephoned to make sure of their suspicions, to check that you were living with me. Remember that day when a woman called and asked for me? You thought it was . . . my wife, my first wife. But she's long gone. I told you the truth about that. It was someone I work with, one of them. You told her we were married, and she didn't like that, and she didn't like the sound of you. You're always so difficult, my darling. She assumed that I must have confided in you and that was why you were angry. She told the others that she was sure that you knew everything and were bound to betray us. That's why things came to a head. I was so frustrated and I . . . I struck out at you. I didn't want to, but you were making it impossible for me to sort out the situation, when all I wanted was to protect you. Since you left I haven't known what to do. I couldn't stand the thought of being on my own again. Now, though, now it's all right, I've told you everything and you're with me. I'll tell the others they can trust you. We know each other completely now, just as I hoped we would. What did we say our marriage would be? The end of loneliness; here's to the end of loneliness!'

Faith did not speak. She lay by David's side, letting him talk for a long time, until he fell asleep in her arms.

How long she stayed in the bed she could not recall, only that she had to be sure that he was deeply asleep. She got up, delicately as a cat; he stirred then and rolled over but did not wake, just took the counterpane with him. She picked up another blanket and smoothed it gently over the side of his head, over his ear, not out of tenderness, but to stop him from hearing. She picked up her clothes and shut the door behind her.

As she left the bedroom she thought that she might faint: a spinning panic disorientated her. She crouched in the hall with her head down until she was sure she would not vomit. In the kitchen, she dressed quickly. She took a glass, filled it with water, gulped it down. She splashed her face and rinsed her hands.

Then, in one instant, she knew what she must do before she left: she needed to find some proof of what David had said, and to make it clear to him that she had the evidence, as insurance. Otherwise, he would recall what he had told her – even though he'd been so very drunk, something so vital would come back to him – and he would understand that she had gone because she was against him and his cause. He would have to tell the others that she'd left him for good; he could not cover it up indefinitely, and they would guess why. And unless they knew that she had something incriminating, which could be revealed at any moment, they would decide that they could deal with the problem best by disposing of her.

In the drawing room, she moved over to the bureau: she would begin there; now that he was living alone in the flat, David might have started to leave his things lying around, without worrying that she might come across them. She went through the drawers, the letter compartments; there was the usual clutter: his ration book, bank deposit book, everyday correspondence, an invitation to a supper party, a theatre ticket, his identity card and his passport. She looked at the passport: there was David's face, gentle, worried, caught slightly off guard; and tucked inside the passport were some photographs of the pair of them – their wedding day, on the steps outside the register office arm in arm; Faith on the Heath with her sketchbook, smiling, shading her eyes from the sun with her hand – and a folded paper.

Faith opened up the sheet. It was a list of facts about David, about his life: his place of birth, the boarding school he'd been to, its location, the number of boys, the names of the houses. Also, details of the village near his parents' home, the type of farmland there and its chief uses. A list of Cornish surnames. The co-ordinates of his army career – call-up, regiment, posting, date of return from the front. Why on earth would he write all of this down?

Faith sat on the sofa, not understanding. She looked around the room again; there must be something to help her to grasp what she was dealing with. She had already searched David's things – clothes, books – looking for information about his first wife. Where else might there be a hiding place?

As she thought this, her eyes settled on the pictures: the three Georgian prints of landscapes near David's family house that he had arranged and hung before she had even seen their flat; then it had seemed unbelievable how cosy and organized he had made the place. One by one she took them down and turned them over, wondering . . . She had prepared enough of her own drawings and watercolours for framing to know what they should look like. The backs of two of them were quite standard, covered in board that was cut to sit inside the rear of the frame and then tacked into place, but one also had thick paper taped across it, and something was filling the space between the board and the paper. You would never notice this when the picture was hanging up. Faith placed it on David's armchair.

Taking the scissors from the bureau drawer, she opened them out and, using one blade, sliced through the backing paper. She heard David cough in the bedroom, and then a groan and muttering. She waited, motionless, for minute after minute, but there was no further sound from him so she carried on, tearing the paper away in small increments, as quietly as she could.

She stood looking at what she had found; no blueprints of factories or ports, no government papers marked *Top Secret*, but two more passports, two more identity cards. She picked up the first and opened it. David's face was there but with another name, Charles Something; no wife or family; a publisher of academic textbooks. In the second passport, David's photograph was accompanied by a different name again, another birthplace; and inside were photographs: a woman – dark-haired, pretty – on a picnic rug, raising a glass of champagne to the person behind the lens; and then one of her sitting before a studio backdrop of fluffy painted clouds, an infant with light curls on her lap. It was odd, but although Faith had never met the family, she felt that she knew the mother and child from somewhere, had seen them before. Another list with the bones of a different life laid bare upon it, a grammar-school education, a job as a bank clerk. She gathered the three passports and other papers together, stuffing them into her paintbox, and left the picture with its ripped back on the chair. David would be certain to see it and know what she had done, what she had taken. She moved rapidly, noiselessly, through the door, down the stairs and away.

Safely back in the hostel, Faith pored over the documents, sitting with them for several hours before she realized fully what they meant, that she had no idea who her husband was, which of these identities was real, if any. Why, then, in his incarnation as 'David Pascoe', had he married her? This caused her agonies. No doubt he had felt his necessary solitude as a burden – the one thing in which he had not deceived her. He desired her, loved having her in bed with him every night, their bodies had never been awkward or unsure. That had given her such happiness at the start of the affair . . . How could such pleasure be empty of meaning?

She began to look with a colder eye at what she had been to David: beautiful Faith, at odds with the world, happy to live in solitude with him. He would no longer be lonely, but he could be as alone as he needed to be. She was absorbed in her work, she lived in her head. And she was a woman from a humble background, seduced by his voice, his manners, romantic tales of travel, of a dream future. He married her because – carried away by his success in manipulating her – he believed himself omnipotent. He had never loved her, only his idea of what she could give him. He knew her so very little that he could believe that he might persuade her to work for the Nazi Empire.

And when Faith shattered David's carefully constructed fantasy, when she rejected the role he had created for her, she placed herself in grave danger. Over the months, as she secluded herself in her Holloway flat, she realized that David was only biding his time, he would catch up with her; he would have to do this, the others would insist because of what she knew about him. But he could not do away with her without also recovering the proof she had taken. And so David had been stealthy and had followed her, obtained her address, come to her room. Meanwhile, she did not know what to do with the documents she had taken. Where could she hand them in so she could be sure that they would not be intercepted by his friends? He had said there were many of them. So she had waited.

But why was David, too, not in a hurry? Perhaps he could not bear to trap her, could not bring himself to act after what they had been to each other? But this was foolish, girlish romance again. The truth was stark, ugly. It was better for him, better for them, if her death happened a significant while after she and David had split up, so that he would not be implicated. Even more convincing if, asking around after she'd disappeared, the police were told by Smith, by Miss Roy, even by the celebrated Dame Laura Knight, that Faith Farr was in a sorry state, separated from her husband, unable to work, failing to feed herself, even to keep herself clean. She might be found as a corpse in a bombed building, or not at all. People vanished all the time these days.

Now, finally, it was over. Faith had rid herself of the packet of passports and papers. David had gone for ever. She could begin to forget. She picked up her paintbox and handbag and left Miss Roy's. The old lady fussed about her going, but did not try to dissuade her, and then folded away the spare blankets quickly with a look of great relief. Faith walked down Camden Road towards the centre of London. She passed a bombsite covered with shoots of rosebay willowherb, a layer of new growth emerging from the ruins.

After she had visited her room in Holloway, packed her suitcase, and dropped it off in the hallway of her parents' house in Blackfriars, Faith sat on the roof of the Odeon, high above Leicester Square, surveying the scene below, the other cinemas, the crowds, the men clearing up bomb damage. She had slipped behind a barrier cobbled together out of cracked bricks, planks and sandbags, and around to the back door. The staircase held the smell of cigarette smoke and bodies. The workmen hammering out smashed windows did not notice as she climbed to the top and out of the door on to the flat concrete. The early spring sun shone over the crown of her head and down her shoulders and arms, loosening her fingers as she looked, choosing her subject. She picked up her pencil and began to draw rapidly, observing, noting from on high the flow of figures up and down the square and, looming above them, the Warner Bros. cinema across the way, its tower still standing defiantly, pointing like an accusing finger at the enemies in the sky.

Chapter Forty

Aubrey Smith sat in his office contemplating his teeth, reflected in the silver cigarette case given to him as a twenty-first birthday present by his mother, which he never used himself as he did not smoke, but would occasionally carry with him in case he found himself in the blessed position of accompanying the type of girl who liked a cigarette. He had brought it into work with him today because he had the feeling that at some point soon that situation might occur; he had a strong intuition that his luck was about to change.

His smile was fine, white and regular, no gaps or discolouration. Not like Minister Bracken's, or Sir Kenneth Clark's, the thought of whose mouths made Smith wince as he pictured them. How could it be that these two eminent men did not rectify their oral deficiencies in the modern era of plastic dentures that so many young people were now sporting? Smith supposed it was because they did not have to bother, they could breathe on you, inflict the painful sight on you as they held forth, and they knew that there was not a single thing that you could do about it. Even the women put up with it without demur.

Smith smiled once more at his reflection, and then again as he glanced around his small office. He was glowing with a feeling so beneficent it was positively festive. Filling the room were the works that had made up the exhibition, ready to be labelled and put into storage. Laura Knight's paintings leant against the chairs. Smith had to admit that Knight had some talent – accuracy of observation, facility of line, boldness with her brush – although he often found her vigour too much, rather . . . vulgar. The painting of the RAF crew had come off very well, though – the young men at their duties, calm and workmanlike as they prepared to fly off into mortal danger – stirring stuff. They hunkered down in the belly of their plane next to the portrait of Corporal Pearson, a terribly homely girl, verging on ugly – Knight, he thought, with her usual lack of consideration, had not made the slightest effort to improve her looks and make the painting more sympathetic to the public. Propped up next to each other, the airmen turned their backs to Corporal Pearson, although she searched the skies for men like them.

Smith was waiting for the arrival of Faith Farr and Cecily Tully, who he had arranged to see together, to save time. Knight – thank the good lord – had telephoned to say that she could not attend a meeting any time soon; something about a poorly husband out in the country. She would be playing nurse for quite a while; there would be no more commissions for her in the immediate future. He could not stop grinning as he thought of this. Farr had, astonishingly, managed to produce another finished work and was to bring it in today for him to view.

But when the office door opened it did not reveal either of the women artists, but the blonde secretary, who stepped to one side to admit Clark.

'I'd never have believed it, but you pulled it off in the end!' Clark said, and then he smiled. 'I underestimated you.'

Smith wasn't sure he could trust his own ears, but Clark was still smiling – there was no question about it – and directly at him.

'Things are looking up all round, I'd say,' Clark continued. 'You know the Germans are in real trouble – Adolf's disappeared, didn't even go to that jamboree they had to toast their decade in charge, he's obviously in a funk about something, and now Goebbels is enlisting *all* women for war work. They like to keep their girls safely in the kitchen . . . or the bedroom, so things must be very bad if they're resorting to such measures. But back to the point – you've proved yourself, man. The Minister's delighted – he's increasing our budget, no less. No need to carry on wasting your time down here – come up to my office after lunch and I'll find something more worthy of you. Perhaps I might introduce you to Henry and Graham?'

Was it Smith's imagination, or had the blonde rearranged her expression and was she now looking at him with interest, even admiration?

Clark slapped Smith on the back heartily and bowled out of the door.

Smith had hardly the time to enjoy his triumph before a knock signalled the arrival of Faith Farr and Cecily Tully. As they moved into the office, he became aware that the change that he thought he had detected in Farr at the private view had definitely taken place. She looked . . . *normal* seemed the only way to describe it. Gone were the shabby clothes, the dishevelled hair and the pallor. Cecily Tully, as ever dressed in grey-brown and radiating a particularly gentle, English type of prettiness, continued a conversation begun outside the door. 'He says he's going to be made an instructor – so no more missions, and we'll be able to live together. I hardly dare to think it, but perhaps the worst is over. I was terrified that I'd lose Richard, that some sacrifice would be required. But my prayers have been answered. Such a weight of doubt has lifted from me. You can't imagine . . .' Faith Farr smiled in reply.

'D'you want us to move these, then?' Faith Farr addressed Smith as she stood with her hands resting lightly on the frame of a Laura Knight.

The improvement in her appearance had not been matched by any corresponding one in her manners, Smith was sorry to find. He flinched at her lack of civility and the taciturn question, and recalled the dramatic, abrupt note Faith Farr had once sent him, refusing to see him. He congratulated himself on a lucky escape. Although he could recall the strength of the old attraction, it was fading. He had removed her note from his inside pocket and returned it to her file. Although it had not been intimate – merely official business – the thought of her fingers pressing on the paper had cast a spell on him, but that had lost its power too. Something – his own acute judgement, a guardian angel? – had prevented him from becoming personally entangled with Farr and had done him a great service. Her gaucheness, truculence and self-absorption – traits that might give her a wayward charm when viewed from a distance – would have been intolerable at close quarters, had he decided to marry her.

'Miss Farr, Mrs Tully, I'm afraid we won't meet again. We should make the most of our time together. Shall we begin?'

Faith Farr opened her portfolio and placed a meticulous water-colour on the desk. She must have climbed up on a roof somewhere to catch this view down on to Leicester Square. You could see a cinema, its façade decorated with muscular art deco sprites still leaping joyfully despite the havoc, around a soaring, optimistic tower, and far below, workmen with wheelbarrows repairing the bomb damage. A timely celebration of man's ability to go about his business with unswerving resolve, bravely to pick himself up and begin again, no matter what the circumstances. At last Farr understood the purpose of her work for the Ministry, and Smith felt tremendous pride that he had made her see sense after such a struggle, such enormous pride in his effectiveness that he judged it appropriate to offer unstinting praise.

'Well, well, well – just the ticket, just the ticket.'

That evening, not far away, Vivienne queued up outside the cinema: her first night of single life. The end of her marriage had been sudden but civilized. She could no longer countenance life at the villa, she informed Sam. But she understood how important Black was to him, to the country, and would raise no objection were he to find another, more sympathetic, helpmeet. After all, they had had eight good years and she was grateful to him. Sam had looked perturbed, but recovered himself by the time she finished speaking. Vivienne knew that he would spend his leisure time now with his motorcyclist; when the divorce was finalized, the girl would move in with him.

Sam drove Vivienne up to London in the Rolls and they had a good lunch with too much wine before they said goodbye. He had agreed to pay her a generous allowance, and had found her a luxurious flat near Regent's Park and an interesting, undemanding job at the BBC. For Vivienne, it almost made up for missing Frido so badly.

Whenever fatigue and loneliness began to overtake her, Vivienne indulged in a daydream that one day Frido would appear at her door, as golden and radiant as a July sun somewhere hot and languorous, somewhere far away from England. But when she felt more like her old self, she knew that he would never come back to her, she had sent him away so coldly. And now there were so many obstacles between them, secrets they could never share. How could she explain to him that she had been blackmailed by Charles but had told nobody, that the assassination plot had failed because of her silence? Frido knew little about her, in truth. She could not even remember telling him her real name. Now that she was free, there was no hope of them being together again as they had been – briefly and rapturously – when she was trapped in the villa.

As she settled into her cinema seat, encircled by couples – soldiers on leave and their girls – Vivienne found that it wasn't altogether an unpleasant feeling, this separateness, this self-containment. If she had to do without Frido she would do without men entirely . . . perhaps.

The Pathé cockerel crowed; women pushed handcarts piled with suitcases, babies and old people along valleys banked with rubble in a place that had once been a city – Vivienne did not catch where; the princesses Elizabeth and Margaret Rose, in dowdy tweed suits and ankle socks, shook hands all the way down a line of nurses.

The main feature began to play. The screen was flooded with luscious Technicolor – such a treat after the black and white world they had put up with for so long. There were bright blue skies, green fields, red and grey uniforms, dark beer and buttery yellow cakes in a café, belle époque dresses with yards and yards of fabric. And there was a woman – a Miss Hunter – involved with two men at the same time, a Briton – brash and larger than life – and an intense, fine-looking German . . . Vivienne sat up in her seat. Miss Hunter was being played by Deborah Kerr, just right, very beautiful. But then, oh dear, as the story went on, she was revealed to be the usual cardboard cut-out of an Englishwoman – repressed, tediously prim and unfailingly upright. And the film was not really about her at all, it was interested only in what happened in the men's lives – as was so often the case. Vivienne had a premonition that it would finish badly . . . for the woman. She left the cinema before the end.

*

Laura Knight stood alone on top of a hill in Worcestershire; the fields spread out below her for miles into the far distance, where they became the same colour as the sky. This was not her natural habitat, and she had been forced to make concessions with her appearance: lisle stockings and brogues, a warm utilitarian skirt, no frills, silks or embroidery. But then – she couldn't resist – she had added at the last minute her scarlet cardigan and a hat with a long curling feather. Just because you were being practical, it didn't mean you had to be a frump! She carried her small portable easel, her travelling paint set, and a hip flask.

She had to admit, she was a lousy nurse. Harold did not complain at all, he made a joke of Laura's lack of patience: her habit of cursing as she counted out the drops of medicine, of making the covers and pillows look more untidy after she'd straightened them, of yawning as she read aloud to him. He was delighted to have her near, and she had detected an improvement in his colour over the past few days, although when she questioned him – in hope – he said that he felt just the same, no better.

While Harold had his afternoon nap, Laura took these daily walks, to try and hold on to her sanity. She carried her art materials to reassure herself, rather than because she had found a subject to paint. The countryside – beautiful as it was – could not interest her. Looking lovely was not enough; there was no human story, nothing at stake. But, still – she was longing to work.

Laura set up her easel, undid her paintbox, and stood scanning the landscape. As she did so, the sound of the wind, of the birds, was interrupted by a familiar rumbling overhead, a noise she could never forget. She put her hand up to her brow, shielding her eyes. A group of Lancasters in formation were cutting through the sky high above. She found herself cheering, shouting and waving. 'God speed! God bless! Good luck! Good luck!' How ridiculous she must look to the airmen, if they could see her. An old lady gone mad, jumping up and down and yelling in the middle of nowhere. She watched as they moved forward together, towards the south, towards Europe, where the course of the war was turning; there were rumours that a counter-invasion would begin soon, that the

Allies would start to push the Nazis back through France into Germany, and Hitler be run to ground in his lair. And a thought came to Laura that it would be wonderful to be part of that, to travel to Europe in an aeroplane and paint what she found at first hand: what a coup, what a subject! No matter that she was nearly seventy: she had always wanted to fly.

Acknowledgements

First thanks go to my agent, Faith Evans, for her belief in *Warpaint*, her wise advice, her hard work and the pleasure of her conversation. I've been lucky to work with a fantastic team at Figtree/Penguin: Juliet Annan, Sophie Missing and Elisabeth Merriman. Andrew Davidson created a wonderful cover. Staff at the Museum of London, the Imperial War Museum, the British Library, the Tate Library and Archive, and the National Portrait Gallery Archive helped with the initial research. I'm also grateful to John Croft, Laura Knight's great-nephew. I've benefited enormously from the perceptive criticism of readers of earlier drafts: John Stokes, Midge Gillies, Dora Mortimer and Lucie Sutherland. Finally, as always, my most profound gratitude to my family, especially to John, our children, Maddie and Zac, and to my sister, Kate Foster, for, variously, their support, the timely distraction they've provided, and their tolerance of my obsessive need to discuss the book I was writing.

Historical Note

There was, during the Second World War in London, a War Artists Advisory Committee chaired by Sir Kenneth Clark, tasked with ensuring the survival of the British art world – and that the 'right sort' of art was being produced. There was also an organization devoted to creating 'Black' propaganda, led by the journalist Sefton Delmer, and based in Aspley Guise, Bedfordshire, near to Bletchley Park. Black made documents, images and broadcasts designed to attack the enemy psychologically, including fake letters from German war dead. WAAC and Black are brought together in *Warpaint*, under the direction of the Ministry of Information, to explore the efforts of those in power to create and control representation, in both its official and wholesome, and its covert and more sinister, aspects.

Warpaint also grew out of thinking about the lives of women artists during the early 1940s. However, it is a fiction, and so the characters that appear – even when they are overtly based upon real historical individuals and their work – are fictional creations. Laura Knight, for instance, as she is depicted in this novel, is my imagined version of her; her inner life, relationships and conversations the product of my writing. The other women – Cecily Browne, Faith Farr and Vivienne Thayer – were developed through research on women of this era, including, respectively, Evelyn Dunbar and Grace Golden who worked as war artists, and Isabel Delmer, wife of Sefton, who worked with him at Black.

Both Dame Laura Knight and Sir Kenneth Clark were public figures in the 1940s, and are still remembered today, and their vivid personae and fame add heft to their presence in *Warpaint*. When I drew upon the work and experiences of lesser-known individuals – Dunbar, Golden and the Delmers – I found myself moving quite far away from their documented histories: I had to; the writing required it. And so it was more fitting to create new names for what had become new characters. Some characters are entirely my invention: Aubrey Smith, Jean Roy, Frido, Charles/David, and George Meredith being the most significant.

As a final note, the border between truth and lies, lived experience and the pictures that we create of ourselves (and others) is embodied in Brendan Bracken, Churchill's close confidant and wartime Minister of Information (1941–5), also publisher of the *Financial Times* and *The Economist*. He was an unforgettable figure, with black teeth, red hair and a repertoire of stories about his difficult youth and the tragic death of a beloved brother – stories which were compelling, moving and, as it turned out, entirely fictional.

These are brief biographical sketches of the women whose lives and work as war artists I have drawn inspiration from:

Dame Laura Knight (1877–1970) found dealing with WAAC burdensome. She did not feel she was getting her due as one of the most successful artists in the country, a Royal Academician whose autobiography, *Oil Paint and Grease Paint* (1936), was a bestseller, and who had sat for the society photographer Bassano. Her work for WAAC can be seen in the Imperial War Museum, and government correspondence in the archive there refers to Dame Laura being 'a little difficult', and to attempts to 'soften her up'. While she did battle with the authorities, her husband, Harold, was content with his portraits and landscapes. In 1946 she flew to Nuremberg to paint the trial of the Nazi war criminals; it was the first time she had ever travelled in a plane, and she was the first woman artist to record such a momentous historical event from life.

Isabel Delmer (1912–92), daughter of a master mariner, trained as an artist at the Liverpool College of Art and the Royal Academy. During the war she worked for Black with her husband, Sefton, but left him during the conflict. His autobiography – *Black Boomerang* (1962) – describes the arrival of a glamorous young woman dispatch rider at his bedside as the beginning of the end of his marriage.

Post-war, Isabel became a legendary figure on the Soho art scene, a friend of, and model for, Francis Bacon. She began to paint again and had a number of exhibitions. One of her paintings is now in the Tate collections. She made two further marriages, both to composers – Constant Lambert and Alan Rawsthorne – and designed for the opera and the ballet.

Grace Golden (1904–93) was from a working-class London family. She trained at Chelsea School of Art and the Royal College. During the war she married, but what caused the breakdown of the relationship very soon afterwards is a mystery. Some of Golden's diaries are preserved in the Museum of London, but those for the period during which her marriage ended are missing: perhaps she stopped writing because of the trauma of what had happened? Maybe she destroyed the journals, not wanting to be reminded of their content? After 1945 Golden worked as an artist and book illustrator. She did not marry again. Her work is in the Imperial War Museum, the Tate and the Museum of London.

Evelyn Dunbar (1906–60) studied at Rochester and Chelsea Schools of Art, and at the Royal College, becoming known as a mural painter and illustrator. She married in 1942 a Flying Officer who was to survive the war; afterwards the couple lived on a farm. She continued to paint and taught at the Ruskin School of Art, Oxford. The Imperial War Museum and the Tate hold her work. Evelyn spent the last two years of her life on designs for murals at Bletchley Park, which had become a teacher-training college.

He just wanted a decent book to read ...

Not too much to ask, is it? It was in 1935 when Allen Lane, Managing
Director of Bodley Head Publishers, stood on a platform at Exeter railway
station looking for something good to read on his journey back to London.
His choice was limited to popular magazines and poor-quality paperbacks –
the same choice faced every day by the vast majority of readers, few of
whom could afford hardbacks. Lane's disappointment and subsequent anger
at the range of books generally available led him to found a company – and
change the world.

*'We believed in the existence in this country of a vast reading public for intelligent
books at a low price, and staked everything on it'*
Sir Allen Lane, 1902–1970, founder of Penguin Books

The quality paperback had arrived – and not just in bookshops. Lane was
adamant that his Penguins should appear in chain stores and tobacconists,
and should cost no more than a packet of cigarettes.

Reading habits (and cigarette prices) have changed since 1935, but
Penguin still believes in publishing the best books for everybody to
enjoy. We still believe that good design costs no more than bad design,
and we still believe that quality books published passionately and responsibly
make the world a better place.

So wherever you see the little bird – whether it's on a piece of
prize-winning literary fiction or a celebrity autobiography, political tour
de force or historical masterpiece, a serial-killer thriller, reference book,
world classic or a piece of pure escapism – you can bet that it represents
the very best that the genre has to offer.

Whatever you like to read – trust Penguin.